The Frenchman and the English Rose

The Frenchman and the English Rose

CAROLANN CAMILLO

Seattle, WA

Published by Camel Press
PO Box 70515
Seattle, WA 98127

For more information go to: www.camelpress.com
www.carolanncamillo.com

All rights reserved. No part of this book may be reproduced or transmitted in any form or by any means, electronic or mechanical, including photocopying, recording, or any information storage and retrieval system, without permission in writing from the publisher.

This is a work of fiction. Names, characters, places, brands, media, and incidents are either the product of the author's imagination or are used fictitiously.

Cover design by Sabrina Sun

The Frenchman and the English Rose
Originally published in 2012 by Camel Press as *Moonlit Desire*
Copyright © 2012, 2018 by Carolann Camillo

ISBN: 978-1-60381-681-6 (Trade Paper)
ISBN: 978-1-60381-682-3 (eBook)

Library of Congress Control Number: 2017953201

Printed in the United States of America

Part I

New York Colony
June 1759

Chapter 1

The only sound pervading the still air came from the incessant rattle of the coach speeding through the night. The horses' hooves plumbed the dry roadway skirting the Hudson River and sent aloft dust particles that drifted beneath the leather window coverings.

Neither the dust nor the constant jostling of the coach disturbed Catherine Bradshaw as much as the man seated across from her.

She had wed Jeremy Flint that very morning after disembarking the ship that had transported her from London. He gave no indication of discomfort. His wiry body swayed as if to the lilting strains of music. The hand resting on the plush gray upholstered seat tapped a slow, steady rhythm. His features were relaxed and unexpressive, save for his dark eyes, which touched her with carnal promise.

"My dear," he said as if she welcomed communication. The commotion on the wharf that morning and the hasty ceremony before a magistrate had left little opportunity for conversation, which suited Catherine's dispirited mood.

"Awaiting your arrival these past weeks put me out of sorts, but finally we are together. Soon you will settle into your new home in Tarrytown. Although I am under no illusion we share a mutual regard, our arrangement suits me well. You chose the correct course."

Beneath partially lowered lids, Catherine studied her husband. His impeccable red coat and buff breeches gave the impression of a gentleman, as did his lightly powdered hair bound in a queue with a silk ribbon. His predilection for snuff might have marked him a dandy. Yet, a crude provincialism lurked beneath the surface. She'd sensed it when they first met, four months earlier. In unguarded moments, his gruff speech and manner lay bare his colonial heritage and suggested he had adopted the trappings of a gentleman later in life.

The coach gave a menacing leap, and Catherine tightened her grip on the strap affixed to the inside wall. Through a chink in the curtain, she searched for signs of civilization. Although the area was heavily forested, she thought she glimpsed a far-off flickering light. Perhaps a colonial settlement lay somewhere in the distance. Or perhaps the savages she'd read about in her history book inhabited these woods. She shivered at the possibility of an encounter.

"Your parents are well, I trust." Flint's concern seemed less than sincere.

"They were in ... passable health when we parted but will sorely miss my company." Knowing she would most likely never see her parents again had tortured her from the moment she bid them goodbye. Two months at sea, confined to a small cabin, had only intensified her longing.

"The bank draft deposited in your father's account the morning you set sail should ease their distress. At least for the immediate future."

This last remark caught Catherine's attention. "Did I not correctly understand that an additional five hundred pounds would be deposited twice yearly upon my settling into this marriage?"

"Yes. However, my generosity depends upon a number of circumstances."

"I have become your wife. Surely that is the only circumstance to warrant consideration."

Coldness crept into Flint's dark eyes. "Let me be clear, then. Should you prove less than dutiful, all payments will cease. The same—and of no small import—will occur should I predecease your father. My agent in London will be notified to take the necessary steps. Also, I expect a fruitful union, in which case you will be adequately provided for in my will. A childless marriage, however, will not sit well with me."

Catherine's fingers clenched. When he had broached marriage, she had been too shocked to concentrate on the conditions that accompanied his proposal. Indeed, the entire matter was basically a coldly calculated business venture; he had, in truth, bought her as if she were a prized brood mare. She had put out of her mind what being wed to a man as arrogant and self-serving as Flint might entail.

"Let us not indulge in premature speculation." His lips parted in a thin smile. "I am certain you will satisfy me in every regard."

Catherine held her anger in check and allowed some moments to pass before she spoke. "It seems you have left nothing to chance."

"You read me well. That should keep our disputes to a minimum."

"Then I must wish you a long and ... pleasant life." Her tone was stiff with frost.

Flint's smile broadened. "That, my dear, has ever been my intent."

The ride continued in silence. Exhausted, Catherine leaned her head against the soft plush and closed her eyes. Then a sudden commotion broke out alongside the carriage. Angry shouts roared above the echoing wind, followed by a loud thud, as if a heavy object had fallen onto the driver's seat. Sounds of scuffling ensued. The coach gave a terrible lurch, careening from side to side, before it slowed and came to a halt.

Flint tore at the window curtain. "What the devil is going on here?"

The door was thrown wide. A man leaned in, a pistol gripped in his hand. He swung the weapon toward Catherine. It came to rest a scant hair's breadth above the neckline of her gown.

She edged back against the seat and screamed. Her heart beat in a wild cadence that robbed her of breath; her stomach threatened to surrender the tiny morsel she'd consumed at her wedding lunch.

Jeremy Flint lunged toward the open doorway.

"Remain still, Flint, or I shall see you a widower far longer than you have been a bridegroom." Darkness shrouded the man who spoke. However, the conviction in his deep, rich voice left Catherine no doubt that he would follow through on his threat.

"See here." Anger contorted Flint's face as he eased back onto his seat. "You have no call to frighten my wife. State your intentions. If it be robbery, then get the filthy business over with and let us continue on our way."

Slowly, Catherine turned her head, straining to see into the darkness. A pair of lanterns anchored to the inside wall of the coach lit the interior, enough to illuminate the man's tall, muscular frame. She found herself looking into a pair of eyes that gazed back at her with unconcealed scorn.

She instantly recalled where she had seen those eyes. Darkened now by shadows, in daylight they were a clear deep green. That morning she had spotted him on the wharf. His unabashed stare indicated he cared little for propriety. His long strides suggested boldness, which was further evidenced when he had drawn close enough to graze Flint on the shoulder. Judging him to be a thief, she kept close the trivial contents of her pocket.

In the night's gloom, his hair seemed even blacker now than first she had thought; his full lips hinted at rakishness uncommon to men of her acquaintance.

The cold metal leveled at her breast caused her fears to mount. Not daring to move, she forced herself to endure the man's scrutiny. Finally, she tore her eyes from his mesmerizing gaze and sent a pleading glance toward her husband. He sat immobile, his breath hissing through clenched teeth. He was clearly impotent with rage.

"Mr. Flint, do something, please."

"Stay calm, Catherine." He returned his attention to the man. "I demand to know why you have waylaid my coach. Am I to understand coincidence has brought us together twice in one day?" When there came no reply, he edged toward Catherine. "I insist you draw down your weapon. Can you not see my wife is in fear for her life?"

The pistol remained in place, touching lightly now against Catherine's flesh. "Your concern for the bride is a trifle late. In your haste to speed her to the marriage bed, you have done her a great disservice. You should remember these roads are treacherous at night."

"Who are you? How is it you know something of my business today? What do you want with us? If you are after money, you are welcome to whatever small amount I carry with me."

"The contents of your purse do not interest me." Waving the pistol aside, the man reached behind Catherine, caught her firmly about the waist and pulled her from the coach.

As she fell roughly against him, she gasped from the shock of finding herself in his arms. Then fear rendered her mute. Sound dimmed, as if she could no longer hear. In all her twenty years, she had never experienced such close contact with a man. This one seemed bent on doing her harm. His tall, well-muscled body spoke of the power he possessed. The arm encircling her nearly cut off her breath. When, finally, her feet touched ground, he loosened his hold, but not enough for her to fully extricate herself from his grip.

Flint sprang from his seat and eased himself from the carriage. "I demand that you release my wife."

"Louis!" The man issued a sharp command.

Another man, hidden by the shadows, stepped forward. Short of stature, he possessed a broad frame and a round face bordered by a thatch of unruly brown hair. Like his accomplice, he wore long trousers and a fringed shirt of animal hide.

"Take another step and I will kill you," Louis said, "although it is my friend, Rive St. Clair, who has earned the privilege." The gleam of a pistol leveled at Flint's head reinforced his words.

Once again, Catherine wanted to scream. Yet who, in this vast wilderness, would hear her? The driver lay sprawled in his seat, motionless. A woman's outcry would never deter the man—St. Clair—from carrying out his plan, which at the moment did not suggest murder. He might have accomplished that earlier on the dock and certainly as soon as he waylaid the coach. If not murder, what did he intend? Then she recalled how boldly he had stared at her that morning.

"Let me go." With one fist, she pummeled his shoulder. The other managed to land a blow to his chest.

Quickly, he secured the pistol in his belt and captured Catherine's hands in one of his.

"The bride has courage, Flint. Or is she just ill-tempered? Whichever, she will learn to improve her disposition before long."

With his free hand, he fingered the coil of hair at Catherine's nape. She twisted her head away until pain stabbed at her neck. One stroke and her pale gold hair tumbled loose. When he reached for the closure of her cloak and gave the cord a tug, she was powerless to stop him. The garment slipped free and fell at her feet.

The color drained from Flint's face. He took a tentative step toward Catherine. However, the pistol pressed against his temple stilled further movement.

"I will pay for my wife's safety. Name your price and it will be yours, provided she is allowed to proceed from here immediately."

St. Clair's dark brows rose. "You are most gallant where it concerns a lady. Yet I remember a day sixteen years ago when you showed no such compulsion. However, this is neither the time nor place to rekindle old memories. My price is steep, but one day, soon, you will meet it. Until then, the bride stays with me."

At his words, an anguished cry escaped Catherine's lips. Her heart hammered against her chest. With renewed effort, she attempted to twist out of his grip. She managed to free one hand, but her blows, no matter how well aimed or forceful, carried no effect. If only she had a weapon. Her eyes lit on the pistol tucked in his belt. No, she had never fired one and knew nothing of its workings. His knife, then. It lay sheathed at his waist and so tantalizingly near. Had she the courage to use it? She had never so much as killed a spider. But, this man, yes.

Without further thought or calculation, she reached for the knife. Her fingers clasped the hilt. A good yank should bring it out of its case. The blade began to slide. Then a hand far stronger closed over hers. With a shake of his head the man disengaged the weapon.

"I believe you would have used that." Brows raised in surprise, he slid the knife back into its sheath and repositioned it against the small of his back.

"Most gladly," Catherine acknowledged.

"Why are you doing this?" Flint rasped. "I have never harmed you."

"Your memory is as short as your temper. In due course, it will return to you. When it does, remember the oath sworn by a twelve-year-old boy as you went about the bloody business of murdering innocent people. Was it for the bounty, I wonder, or did you simply relish your role?"

"You have mistaken me for another man."

"Another man does not bear that scar. I think that before long, you will remember me well."

Flint touched the puckered line that cut just below the right side of his jaw.

For a moment, the two men locked eyes. Then Flint's widened in slow recognition.

"Louis, I think we are done with Mr. Flint."

Working efficiently, Louis bound Flint's hands, thrust a gag into his mouth and shoved him into the coach. St. Clair released Catherine long enough to cut loose her two small trunks lashed to the roof and throw them to the ground. He sprang the locks and emptied the contents.

He pulled a plain, rose-hued muslin gown from the pile and tossed it to her.

"Change your clothes. You will have little need for fashion where I am taking you."

She backed away until one of the coach wheels stopped her. The cold that had gripped her body gave way to an intense heat, which enflamed her cheeks. Did he expect her to strip before his eyes? To stand before him in her stays, hoop, linen shift and hose, all she wore beneath her outer clothing? Modesty, ingrained in her since childhood, sent her hands fluttering to her bodice. No doubt, he would have shed his garments and paraded in front of her as bare as the day he entered the world. She could do nothing beyond stare at him. She felt closed off from civilization, lost in a universe where reason no longer ruled. Fear stabbed at the pit of her stomach. Where did he intend to take her? What would he do to her?

"Don't be stubborn. I'll not ask you twice."

"No." To capitulate was unthinkable.

I must not capitulate.

"If you require the services of a lady's maid … that is a duty I shall gladly perform."

For a moment anger replaced fear, and she tossed aside the gown.

"Temper, Catherine." His tone was deceptively light-hearted.

For him to use her given name was an insult. She refused to obey. After surviving an arduous sea journey and a marriage that made a mockery of such a noble institution, she would suffer no man—whether sinner or saint—to strip the clothes off her back. Bravery, she reminded herself, played not the least part in valor.

He stepped close and slid his knife from its sheath. With the tip of the blade, he severed one of the ties that anchored an unadorned deep blue stomacher to the bodice of her wool gown.

"We have little time, and I am losing patience." The tip of the knife slashed through another tie and then another. "Shall I continue?"

Catherine glanced down to where her stomacher lay askew, exposing her shift and, from beneath the fine oft-mended linen, the outline of her breast. She hastened to cover herself with her hand. The fear she had so gallantly bitten back resurfaced.

"Go behind the coach and change your clothes. Now. Or I will do it for you." His affable tone did nothing to temper his warning.

This was no halfhearted threat. If she did not want the garments torn from her body, she must do as he ordered.

Tears threatened, but she forced them back.

With the tip of his knife, he scooped up the muslin gown and extended it toward her. "Keep in mind our journey will offer few of the comforts of a coach. So, dress accordingly."

She followed the line of his gaze. There was no mistaking his inference; her hoop must be left behind. She clenched her teeth and reached for the other gown.

He walked with her as far as the rear of the coach and leaned back against the dark wood.

"Three minutes … Catherine."

Biting her tongue, she hastened behind the coach to a spot close to the front wheel. At least it afforded some privacy. It occurred to her to bolt into the nearby trees; however, she knew he would be ever vigilant—he, or his accomplice. One of them would spot her. No, she must bide her time, wait for him to become less watchful.

She removed everything but her shift and stays fairly quickly—considering all the ties and hooks—and slipped the muslin gown over her head. Her hoop lay near her feet. On impulse, she reached under her gown, unlaced her corset, and tossed it onto the pile. Somehow, she must find a way to escape her captivity. That would require shedding the hated garment that bit into her flesh and made bending from the waist nearly impossible.

After fumbling with the bodice laces, she finally accomplished the task of dressing. None too soon. Without warning, he stood beside her.

"You see, I can be reasonable when I am obeyed."

"You know nothing of reason." Although she experienced a resurgence of fear, she could not entirely still her tongue.

He wore an expression of quiet amusement as he reached for her, his fingers gently encircling her arms. "Come, it is time to leave."

Catherine stiffened and stood her ground. Past adversity had bred strength in her. There was no better time than now to call upon it. If she didn't stand up to this man now, her situation would become completely intolerable.

"I will not go with you. I cannot."

"Yes you can, and by God, you will."

"No."

"Obey me." His steely tone implied that she had little choice.

"You, sir, are thoroughly uncivilized." How she still managed to challenge him astonished her.

He laughed, a low sound that drifted into the moonlit night. "All the more reason you should obey. In time you will learn to do as you are bid."

She balled her hand into a fist, took aim and almost caught the side of his face.

He easily dodged her intended blow.

"Who is uncivilized now?" He captured her wrists and pulled her against him. Then he lifted her into his arms. She pummeled his chest as he carried her to where his chestnut horse grazed by the roadside.

"You will have ample time to refine your manners." He tossed her onto the saddle and sprung up behind her. Wrapping an arm around her waist, he held her close. "I suggest you start now."

He urged the horse forward, stopping at the open doorway of the coach. Gasping for air, Flint struggled to free himself from his bonds. His face had taken on the hue of a ripe pomegranate.

St. Clair reached down and yanked the gag from Flint's mouth.

Almost at once, Flint raged. "I'll hunt you down and kill you for this."

"Few are given a second chance. You know where to find me." St. Clair wheeled the horse around, dug his heels into its sides and raced into the forest.

Chapter 2

In the profound darkness, Catherine lost all track of time. There was no way to gauge their direction. The trees had closed about them almost at once. As they penetrated deeper into the forest, the moonlight diminished. Save for the soft plodding of the horses' hoofs, she found herself cloistered in a world of silence, for neither the man nor his accomplice, who rode closely behind, exchanged a word.

Cramped and bruised, she shivered from cold and fear. When he wrapped her shaking body in his arms, she accepted his warmth. More than ever, she was determined to survive the night.

When they finally stopped, shadows crouched upon the lightly dewed earth. St. Clair lifted her down from the horse, loosened the saddle, yanked free a blanket, and tossed it to her. It smelled of horse and mulch, but she welcomed it anyway. She wrapped herself in it and sank to the ground. With no one to protect her, she fought the urge to sleep, but eventually succumbed to exhaustion.

Sometime later, she awoke to the sound of voices. They were camped in a meadow ringed by tall trees. The moon glowed silver against a black sky pricked by countless stars. A carpet of wildflowers mingled with the grass. The night breeze carried the fragrance of early summer, but the arrival of her favorite season offered no comfort.

A gush of water suggested a stream flowed nearby, or perhaps a river. Her parched throat reminded her that many hours had passed since she had drunk anything. As she thought about water, she could almost imagine a refreshing trickle moistening her tongue. She must keep her thirst to herself. She would make only one demand—to be set free.

The two men sat a short distance away, their silhouettes barely perceptible in the gloom. They conversed in French, which surprised her. Although Louis's speech hinted of French descent, the man known to her as Rive St. Clair had spoken in unaccented English. She managed to catch snatches of their conversation, since she had some familiarity with the language. Although an apt pupil during her school years, she found her skills limited by too few opportunities to practice them. During the past eighteen months, as her family's financial situation deteriorated, she'd had no opportunity to practice at all.

"No one would deny you … conscience … frightened her half to death."

His choice of words and gruffer tone told Catherine it was Louis who spoke.

"Better only by half … circumstances … took advantage … stays with me."

St. Clair for certain. He had a surprisingly cultured voice, not what she would have expected of a common outlaw.

Louis had used the word "conscience" to his friend. Was it possible he possessed one? No, his behavior proved him to be as unprincipled as the basest criminal.

He continued, "The murdered avenged … justice …."

"They are at rest … take comfort … the wharf … chance this morning."

"Too public …."

"A quick strike."

"Not suit my purpose … must answer not just to me …."

He raked his long fingers through the midnight-black hair that fell from near the line of his jaw halfway down his nape. Then he placed an arm about Louis' shoulders in what struck Catherine as a companionable gesture. Apparently, he took no offense at his comrade's criticisms. A common thug might have shown his fist, or worse, his knife. That he possessed a somewhat agreeable disposition surprised her. She would not have guessed that tolerance was a part of his nature. The discovery made him seem almost as perplexing as frightening.

"My decision." Then he rose and stretched. "I need sleep … my word no harm … befall the bride."

As he walked toward her, Catherine closed her eyes. How much could the word of an unprincipled man be worth? This one spoke of justice and murder in the same breath. Lying down beside her, he looped a thin strip of something soft about her wrist. She needed no visual proof he had bound her to him. After having accomplished her abduction, he would never chance her escaping in the night. A short while later, she heard his deep, even breathing.

For her, however, sleep proved as elusive as freedom. Even when she forced herself to put aside her predicament, she dozed only in snatches. For a good part of the night she stared at the dark sky studded with its myriad of stars. The aromatic, woody scent of the air did nothing to dispel her anxieties. She lay still, consumed by one thought: she must find a means to escape. Somehow.

She next awoke to sunlight and found him standing over her.

"Good morning." He sounded almost cheerful.

Her gaze met green eyes intensified by a sun-darkened complexion. A lock of dark hair lay across a wide and yet unlined brow. Now that his features were no longer enshrouded by night, she could see that his nose, if not quite straight, fit comfortably between strong cheekbones. Indeed, she thought him a man of uncommon beauty, if the term could be applied to the masculine gender. His beauty made him even more dangerous, for never must she stop thinking of him as anything other than an ogre. She sat up and edged away.

"You must be hungry. I know I am." He didn't wait for a reply. "Do you like rabbit? While you slept, I snared a plump one."

Louis was nowhere in sight.

Catherine scrambled to her feet and watched him with a wary eye. No longer bound, her hands, partially concealed in the folds of her gown, curled into fists. In spite of passing the night with him without incident, she considered him no more trustworthy than a cutthroat.

"I'll assume from your silence that you have no distaste for rabbit."

Finally, Catherine found her voice. "Who are you? Why have you committed this despicable act?"

He stood, thumbs hooked in his belt. His ease suggested that her harangue in no way intimidated him.

"I will gladly answer your first question. My name is Rive St. Clair. Since I know you are called Catherine and have already been referring to you as such, I ask you to use my given name, as well. Again, it is Rive. That should not be too difficult for you to master. Try it."

He had the gall to smile.

Catherine breathed deeply in an effort to contain her outrage. "Rive," the French word meaning bank or shore, a place of safety, of refuge. In his case the name was an obvious misnomer.

He cupped a hand behind his ear. "I didn't hear you."

"I said nothing."

"Exactly."

Her brow furrowed as if he had posed a riddle.

"My name. Say it."

She pressed her lips together.

He stepped closer. As she tried to back away, his hand snaked about her waist. He lodged a curved finger beneath her chin. He tilted her head up so that her eyes met his.

Panic set her pulse fluttering. Her brief moment of defiance dissipated like a wisp of smoke. She dropped her eyes. "Rive."

He freed her with a triumphant grin.

"See, that was not so difficult. Now that is settled, we can proceed to other matters. I'm going to assume you are famished. I know I am." He spoke as if she were not his prisoner but a willing partner in some adventurous romp. "However, if we are to breakfast, we shall need a fire. Why don't you collect some wood while I skin the rabbit?"

Catherine stared in disbelief. "If you meant that as a jest, I find no humor in it."

"I rarely jest when I am hungry. If I must repeat everything I say, we shall lodge in these woods well into summer. A prospect you might wish to avoid."

She steeled herself to ignore his demands. "If you were dying of thirst, I would not fetch so much as a cup of water for you. I am a lady, not a lackey pressed into your service."

"Are you? I hadn't noticed."

"I happen to be educated, sir."

His dark brows lifted. "Indeed." His neutral tone made it difficult to decide if he were mocking her. "Which subjects besides needlework and the other … womanly arts would interest such a lady?"

He was beyond infuriating and *somewhat* less threatening, perhaps because darkness no longer cloaked the scene. The bright morning sun bathed the ground in luminous rays and brushed her skin with gentle warmth. High in the trees birds trilled a merry chorus. An intense blue draped the sky, as if to defy a painter to reproduce it on canvas.

In answering him, she was not above a small boast. "I am well versed in history and mathematics. I play the pianoforte, have read extensively and am somewhat familiar with the French language." He seemed to ponder her last bit of information. She wondered if he were rethinking last night's conversation with his friend and weighing how much of it she might have heard.

"By your own admission, you are an accomplished woman. Who, might I ask, instructed you in those subjects?"

Catherine fixed him with a smug look. "I had a tutor."

"A tutor. Your mother, then? What did she teach you? I shall assume manners among other things, although I have seen no evidence."

She hesitated, the subject of her mother's greatly reduced circumstances being all too raw. At first she thought not to answer him but, upon further contemplation, changed her mind. "She taught me that if I must make my own way in the world, to do so with dignity and honor."

He let the silence stretch out between them, as if he had lost interest in the conversation. "You have made your way into a world that, shortly, would have stripped you of all dignity."

"I did not willingly enter your world."

"I do not speak of myself."

Flint. Consumed by her predicament, she had not entertained a single thought of him. In contemplating escape, she had dwelt on the need to save herself from whatever affront this man might impose upon her. Now, with her mind clearer, her desperation became more acute. Would her husband mount a rescue or deem it too dangerous? Either way, she must find a way to reunite with him. Failing to do so would mean disgrace and destitution for her family, surely prison for her father. Dignity? She'd surrendered it the day she agreed to Jeremy Flint's marriage proposal.

"Are you always so difficult?" Rive asked. "You'll make both of our lives more tolerable if you obey me, especially since you no longer have Louis to plead your cause. He was most concerned for your welfare."

"If I refuse?" For the life of her she could not imagine what had prompted such a provocative statement.

Rive smiled even as he shook his head. He guessed her conflict, evidenced in the wide blue eyes that met his gaze without faltering. At the same time, she seemed unable to control the slight trembling of her lower lip. She was determined to defy him. This he understood, although it vexed him greatly. She feared him, too, and this he also recognized. Only God knew what she thought he was going to do to her.

He knew what he wanted to do. He would start by taking that stray curl that rested against her brow, coiling it about his finger and bringing it to his lips. Then he would brush her cheek and, next, the sweet line of her long, slender neck, which he would follow to the little hollow at the base of her throat. There he would pause briefly before venturing to the pale flesh that lay hidden below the neckline of her gown. He wanted to explore every part of her—from the tip of her delicately pointed, defiant chin to her toes—without haste. He would give special attention to all the soft, secret places concealed by a thin veil of dress fabric.

He was becoming aroused. To follow thought with deed would be unwise, if not dangerous. Earlier he had wondered what kind of woman would consort with the likes of Flint. The word that came to mind was one not spoken lightly and only in the company of men. Twelve hours later he conceded the woman he ached to possess was indeed a lady.

Why must life be so complicated?

With a sigh, he admonished himself to deal with the part of his anatomy that, at the moment, made it extremely difficult to adhere to his higher instincts. And to do it in all haste.

He needed a task. The rabbit lay on the ground where he had tossed it earlier. He waited a moment for his body to ease, before he walked over and snatched up his catch. He held it aloft by its hind legs.

"Would you rather help prepare the meat?" He unsheathed his knife.

"You are a brute and an unconscionable heathen."

He watched her lips tremble with indignation. Lush, full lips that made him want to trace their contour with his thumb. Perhaps later. No, definitely later when they were settled in and awaiting Flint.

"Does that mean no?" With what she now realized was inherent stealthy grace, he was beside her in an instant, holding out his offering. As he expected, the sight of the poor dead creature produced the desired effect. Her face pinched into a frown. She looked as if she had swallowed a spoonful of rancid stew.

"You are—"

"Yes, I know." He cut short her litany. "I am a brute, a savage, a beast and inhabit at least half a dozen other incarnations, all of which offend you. Remember, I am in charge here." His tone bespoke utter conviction. "Or do you need further proof?"

Chapter 3

Catherine recognized that if he chose to demand her submission, he had the will and strength to accomplish it. He must know something of her, too. She would not easily cave under his pressure.

He had moved very close to her. Too close. His restless gaze shifted over her body as if, mentally, he was stripping away her few garments. Although modestly clothed, she was gripped by the feeling of standing naked before him. Her pulse quickened and an odd sensation of heat settled deep inside. A sensation she had never before experienced, but whose meaning even a woman of sheltered upbringing could fathom. The knowledge that he could bring this about horrified her.

"Catherine?"

She took a moment to collect her senses. "The kindling …." Then she turned and hurried away.

"Don't wander from my sight. Make certain the wood is dry and a decent size. I have a most fearsome appetite this morning."

His last words sent her off with even quicker steps.

Seconds later, she skirted the edge of the meadow. The forest loomed thick with towering fir and pine trees, along with a smattering of maples. She yearned to run, but a glance over her shoulder confirmed that he was keeping a watchful eye. She did feel almost faint from hunger. The thought of rabbit roasting on a spit had her almost licking her lips. Common sense dictated she would not venture far before he tracked her down. She must first regain her strength and then wait for him to become careless.

The freshness of the air mingled with the woody scent of bark and foliage.

She noted that they were in a hilly, even mountainous region and tucked that bit of information away. In the future, it might prove useful.

She tried not to torture herself with worries about the future: the peril to her family if a disaster were to befall Jeremy Flint. Perhaps he had already decided he valued his life far more than his desire to possess her. What past involvement with Rive had induced him to abduct her? By now, her husband might have sent word to his agent to cease subsequent deposits to her father's account.

What if she confessed everything right now—the circumstances that had led her to marry Flint and how the man had endeavored to win her hand?

They had met at a piano recital given by Catherine's only pupil. Flint, passing the Season in London, had introduced himself and thereafter never strayed from her side. Although polite, there was something disquieting in his demeanor. It went beyond his braggadocio and all too familiar manner. When the hour grew late, he insisted on escorting her home in his carriage.

Social invitations followed, each met with polite, but cool, refusals. Shortly thereafter, she began to encounter him in the street with alarming frequency.

He would show up at her home, uninvited, each time bearing gifts of wine and sweet cakes, cheese or fresh fruit—luxuries her parents could no longer afford since her father's failing eyesight had forced him to abandon his surgeon's practice. For their sake, Catherine tolerated it.

The night before he sailed for New York, he paid his final call. The moment her parents retired, he made clear his intentions.

His inquiries had confirmed her family's financial distress. He could alleviate it, should she consent to become his wife. The thought of being bound to Flint was repugnant, but she was left with no other recourse. She agreed to the marriage; however, when she refused to set sail with him the next day, he made one concession: she would follow on his ship, West Wind, due to leave for New York in a month.

Would Rive set her free if she were to confide in him? Would he even care? He hated Flint. No, he would never free her.

Pine needles covered the ground and muffled her footsteps as she went about the task of collecting the kindling. Other than a darting squirrel, she neither saw nor heard another creature. City-bred and used to throngs of people, bustling markets, street performers and vendors, she was frightened by the isolation almost as much as the man who held her prisoner.

Her supposition about a stream proved true. Clear water gushed over rocks worn smooth by its flow. Fierce sunlight glinted off the surface. Was it possible the stream led to a not-too-distant town? She stepped closer, listened, but heard only the softly burbling water.

She heaved an anguished sigh.

I can count on no one but myself to reverse my plight.

Retracing her steps, she reentered the clearing and dumped the wood at Rive's feet. He had already skinned the rabbit and fashioned a makeshift spit.

"If you expect me to light the fire, as well, then you are in for a disappointment."

Before he could respond, she turned and dashed back to the stream. She would give her last farthing—if she possessed one—for a bath and a change of clothes, even a simple brush or comb. She ran her fingers through her disheveled hair and tugged at the knots, repeating the exercise until she had worked out the tangles. As she pulled off her shoes, she felt his eyes on her back. Reaching carefully under her gown so as not to compromise her modesty, she removed her torn hose.

Because she was within his sight, she resisted the impulse to hike up her gown and wade into the stream. She settled for a mere fraction above her ankles—a choice certainly not provocative enough to stir a man's imagination—and stepped into the water. The numbing cold raised goose bumps along her skin. She tugged at one of the ruffles that edged her shift's sleeves and tore it loose. Then she moistened the bit of lace and leisurely went about refreshing herself, dabbing at her face, arms, and throat, in no hurry to rejoin her captor. The sun, rising steadily overhead, warmed her while she continued to accomplish her simple toilette. When she finished, she left the stream and sat upon the grassy bank. Listening to the gentle murmur of the flowing water, she discovered a newfound appreciation of the pristine beauty all about her and was nearly able to free her mind of the circumstances that had brought her there.

Time passed, and eventually she heard him call. Resigned, she tucked the wet lace into her bodice, donned her stockings and shoes and went to him.

He was stretched out on the grass, picking at a piece of succulent meat. The sight of it only intensified Catherine's hunger pangs. The rabbit, gutted and spitted, roasted over a low fire.

"Here, help yourself." He offered his knife as if they were dining in mutual camaraderie. "You're in luck, for this is one of my better efforts. It could not be tastier had the royal cooks prepared it in the kitchens at Versailles."

She stared at the knife. What devilish trick was this, and to what purpose? Her eyes narrowed in suspicion.

It was on the tip of her tongue to tell him she'd rather starve than accept food from him, but the sight of the juicy meat, roasted to a golden brown and dripping fat, along with the appetizing aroma emanating from it, reminded her she was ravenously hungry. When he pulled her down beside him, she didn't protest. She accepted the knife and sliced a piece of meat off the breast.

While they ate, it occurred to her she would rather plunge the blade into his heart than the rabbit, but she was already acquainted with the quickness of his movements and knew he watched her closely. So, instead, she helped herself to a liberal portion of the tender meat. He too concentrated on his food, cutting and eating small quantities. His show of etiquette surprised her.

At the moment, he seemed to pose no threat, and her tension eased. She wondered at his reasons for hating Jeremy Flint. Rive had spoken of murder, but whose? Someone close to him, certainly. He had made reference to a boy's sworn oath—his, she assumed—and thought her abduction the result of a long-standing vendetta. Apparently, the wound, still fresh in his mind, kept him bent on retribution.

The companionable silence continued, and Catherine decided to take advantage of it, along with his seemingly good mood.

"Why have you done this?" She fought to employ a neutral tone.

Instead of answering, he leaned toward her and placed a finger lightly against her lips.

She edged back. "I have a right to know."

"Do you? So you will, in due course. Meanwhile, you are in no danger from me. If harm befalls you, it will come through your own miscalculations."

Either his threats had lost some of their sting, or she was becoming inured to them. Therefore, she sliced off another piece of meat and continued to challenge him. "My curiosity is natural, don't you think?"

He shrugged. "It is misguided, however."

"At least tell me who you are. I know your name and precious little else. Surely it can make no difference if I learn about you now, or later, when you swing at the end of a rope."

He laughed and slowly shook his head. "I thought we had settled the question of my ancestry. I am a brute. You said as much yourself." He uncoiled his long, lithe body and rose to his feet. "Shall I prove it further? There is at least a half hour before we depart."

"No." Again her voice betrayed her. It emerged as a squeak, when she meant to employ a far more forceful tone.

"Then eat." He settled back down.

She nibbled on another morsel, but more than ever found her curiosity piqued. "You are French?"

"I come honestly by the name St. Clair. Yes, I am French. Does that reassure you?"

"Hardly. Not when our countries are engaged in a war over Canada."

It had begun with disputes over territory in the Ohio Valley. By 1756, war had been declared between the French and British. As it entered the third year, Catherine had devoured every newspaper account, which lately had touted her countrymen's successes. French forts continued to fall, leaving

Quebec—the center of French power in North America—vulnerable. If the British were to seize Quebec, they would control Canada.

"The war has nothing to do with you. As a Frenchman, I bear you no ill will."

"You do Mr. Flint. Why?"

"This is not the time to discuss it."

She exhaled in irritation. "I can think of no better."

"You will know everything soon enough, when your husband and I meet again."

"You sound certain you will."

"Unless he is a fool, and I don't believe he is, he will come for you."

Would he? Perhaps he had no stomach for a confrontation. Her ignorance of the circumstances tortured her, just as it troubled her that she might never learn the truth. She was certain Rive intended to kill Flint. Would he succeed? She thought it probable. The passage of time already boded ill for her rescue. She must escape before they traveled any farther.

The possibility continued to tantalize her. The night before, from the coach, she thought she had spotted pinpricks of light. Did these suggest the existence of a settlement? If one existed there, then why not somewhere near here? She closed her mind to the dangers of the forest—snakes, wild boar, bears and who knew what manner of men who made their living in those woods. Yet, she must risk it.

"It is getting late." Rive tamped down the fire and crossed to where his horse grazed. The saddle lay on the ground, the blanket he had wrapped her in the previous night beside it. It would still require several minutes for him to prepare for their departure.

Now, she resolved, while his attention was diverted.

She backed away slowly, then turned and dashed toward a thick copse of trees. Her plan was to follow the stream, but her shoes, with their low slim heels, made running difficult. Still, she kept up a swift pace, slipping and skidding over small stones, dry pine needles and rotting leaves. Thick roots rose up in a tangle to trip her. When her skirt caught around her legs, she hitched it up to her knees. Modesty had no place on this day. For now, her one goal was to make good her flight.

More than once, she tripped and fell, skinning her palms. Thistles clawed at her arms. Even after her breath became labored, her lungs threatened to burst and pain knifed into her side, she fled blindly. Finally, necessity forced her to slow. The only sounds, other than her wheezing breath, were her footfalls. Yet she knew he was searching for her.

Screened by the trees, the sun provided only dim, filtered light. Shadows patterned the ground. Anticipating the dangerous pitfalls that seemed everywhere about, she kept her gaze lowered.

Then, suddenly, a man stepped directly into her path.

Chapter 4

R IVE PULLED HER TO HIM AND held her in a crushing embrace. Her heart beat with a fierce rhythm and pounded against his chest. Time passed, a minute, possibly two, and he made not the slightest effort to release her. For all he cared, time could have stopped altogether. Embers that had lain long dormant flared to life, and a surge of heat pulsed through his body. Her eyes registered genuine shock, but not even his concession she was well-bred could persuade him to let her go.

Her pale hair tumbled about her shoulders, and he allowed himself the lightest touch. It lay as gossamer as a web against his palm. A tiny twig had lodged in a tress curled above her ear, and he plucked it out with utmost care. Then his fingers glided to the soft, moist, flesh at her nape. She gasped and her breathing quickened—after all, the merest touch from him no doubt rekindled her fear. Her skin reminded him of the smoothest satin and to explore it further would give him the greatest pleasure. His gaze fell to her perfectly formed breasts and slim, uncorseted waist. As to her legs, he made up his mind that one day soon he would judge their perfection for himself.

He threaded the fingers of one hand through her hair and let them glide along her scalp before lightly cupping her head. She shivered, but he guessed not from the coolness of the forest. Certainly not in ecstasy from his touch.

What if his touch had moved her? That would add a devilish complication to an already risky plan.

Tiny beads of moisture formed a delicate sheen on her forehead, and he used the back of his hand to gently brush them away. Her cheeks, still flushed from her impulsive dash through the woods, invited touching as well. Her lips, full and ripe, remained parted as she fought to catch her breath. They offered, if not an invitation, then surely a temptation any man in full possession of his senses would find impossible to resist.

Yet he forced himself to call upon restraint—not out of nobility, but necessity. To continue meant not only provoking her wrath but also threatening her virtue, for she was bringing him to the brink of arousal again. Unless he intended to bed the lady here and now, it became circumspect to put at least some distance between them.

He pressed his hands to the small of her back, which allowed him to keep her in his arms. Her courage astounded him. Her beauty sent a torrent of heat tearing through him. Her recklessness made him want to turn her over his knee and give her a good old-fashioned drubbing.

A SHIVER RIPPLED THOUGH CATHERINE'S BODY, a shiver having naught to do with the lack of sunlight or the cool, damp air. She had responded to *him*, and she could no longer deny it. It had something to do with the tilt of his mouth when he smiled and everything to do with his touch, now so surprisingly light, considering that he must be furious with her. When he threaded those long, sculpted fingers through her hair, her scalp prickled with the most delicious sensations. She wondered when he would stop, was afraid to contemplate *where* he would stop. It took all her willpower to smother the moan that was forming dangerously in her throat. She could still feel his body imprinted against every part of hers.

It also took a considerable dose of common sense, combined with a stout mental kick to the posterior, to gather her defenses. Admittedly, he treated her with some respect. He touched her, but in a far less intimate way than he might have done, and had been generous in sharing his breakfast. Still, she was loath to think of his actions as gallant. She had no guarantee he would continue playing the role of a gentleman if they were to spend many more days and nights together. Her body's betrayal frightened her, and she resolved to give him no cause to abandon all decency.

After what seemed an eternity, he said, "Don't ever do that again. There are dangers about far greater than any you will ever suffer from me."

She pushed against his chest with her arms. "I cannot breathe."

He tipped her face up and gazed into her eyes. "I cannot trust you. So, Catherine, it seems I had better keep you close."

He lifted her into his arms and carried her to the stream, setting her on her feet at the water's edge. A flock of wild geese flew overhead in a V formation. On the opposite bank, a doe and her fawn stepped out of the trees and approached the stream. Rive placed a finger against his lips, and together they watched the animals drink.

Having experienced such an idyllic scene only in books, Catherine stared, enthralled. The doe raised her head and stood perfectly still for a moment before she turned and bolted for cover, followed closely by the fawn.

Rive slipped free the lace ruffle Catherine had tucked into her bodice, dipped it in the water and dabbed at the tiny cuts on her arms and hands. Throughout his ministrations, she stood as still as one of the surrounding trees. Spent from her flight and desperately in need of refreshing, she let him cleanse her wounds. While he did, she deepened her resolve to allow nothing he said or did to affect her in *that* way.

The task completed, he led her to where he left his horse, saddled and ready to ride.

"Madame's transport awaits." Then he lifted her onto the horse's back, gathered the reins and bounded up behind her. Looping one arm about her waist, he murmured against her ear, "Yes, from now on, I intend to keep you very close indeed."

Chapter 5

Catherine pulled the leather slipper from her foot. An examination of the sole confirmed her suspicion. It had finally torn loose. With an exclamation of disgust, she pitched the useless footwear, along with its mate, into the nearest bush. Rive had encouraged her to walk beside him for an hour each morning and afternoon to stretch her legs, and she gladly acquiesced. Hence, the punishment to her shoes. Days earlier, she had abandoned her near-shredded stockings, and some of the stitches in her hem had unraveled. Her dress was soiled with dirt and sweat.

"You will have to ride from now on." Creating a stirrup with his hands, he boosted her up onto the horse's back.

Time seemed to pass in an endless cycle, but she kept careful track. During their five days of travel, she'd had only a few moments of privacy. The second morning following her abduction, before they broke camp near one of the many sparkling lakes in the region, he suggested she strip off her clothes and bathe. Her look might have shrunken another man down to the size of a withered shrub. His only reaction was a shrug. But later, as if recognizing the imprudence of his suggestion, he hung a blanket from the lowest branch of a tree near the lakeshore.

"This is the stoutest barrier I can provide. Have your bath. I shall respect your privacy. You have my word." He turned toward where the fish he caught earlier lay on the grass and proceeded to build a fire.

Desperate to cleanse and soothe her body, she decided to trust him. Backing away, she slipped behind the blanket. With her gaze fixed on the slender barrier lest he have second thoughts, she quickly shed her clothes. Making further haste, she waded into the lake, shivering as the first jolt of icy water lapped against her legs. When immersed up to her hips, she sunk down and turned her face toward the waning sun. Modesty, perforce, fell to a low rank in her list of priorities.

Each night she slept wrapped in the blanket. Rive lay beside her, his wrist bound to hers. Once, having awakened, she discovered he had slipped the knot and was headed to the lake. As he pulled off his clothes, her mouth opened in shock, but she could not prevent herself from staring at him. His shoulders and back showed well-defined muscles; his waist tapered above buttocks and hips so taut it seemed his body contained not a spare ounce of flesh. Did he not possess the longest legs in the universe? A full moon lit the night sky. Bathed in its incandescent glow, his skin took on an ever-deeper tone. He appeared more like a figure cast in bronze than a mere mortal.

The sight caused her breath to catch. Apparently, he also possessed acute hearing. Before plunging into the lake, he called, "Go back to sleep, Catherine, or come and join me."

She did neither. Burrowing deeper under the blanket, she lay awake for the better part of the night, wondering if her heart would stop its wild beating before it completely gave out.

Now, sitting astride the horse and rocking gently to its gait, she examined her fingers, stained purple from wild blueberries. They had picked them the previous day in order to supplement their diet of fish and small game. Would the stain, another visual reminder of her unkempt state, ever fade? Would she ever again sit down and eat a meal without using her fingers or perform her toilette in front of a mirror rather than behind a blanket or a bush? None of this seemed to bother Rive, and she no longer wasted her breath complaining.

More important topics occupied her mind, the most vital being their destination. She was as ignorant now as when they began their journey. So far her attempts to wring even the smallest scrap of information from him had gone unrewarded. Her repetitious questions irritated him, or so he claimed. His most effective strategy in silencing her was to place a finger against her lips. Too often, it strayed to the warm, moist flesh within.

A wave of heat would build slowly inside her and her skin would prickle from her toes to her scalp. To her dismay, her nipples would peak, and the only way to stop this wanton reaction was to bat his hand away and excoriate him for being such a scoundrel.

She turned her face to the sun. It splashed through a break in the trees and onto the path they followed. Every part of her exposed flesh had turned a light brown. Was it just a few short days ago her skin had been as pale as milk? Surprisingly, her new sun-tinged hue did not discomfit her. The sight would have shocked her parents.

As her thoughts strayed to them, tears misted her eyes. How she longed to see her parents again, to sit in their tiny drawing room and read aloud to her father or even perform some needed task to ease her mother's day. From her mother, she had inherited the virtue of good common sense, which helped immeasurably as the family finances dwindled. Never profligate, she learned to become downright thrifty. Nothing went to waste. She found uses for every bit of fabric and devised ways to make even the meanest scrap of meat palatable. She had become expert at bargaining in shops.

From her father, she had inherited her love of books and music. For her seventh birthday, he had bought her a pianoforte and engaged a teacher, who came to the house twice weekly. Her father loved to hear her play, and she had enjoyed giving little impromptu concerts.

Now, thinking of her parents and the danger her abduction had placed them in emboldened her to seek some nugget of information from Rive. She was dulled to consequences. "If you won't give a reason for this unforgivable act, at least tell me where it will end. It costs you nothing."

He continued expertly guiding the horse around thickets whose dense and thorny spikes reached out like talons to pluck at Catherine's dress.

Her gaze settled on his broad back, slim hips, and elegant swagger. Minutes elapsed and it became evident he wished to ignore her query.

"Why must you be so secretive?" His silence only made her press further. "Are you afraid you will prove yourself a worse villain?"

Finally he broke stride. When he turned to look up at her, the hard set of his jaw and the expression in his eyes bespoke his irritation. She blinked against the sun but otherwise kept her gaze steady. She wished he would put aside his annoyance and understand that she needed him to ease her fear and uncertainty. He muttered under his breath, a small exasperated sound. Then he climbed up into the saddle behind her.

"You seem anxious to complete our journey. Only, be warned that it might not end to your liking, and that you will have just cause to regret the day you married Flint."

They sat so close that her body seemed to melt into his, where it met the broad sweep of his chest and abdomen. His arm encircled her waist; his fingers rested on her hip.

She pounded his thigh with her fist. "I won't put up with your insults."

"You will put up with a lot more before I free you. In the meantime, exercise care lest your sharp tongue tempt a man to take you for something less than the genteel lady you claim to be."

"I claim nothing except my right to freedom."

The hand that had clasped her hip now found its way to the underside of her chin. He tipped her head back, and his lips brushed her ear.

"No."

She bristled under his forceful tone and knew he wished to end the discussion.

"How can you be so unfeeling?" She turned her head and glanced up at him. "Do you respect no human life?"

"That is a question best put to your husband when next you see him."

"Why won't you answer a civil question?"

He shrugged. "Perhaps one, if it is asked with a civil tongue."

She waited for her anger to subside. "Where are you taking me?" Although it rankled, in compliance with his terms, she injected her tone with what she considered deference. "It is a simple question and deserves an honest answer."

Rive clasped her around the waist again and spurred his horse into a trot. "We continue north to where I lived for two years as a boy."

His vague reference left her as confused as ever. "Are you speaking of Canada?"

A quizzical expression crossed his face. "What makes you ask that?"

"You are French, or so you say. New France lies in the direction you stated." Perhaps the war over Canada sat at the root of his hatred for Jeremy Flint. As a British subject, Flint might at one time have been pressed into service for the Crown. In years past, the two might have met at any number of battles. Yet she was reasonably certain their initial encounter harkened back to when Rive was a boy.

She was about to pose a question to that effect when the horse stopped. A moment later, Rive slipped to the ground. He cocked his head as if listening for some far-off sound.

Alert to the possibility of danger, Catherine listened as well. A reassuring stillness lay in the air, broken only by a soft, rhythmic trill not unlike some arrogant bird caught up in the ecstasy of a mating call. She searched the trees but could find no sign of one. Then Rive placed his hand beside his mouth and repeated an exact imitation of the sound.

Puzzled and amused, she grinned at his silly antics, which were so completely out of character. Indeed, his call was so realistic she almost expected him to take flight. The image made her laugh. About to comment, she stopped when a man appeared in her line of vision.

Except for a square of animal hide that barely covered the area below his waist and a pair of moccasins, he was naked. A good deal of his scalp was totally devoid of hair. What did remain hung braided and adorned with a spray of feathers. Tall and muscular, he was even more deeply bronzed than Rive's. At first sight of him, she felt herself blush. That soon gave way to fear as the Indian—she assumed that was his ancestry—approached. He carried a musket slung through the crook of his arm. After studying her for a moment, he addressed Rive.

They spoke neither French nor English, but in what had to be the savage's tongue. Whatever they discussed, the bold way the Indian stared at her made her reasonably certain she was the main topic of their conversation.

Terror, more intense than anything she had experienced so far, sent blood pumping wildly into her head. She had read that the North American Indians sometimes made it a practice of selling captive women taken in raids on colonial settlements, or, even worse, keeping them. Unable to tear her eyes away from the two men, she was now convinced they were bartering for her. A chill swept through her body.

When the brief exchange ended, the Indian slipped away into the forest as suddenly as he had appeared. Although his leave-taking brought Catherine some relief, it did not totally calm her anxiety.

Rive gathered the reins, and they continued on in silence, dashing her hopes of an explanation. Although suspecting this was a chance encounter, she was almost certain Rive knew the Indian. Eventually, her curiosity replaced her fear.

"What did he want?" she ventured.

Rive glanced up at her. "Nothing. Or did you think he wanted you?"

"It crossed my mind."

"Well, he didn't."

His tone suggested he spoke the truth, but believing him was akin to trusting him. If she had learned one lesson, it was to guard against the danger trust might pose. She shook her head as if to chase away dark thoughts. "Since he wanted nothing, what did you say to him?"

He heaved a weary sigh. "I told him he could have you anyway, as you are a scold and a nuisance whose penchant for questions could turn a sober man to drink."

"I hate you."

He smiled. "I would never have guessed it. However, there will be time, in the long nights ahead, for you to change your mind."

Chapter 6

They reached an Indian village just before sunset. The sky was streaked with orange and red, and the waning sun cast a fiery glow on the surface of a nearby river. Catherine's first fleeting impression was of dome-roofed huts covered with tree bark and arranged haphazardly in a clearing. Canoes lined the riverbank, fish and spitted meats roasted over cooking fires, green melons grew in clusters among vines. Dogs ran loose. The natives themselves—expressions dour, eyes continually focused on her—were cause for some anxiety. Rive may have brought her here intentionally, but that did not mean these people welcomed her. Perhaps this was the tribe of the savage they had met along the trail. She hoped their stay would be brief.

There were perhaps sixty men, maybe half as many women and children, each one as brown as the Indian she had encountered in the forest. Some men wore odd-looking trousers made of animal hide, with a deerskin strip sewn front and back. Others sported only the scanty attire that had shocked her earlier. The smaller children, though completely naked, were utterly without shame. Upon studying the women, Catherine understood why.

Buckskin draped their hips, leaving their legs exposed to the knee. Some wore loose-fitting garments of the same hide above the waist, others homespun shirts. A few sported only strands of beads or feathered ornaments. These offered little in the way of concealment. Instinctively, Catherine's hands flew to her bodice, as though to reassure herself that her own modesty was preserved.

As she and Rive progressed slowly into the heart of the village, the natives followed in a loosely knit half-circle. They spoke little and then only in hushed tones. Although their language was indecipherable, the looks directed at her confirmed Catherine's suspicion: they spoke of her.

The procession halted before one of the huts. The deerskin flap that covered the doorway was thrown back, and a man emerged. He was well advanced in age, judging from the deep creases in his sun-scorched face. However, when he straightened, he stood as erect as the youngest man. He wore what seemed to be the traditional garb of buckskin trousers. Gray strands threaded his black hair, worn in two braids and adorned with a trio of black and white feathers. Necklaces of what looked like stone beads draped his bare chest. Like his arms, his chest bore many healed scars. A beaded strand, ending in a metal disk, hung suspended from each ear. Catherine stared at him, transfixed.

He extended an arm, which Rive stepped forward to clasp. The old man smiled, pleased at the sight of his visitor. Catherine could think of nothing to explain the relationship between the two. They began to speak in the same strange tongue she had heard earlier, unintelligible except for one word that raised goose bumps on the back of her neck: Flint.

The old man's attention shifted to her. She could read nothing in his expression, neither welcome nor distaste. Then Rive lifted her down from the horse.

Questions rose to her lips, but she remained silent. Apparently, Rive was acquainted with these natives, and they knew about her husband. Perhaps, whatever once brought them together had happened right here. Something deadly and demanding restitution, judging from Rive's hatred of Jeremy Flint. She could not deny Flint's cruelty.

She remembered the night of her abduction. Rive had reminded Flint he would know where to find him. Had he referred to this village? If so, was this the end of their journey?

Finally, Rive turned to her. "Go with the women. They will take you to a lodge."

Before she could ask the purpose, she was immediately surrounded. Ignorant of what lay ahead, she felt a wave of apprehension. She had no friends here. The one man who could have allayed her fears had turned his back and walked away.

Resigned, she followed the women. Several, tentatively at first then more boldly, reached out to touch her arms, gown, and hair, chattering away in their own language. Whatever the gist, it inspired nods from the older women and fits of giggling from the younger ones.

At the entrance to the lodge, most of the women fell back. A half dozen of the elders remained in charge. Catherine stumbled through the low doorway, followed closely by her escort. Only a weak shaft of light spilled from a small opening in the roof, making it quite dim inside. Before she had an opportunity to study her surroundings, a gentle push urged her farther into the interior.

"Please." She held up her hands, palms outward. "If I may just rest alone for a moment …." She hoped, on the odd chance, one amongst them understood some English. "I'm really quite exhausted."

Her protests were greeted by short bursts of laughter. Perhaps they found something amusing in the situation. She might take their good spirits as an encouraging sign if she wished to stretch her imagination. However, her distress made that impossible.

While three women held her firmly, two others began to remove her gown and shift. There seemed no point in resisting—her clothing had already suffered enough abuse—and she thought the wisest course was to ensure her garments survived in one piece. As she stood naked, she could read the looks of disapproval in the women's eyes. Compared to their ripe figures, her slim frame must have appeared woefully undernourished.

Another woman entered with a deep clay bowl, its rim etched with simple animal designs. Catherine had no need for instruction. Cupping her hands, she splashed the cool water it contained over her body. Gradually the liquid sluiced down her arms and torso, and some of her tiredness dissipated. While it was the most primitive bath she had ever experienced, it was also one of the most welcome. No further amenities followed, only the warm air to dry her.

During this bathing ritual, a short, thickset woman gathered her hair. Another produced a sharp instrument resembling a comb and pulled it through the knots. Each yank made Catherine's eyes water and her scalp tingle from the unaccustomed harshness. Still, it was worth suffering their ministrations just to feel refreshed again.

As they worked, no one spoke. Then another woman entered the lodge. She carried a small bundle of clothing like that worn by the natives. She draped a garment of pale doeskin around Catherine's hips. Three rows of red and black beads weighted the hem, but it left a vast expanse of leg exposed. Catherine's cry of dismay was quickly silenced with an admonishing wag of a finger.

Resigned, she stood silently, while another garment, as soft and pale as the first, was slipped over her head. There were no sleeves, and the beaded hem stopped several inches above her waist. She felt a hot flush suffuse her face. Was she not to wear her own clothing? Surely, no one expected her to show herself before the others dressed in this fashion. She looked about for her gown, but it was nowhere in sight. It seemed hopeless trying to explain "modesty" to these women. Hopefully, while she remained in this village, she would be kept in this lodge and away from the inhabitants.

Finally, three necklaces—each strung with smooth, highly-polished cream and black stones interspersed with downy white feathers—were draped about her neck. The women stepped back, nodding and whispering as they surveyed their work.

Catherine kept her arms pressed to her sides and endured their inspection. Their expressions were difficult to read. Their eyes offered none of the warmth of friendship, their lips a mere glimmer of satisfaction. She wondered why they cared at all. Before long the answer presented itself. The deerskin flap covering the doorway was brushed aside, and Rive slipped silently into the lodge. He was greeted with squeals of delight.

A sudden thought made Catherine almost leap out of their circle. The ritual had brought them pleasure because they had not done it for her, but to please him.

With a few whispered words, he shooed the women from the lodge, then slowly approached, a shadow vision, nearly naked except for the abbreviated strip of deerskin that covered his loins.

Catherine swallowed against the hard knot in her throat. An amber flame swayed in the clay bowl he held, sending shadows leaping across the walls and down the hard, muscular expanse of his bare chest. His eyes, vivid green shafts of color, impaled her, lingering on the soft, rounded curves barely concealed by her scanty garments.

She could not tear her eyes away. For days she had ridden with him, their bodies pressed so close she thought she knew every angle of his. At night they had slept side by side. With their wrists tethered, the slightest movement often brought his hand brushing against hers. They had eaten together and shared embarrassingly intimate moments. Each line and plane of his devilishly handsome face was committed to memory, and yet, none of these now seemed familiar. New images were transposed over old ones, redefining and reshaping what she had only thought she knew. She waited for him to speak, to break the silence that filled the air.

For the moment he seemed content just to stare. The slight upward curve of his lips told her what he saw brought him pleasure. She pulled at the doeskin skirt in a vain effort to extend its length.

"Don't cover yourself." His words were as familiar as a lover's. "You are even more beautiful dressed this way."

Still, Catherine's fingers clutched at the skirt. Managing to pull her gaze from Rive's, she dropped her eyes to the flame that licked at the edges of the bowl. Then, finally, she found her voice. "You are a scoundrel and a knave."

"You have a charming way with an insult." He placed the bowl on the floor. "Although 'knave' is a bit archaic, don't you think?"

"Perhaps 'savage' suits you better."

If he craved something more in keeping with their surroundings, she would gladly provide it.

He nodded, and his features softened in the flickering amber light. "Ah, yes, that, too."

Confusion and a new wariness guided Catherine's next words. "Are you one of them?"

"By birth, no, but in spirit, always. These people saved my life once and gave me a home and hospitality for two years. They are a proud people, and if that were the case, I would feel no shame in admitting a common ancestry with them."

She wished desperately for him to shed more light on his past, give her a reason for the blood feud between himself and Jeremy Flint.

"Does your association with my husband stem back to the time you just mentioned?"

"Let us not speak of the past tonight." With the lightest touch of his fingers, he traced a path that started at her shoulders and ended in the palms of her hands.

Heat suffused Catherine's skin. The flickering light that enveloped them in dusky shadows did nothing to blunt her awareness of his near-nakedness. Nor did it still the pulse beating in a wild, steady rhythm in her throat. His lips mocked her with their closeness, and his warm breath fanned her face, waking her to the heated promise of his manhood.

THROUGH THE OPENING IN THE LODGE roof, the night sky shone with a million stars. All Rive's life, the constellations had intrigued him. Tonight he barely noticed them. Instead, he watched the play of light on her flesh. It caressed her cheeks, sun-darkened from a warm peach to a rich, glowing brown. Then his gaze slid over her slender arms and—as he had suspected—the pleasing curves of the shapely legs that unsteadily supported the whole fragile structure. Her eyes were large with fear, and her chin—jutting forward at a defiant angle—trembled with it. Yet she stood her ground. She had armed herself behind a brave front, he guessed, and it took every ounce of her will. She was truly beguiling.

He drew her to him, and the contact of her breasts, hips, and slender thighs against his flesh wreaked havoc on his heart. Her hair fell in thick, golden waves. He captured a handful and brought it to his lips. Then his mouth continued its exploration—first the pulse that beat in her throat like a fluttering leaf, then the indentation just visible above the doeskin draping her breasts. He felt no compulsion to hurry, not even when his tongue left a moist trail along the column of her neck, and the tiniest taste of salt clinging to the dewy moisture of her skin inflamed his senses.

For a long moment, he held her against him. Then, slowly, he began to savor the velvet-soft flesh hidden beneath the tunic draping her back. With a delicate touch, he followed the line of fragile bones, teasing, stroking, as if coaxing a sweet tune from the finest instrument. His senses, greedy for the touch and taste and scent of her, led his body down a path as familiar to him as it certainly was alien to her. She aroused him to the brink of torture.

"Come." He swept her into his arms as if she weighed no more that a goose-down pillow. In the back of the lodge, beyond where the opening in the roof ushered in cooling night breezes, a mound of furs lay strewn on a low wooden platform. He carried her to the bed, laid her down, and knelt beside her.

"Now I will teach you to be a woman."

Chapter 7

✧

Catherine luxuriated in the embracing warmth of the pelts. Rive lay at her side, propped on one elbow. Despite her innocence, she was not ignorant of a man's desire. She knew Rive wanted her, indeed meant to *have* her. He bent lower, fingered the necklaces draped across her breasts and slowly removed them. One barrier gone. His hand brushed the hem of her skirt, which had crept above her knees. She shook her head so violently the ends of her hair whipped against his face and throat. It seemed to have no adverse effect on him, but at least it roused her from her near dreamlike state.

"Why do you hate me? I have done nothing to warrant it. You say your quarrel is with my husband …."

He pressed a finger gently to her lips. "Husband? No, I think not. He bears the title in name only and not in deed. That, Catherine, is something I have every right to reserve for myself."

He bent closer, his face only inches from hers. With one hand he traced the curve of her cheek; his other hand became lost in the spill of hair swept back from her brow. Heat blossomed where his thumb skimmed lightly along her chin. Her skin prickled and tingled, and his touch sent the blood rushing in a torrent to her head. His lips brushed the corner of her mouth, and his tongue teased the line drawn tight against his unhurried assault. Then he slowly parted her lips.

She gasped and was immediately silenced by his mouth. His hands took command of her body. A leisurely descent from the nape of her neck and down her bare arms tortured her flesh. He hooked a thumb under the hem of her tunic and lifted it slowly. His mouth left hers to explore the newly uncovered flesh, then moved higher until the tip of his tongue found the underside of each breast. Sensations—unfamiliar and never before contemplated—invaded her body. She felt herself beginning to respond as if something unfathomable inside her craved the things he was doing to her, as if the blood pounding against her temples in an insane and uncontrolled rhythm didn't matter.

"No!"

How to mobilize her forces? How to meet each thrust and parry of his tongue, to counter the exquisite sensation that swept through her as his palm massaged first one nipple, then the other, leaving them stiff and engorged? How to stop this madness? She knew it would cost her very soul to tempt the devil into saving her from a most certain fate. Rive had come to her as a lover, his desire evident. Never would she willingly offer her body to him. Nor would she give the devil his due tonight. If she must lose her virtue to a savage who dared call himself a saint, then she vowed to see it done without bargaining or detestable fits of weeping.

"Yes!"

He swept aside the tunic, fully exposing her breasts to his view.

"Let me go. I cannot breathe!" She struck at his arms. Her blows glanced off his body, accomplishing nothing. They did at least bolster the charade that she was capable of putting up a spirited defense.

"If you can talk, my sweet, then you can breathe." He looked into her eyes. "You have a vexing tendency to talk too much."

She stole a fleeting glance at his face then dropped her gaze, shutting out the heated passion in his deep-set emerald eyes. The flame still burned in the clay bowl and cast a muted glow. Flickering shadows danced against the rough walls of the lodge like hazy figures in a dream.

"Look at me, Catherine. Let me see your eyes."

She pressed her lids closed, ignored his command. Even so, his face, the individual features of which came together to form a perfect whole, seemed impressed indelibly in her mind. That such a face must have had an extraordinary effect on women—and was she not to be counted in their number?—was not difficult to imagine. She bit her lower lip, angry at herself for responding to him.

"You look as if you are about to be tortured, but I assure you that is not my intent."

"Then your definition is contrary to mine. We share no common opinions."

He caught her lower lip and teased it lightly with his mouth. Then he drew back. "Shall we put it to the test and see? Time, I suspect, will prove you wrong."

"What we shall see," she muttered through clenched teeth, "is how long it will take you to die at the end of a rope."

"That again?" He gave a low laugh, as if her barbs delighted him. "You have threatened me so often with the noose, it has lost all meaning. I promise, the torment you are imagining can be of a most sweet nature."

Before she could distract him with words, he silenced her by capturing her lips with his and leisurely exploring her mouth with his tongue. She made a gallant attempt to strain away from him, but he cradled the back of her head with his strong hand and held her that much closer.

Twisting beneath him, she tried to break the deepening kiss, to escape the slow movement of his palm as it curved about her breast. Her lungs filled with air, and for the life of her, she could not seem to expel it, or to reconcile the insidious thrill that swept through her body. The more he touched her, the more the sensation built and intensified. Once again, she felt an exquisite heat between her legs. This, then, was what urged a woman to seek a man's bed, for to experience such a feeling and find no release would be torture indeed.

She shivered, in part from the awareness that he could turn her body against her, but more from what he was doing with his hand. It had moved from her breast to the inside of her thigh, where the deerskin covering offered so little protection.

"Please, don't." Drawing from somewhere deep within, she made one final effort to harness her wayward emotions.

Her body stiffened, and with hands that were anything but steady, she pushed hard against his chest and eased as far from him as the circle of his arms allowed.

◆

HE GAZED DEEPLY INTO HER EYES. His hands now moved in slow seduction up along her sides, over delicate ribs, his thumbs furrowing her skin grown hot and moist to his touch. He stopped only to cup her high, firm breasts. Her body reminded him of a slender reed, yet she was very much a woman as evidenced by her instinctive response to his lovemaking. When she moved, he pulled her against him and molded her body's soft contours to the strong, angular planes of his.

Now, more than ever, he sought acquiescence from her. Yet, to his great disappointment, he found none. A measure of fear, yes, but more so, a steely determination to resist him. Perhaps he had been a fool to expect otherwise. She was chaste, he was certain, but passionate. He had discovered that with his lover's tricks. He suspected, too, that if he were to ignore her plea, her body would eventually yield. Not her heart. There would be no affection in her coupling with him, and very soon thereafter she would come to hate him. Her disdain, more than anything, he did not wish.

He pulled away from her and sat up. With legs bent and elbows resting on his knees, he raked his fingers through his hair. It took some minutes, but finally his breathing eased, and some of the tension left his body. Only then did he turn to her and plant a brief, chaste kiss upon her brow. With a sigh, he moved away and gained his feet.

"Ah, these hollow victories." He gazed down at her. With a weary smile, he went to the doorway and pushed aside the deerskin flap.

He stepped outside to a night sky that blazed with stars. One streaked across the heavens in a white-hot arc only to burn itself out a moment later. The perfect metaphor for his mood.

Chapter 8

Catherine awoke to sunlight spilling through the opening in the lodge roof. Sounds reached her from outside—a woman's laugh, children's excited yells, a dog's bark. The air smelled of smoke and the aroma of cooking meat. Last night, in spite of the luxurious comfort of her bed, she had lain awake for what seemed hours and then only managed to fall into a fitful sleep. Rive had not returned, and mercifully, she passed the night alone. Now, the warmth of the air suggested it must be well past dawn. She sat up and took stock of her surroundings.

Besides the bed, the conical-shaped room held few furnishings. Several woven baskets of varying sizes and shapes hugged one wall. A crude table, little bigger than a footstool, supported a handful of stacked wooden bowls and a long-stemmed pipe. A deerskin pouch rested against one leg of the table. The mats mostly covering the hard-packed dirt floor appeared woven from sturdy grass; interspersed with those were several fur pelts like the ones on which she lay. Leather strips, intricately patterned with black, white, and red beads, hung against the wall, along with half a dozen carved wooden masks of fierce countenance.

It was all quite primitive and unsettling. Her studies had made her aware that many natives roamed Colonial America. She had been curious as to what extent their lives and customs had been disrupted by the steady flow of Europeans who now lived in towns, cities, and farms that encroached upon their lands. Certainly, the natives bore the colonists some resentment. So far, the people of this village had treated her with no disrespect. Apparently they knew her recent history and shared Rive's view on the subject of Jeremy Flint.

Even a fleeting thought of Flint was enough to ignite her anger. Because of his deceit, she had been abducted and almost bedded. Heat burned in her face at the memory of it. Nothing short of Divine Providence must have intervened to sway Rive from taking what he so bluntly declared as his right. She was the prisoner of a man who possessed the power to do as he wished with her. Yet he had left her with her virtue intact. But that was last night; this morning he might already have regretted his decision.

Such a disturbing thought hastened her from the bed. The grass mats beneath her feet brought a welcome coolness, and on one of these she found a neatly folded garment and a pair of deerskin slippers. The garment was a homespun shirt, apparently clean and of a not too expansive size. Obviously it had been placed there for her use, which puzzled her. The abbreviated tunic she wore might certainly have been considered adequate, since some of the Indian women wore little above the waist.

She slipped out of the tunic and quickly donned the shirt. After tucking it under her skirt, she pulled it down until it extended past her knees. Its purpose, she guessed, was to act like a shift. The sleeves' ragged edges reached just below her elbows. Someone had made concessions to her modesty, but not the women who dressed her the night before. That left only one person—Rive.

She sighed. In spite of her education, which fed her inquisitive mind and provided at least a rudimentary understanding of the world, she did not possess the tools necessary to understand *him*. Last week he had cold-bloodedly planned her abduction; then, with no one to stay him, he could have ravaged her with the same callous disregard. *Yet he had not. Why*?

The answer was as complex as the man. This morning she felt no inclination to unravel the mystery.

Instead, she continued dressing, stepping into the slippers, which fit well enough, grateful to have something to protect her feet. Further investigation turned up a wooden bucket filled with fresh water and a primitive comb such as the one the women had used on her hair. She settled on a mat and washed her hands and face, relishing the coolness of the water. The comb worked surprisingly well, and she pulled it through her hair until her scalp tingled.

She supposed she should thank Rive for the clothing. When he chose, he could be very considerate. He had proved it often during the time they had spent together in the forest. He kept her well fed each day and as comfortable as possible at night. She had happily accepted the makeshift bed he always made for her. He respected her privacy when she performed her simple toilette, and there were times when she had almost forgotten his treachery.

Then there was last night ….

"Madame?"

The voice calling from just outside the doorway brought Catherine to her feet. It was a man's voice, familiar, but not Rive's.

"Who is it?"

"Louis Villet. I have brought you something to eat." There was a pause. "May I enter?"

Louis. Rive's friend and accomplice, the man who had pled her cause that first night. Had he wondered if Rive had taken his words of caution to heart? Surely he knew his friend well enough to recognize he sought no counsel other than his own. Hence, Louis might naturally assume she had spent the night in Rive's bed. What could she say to dispel the notion without adding doubly to her embarrassment? She knew she must appear like a vagabond in this odd assortment of clothing.

She could pretend she didn't hear him. However, her stomach felt as empty as a beggar's purse. She needed nourishment.

"Yes. Come in."

He looked exactly as she remembered him from the night of her abduction—compact, sturdy, and exceedingly bowlegged. His eyes bore a gentle expression.

"Rive asked me to bring you something to eat. It's simple fare—venison, blackberries, nuts, and a corn cake. I think you'll find them to your liking."

A peace offering? Was it possible Rive did actually possess a conscience? If so, could this be his way of acknowledging his guilt?

"He rode out at sunrise and did not want to disturb your rest. It is not too early for you, I hope."

"No." Catherine took the bowl of food and set it on the bed. Later she would devour it, but first she must speak with Louis. From the conversation she overheard the night of her abduction, she believed him sympathetic to her plight. She had so many questions. Perhaps he would not be as parsimonious with his answers as his friend.

Where, however, should she begin? Not having anticipated his arrival, she'd had no time to plan. He seemed ready to leave her to her breakfast.

"Have you known Rive long?" It was the first thought to spring into her mind.

"Oh, yes, since he was a boy." Louis' face split into a wide grin.

"You have great affection for him."

"But of course."

"You met in France?"

For a moment, he looked puzzled. "I have never been to France, Madame. It is here I first made his acquaintance."

Now it was Catherine's turn at puzzlement. "Here?" She sensed he meant this Indian village.

"Did you meet during the two years when he lived among these people?"

"He has spoken to you about those years?"

She could not decide if he was surprised or relieved to think Rive had confided any of his personal history to her. Clearly, if she led him to believe he had, she could more easily draw him into her confidence. Yet, she could not bring herself to trick him. Not just because he would eventually discover her deception, but because it was not in her nature to deceive. Also, she needed an ally. Louis, she hoped, would assume that role.

"He spoke of his affection for these people, who saved his life and offered him a home. He never told me of the circumstances. In truth, I know nothing of your friend. I am not even sure what kind of person he really is."

Louis smiled. "He has grown into a man of many contradictions. But he is a man of honor. Believe me, Madame. He has a keen sense of justice. He possesses a strong character."

So far, she had seen nothing of his justice. As for honor and strength of character, perhaps a ha'penny's worth at best. She replied, "Those are lofty aspirations for someone of rough colonial heritage."

This earned a laugh from Louis. "Colonial? No. The St. Clairs are not what you imagine."

Catherine seized upon this information. "Are they not? I assumed as much, since this continent is still largely untamed—"

"Yes, of course, but the St. Clairs are a very prominent family. Rive's Uncle Hubert, with whom he lived for many years in Paris, is a man of wealth and refinement, as is his Uncle André in Quebec. They are merchants and bankers. They own a fleet of ships and are very active in the fur trade."

Grateful for the information, Catherine was nonetheless even more confused. Rive was the product of a wealthy family. Was it money, then, that lay at the root of his hatred of Jeremy Flint?

"The St. Clairs are an extremely tightknit clan. They are in no way provincial. Rive does not lack sophistication. The education he received at the Sorbonne would place him on a par with any man educated at King's College in the City of New York. He has also studied at Oxford University in your country. Although it might appear otherwise, he is no stranger to social niceties. He has been to court."

Court? Catherine's jaw dropped, though she quickly recovered. Were they speaking of the same man, the one who snared rabbits and snagged fish with his bare hands?

There was a long pause. It appeared Louis had nothing further to say on the subject of the St. Clairs. He had left a gaping hole in Rive's lineage, however, and one she dearly wished to fill.

"You have not spoken of his parents. Do they also live in Paris or Quebec?"

An immediate change occurred in Louis. His whole countenance seemed to take on an air of sadness. "Unfortunately, Madame, they are no longer alive." Then almost abruptly, as if to avoid further questions, he backed toward the doorway. "I will leave you to your breakfast. I have already taken too much of your time."

"No, not at all."

It was too late. With a nod and a slight bow, Louis left her alone to ponder the enigma that was Rive St. Clair.

Chapter 9

Rive sat with his back against the granite face of a boulder, high on a ridge overlooking the village. Two long whistles followed by one short signaled his presence to the young braves stationed on the mountainside guarding the entrance to the valley. When the sun rose high overhead, he would move into the shade to eat his solitary meal of smoked fish, corn cake, and melon, all the while continuing his surveillance. No sound escaped his ears, and his eyes remained as sharp as those of the hawks that glided high above on the air currents. If any man ventured forth, he would know it. His pistol was always primed and his knife sharpened to a fine edge.

He began the day with high expectations, certain that soon his vigil would end. Then grim reality intruded. Perhaps he had misjudged Flint. Yet, had Catherine been his wife … the thought of her always reassured him, for it was inconceivable how any man could allow such a woman's abduction and make no attempt at rescue.

Shading his eyes with his hand, he scanned the valley below, and beyond that, the horizon. Except for a brown bear foraging in the shallows of the river, he could detect no movement. Silence enveloped him, broken only intermittently by the high-pitched call of geese.

Leaning back, he closed his eyes against the mid-morning sun. The warmth that seeped into his sore muscles rejuvenated him. His mind, however, remained in turmoil. Since rising before dawn, he found his thoughts continuously returning to the woman he had carried to bed less than twenty-four hours earlier. He had intended to bend her to his will, to ignite her passion, and to make a mockery of a marriage in which he had taken no part.

He shook his head. He might just as well have tried to capture the moon and lay it at her feet. Last night he had fought a battle with his desires and chivalry had prevailed. He had spent the better part of the night pacing along the riverbank, debating whether his decision to acquiesce to her wishes had been wise or foolish. At least when he slipped into her lodge at dawn to leave the clothing, he had found her asleep, seemingly at peace.

Opening his eyes, he resumed his lonely vigil, searching the valley for signs of Flint. Almost at once, he heard movement and was certain someone approached. He pulled his pistol from his belt and crouched low in the shadow of the rock where he could not be observed. Only it was not Flint who came into view, but Louis. Stepping into the open, Rive signaled to his friend, then settled back into his earlier position.

Louis scaled the slope and hunkered down in a patch of shade. "It has been quiet?"

"As I expected, Flint has probably used the time to muster help. Perhaps he will make his way here tomorrow. Or the next day or the one thereafter. Eventually he will come for her."

"You seem certain."

Rive kicked lightly at the ground with his heel, sending a shower of stones skittering down the mountainside. "What man would not?"

"Flint, perhaps? He has no scruples."

Rive shook his head. "His arrogance will not allow this to go unchallenged. He appears to have wealth and position now. Somehow, he found himself a young and very beautiful wife. No, I expect that before too long, he and I shall meet again."

He pulled a long blade of grass from the ground and twisted it between his fingers. He lowered his eyes and, once again, his thoughts spiraled back to the day he had first met Flint—just as they had a thousand times over the course of sixteen years. No detail was too small not to be recalled—the reek of gunpowder, the screams of the women and children who never found safety, the fiery torches exploding beneath the dry bark and grass that covered the lodge roofs, the crimson flames leaping against a dull pewter sky. The army scout, Flint, had led the soldiers and militia to the Indian village. How eager he had been to display his skill at extracting information from women and young girls. Especially young girls.

At the first crack of musket fire, Rive had dropped the beaver pelts he was loading into a birch bark canoe. A group of men swept by. Only through skillful dodging was he able to avoid being trampled beneath the horses' hooves. He ran toward the chief's lodge, where last he had seen his father.

"What have we got here?"

Rough hands pulled at his shirt. He lashed out with his fists but was no match for the taller man, whose close-set brown eyes exaggerated the cruelty imprinted upon his pinched, narrow face.

"Yer worth ten pounds to me, boy, dead or alive." The man, dressed in buckskin, brandished a knife. "Makes no difference to me one way or t'other how I collect it."

"You, Flint." A soldier wearing the red coat favored by the British called to the man who held Rive. He thrust a young girl forward. "See if you can get this one to talk."

The chief's granddaughter was tall and slender, with thick black hair that reached to her waist. Rive suspected she was little older than he, yet her body had ripened into that of a young woman. For four years, he had accompanied his father to this Indian village in early spring to trade for pelts. Each day, he followed the girl with his eyes, too shy to speak with her. *Next year*, he promised himself. One day, when he entered manhood, he would ask the chief's permission to make her his wife. On that day, when Flint and the soldiers came to the village, terror had turned her dark eyes to stone.

Flint thrust Rive into the arms of a soldier, who held him in a steely grip. Then he addressed the girl in her own tongue. "Where are the men?"

Her terror had rendered her mute even after Flint used her and then began to torture her with his knife.

Rive shook his head. Memory receded and now there was only the present. "He will want to finish his business with me. His pride, and perhaps, his reputation—if word of this gets about—will demand it. She is his wife."

The look that passed across Louis' face made his thoughts transparent.

"The bride's virtue is still very much intact," Rive assured his friend. "I doubt Flint had the opportunity to exercise his marriage rights."

"Which you thought to usurp for yourself, no?"

Rive shrugged, then laughed softly at his unexpected decision to play the knight.

"It seems I have abdicated all right." The decision did not rest easily with him, nor could he guarantee its finality. He could still feel the curve of her hips and the gentle swell of her breasts as vividly as when she lay against him. Even if he lived long into the century, she would forever torture his dreams.

※

As the day grew warmer, Catherine longed for fresh air. Her breakfast long since consumed, she grew increasingly restless and in need of activity. She remembered the river and its close proximity. Would anyone deny her a short walk along its bank? There was only one way to find out.

She approached the doorway. With some trepidation, but determined to end her forced imprisonment, she pushed aside the deerskin covering.

The sun's harsh glare almost blinded her. Using her hand to shield her eyes, she navigated the opening and almost collided with an Indian who stepped directly into her path.

"Oh." She took a deep breath and stared up at the young man she recognized as the one she and Rive had met along the trail the previous day. Puzzled by his presence outside the lodge, she studied his face. If her sudden appearance made any impression on him, he kept it closely guarded beneath a stern countenance.

She stepped forward, fully expecting him to unblock the way. Instead, his arm shot up, posing a hard, muscular barrier.

"You ... stay." He formed the words in halting English.

Suddenly, his purpose became clear. Rive had placed her under guard.

"It is too hot inside." She did not know if the Indian understood her or not. To make her point clear, she fanned her face with her hand. "Hot."

The guard did not move or change his expression.

"I must have air." She attempted to circle around him.

Instantly, his hand reached for her shoulder as his other one uncovered the doorway. With a shove, the Indian propelled her backward, through the opening. She landed bottom first on the hard floor.

Too stunned to move and more angry than frightened, Catherine stared at the deerskin pelt the young man had dropped back into place. Ineffective by itself, when combined with the guard who stood on the other side, it might just as well have been fashioned from the sturdiest wood. She was indeed a prisoner.

With an exasperated sigh, she stood and straightened her clothing. At least some fresh air came down through the opening in the roof. Also, she could hear birds chirping. How she envied their freedom. She paused and listened to their song. So sweet and musical, it reminded her of the day—her ninth birthday—when her father gave her a yellow canary. She awoke to find it perched in a small cage. A shaft of sunlight slanted through the window and caught the bars, turning them into a golden prison. The bird fluffed its wings as if about to take flight, but the bars stood as a silent warning. After a while, it gave up the pretense. The sight had saddened her, and she opened the small door and set the creature free to swoop about the room. This became their routine every day for the reminder of its life.

She moved into the center of the lodge. How long must she stay confined in *this* prison? Until her husband rescued her? In the early days of her abduction, she naturally thought he *would* rescue her. Now seven days had passed, filling her with doubts. Why should he risk his life? Who would blame him if he chose not to? Even now he could be sending word to his agent in

London. Then what? She felt a sudden chill as her eyes strayed to the gold band that encircled her finger.

Oh, the irony of it. To pray for rescue from a man she so despised.

She needed to push the dark thoughts from her mind. As she looked about, searching for something to distract her, her gaze settled on the deerskin pouch she had discovered earlier. She opened the flap and peered inside. The contents proved somewhat meager. They included two creased sheets of parchment, one completely blank. The other, when unfolded, displayed a neatly defined map. Someone had circled the names of two important cities in New France: Quebec and Montreal. A line traced a route from Quebec in the north through Montreal, then through the American city of Albany. It ended some distance south in New York City. There were other markings mysteriously marked with an X.

The pouch also contained a quill pen and small inkpot, along with two thin leather-bound volumes and a slightly thicker one.

She moved into the spot where the sunlight shone through the opening in the roof. The books' leather covers were worn in places, as if the owner had perused them often. One was written in French. Upon closer inspection, it appeared to be, of all things, poetry. The second proved the same. Then she opened the third, thicker volume with a strip of leather marking the place.

It was also written in French. Scanning the page, she discovered to her dismay that it was a military journal. The text was illustrated by rough sketches of cannons as well as muskets and other firearms. Notations dotted the margins on either side of the page, the script neat and concise, obviously written by a practiced hand. She suspected the pouch and its contents belonged to Rive. She recalled the skill with which he wielded a knife, so perhaps his expertise extended to a pen as well.

What need had he of such a journal? She perused the unfamiliar writing, hoping to gain insight. Perhaps the notes held further clues to his nature other than the audacious and stubborn sides he had shown. Grateful now for her tutors and the hours she had spent at her lessons, she sank onto a mat with book in hand. Although her vocabulary for this sort of material proved limited, it was not impossible to make sense of it. Time passed, and she became deeply absorbed in her reading.

Then a voice broke the spell.

"I see you have found something to occupy your time. Are you interested in the art of warfare?"

He had entered as silently as a cat, so his deep voice was the first Catherine knew of his presence. With a startled cry, she looked up from where she lay on her side, head propped against her palm. Rive, hands on his hips, stood over her. She quickly drew in her knees and sat up.

"I find my interest piqued of late, but only on a limited scale … as needed."

"Ah, last night." Stooping, he took the book from her hands. "Did you hope to sharpen your skills with this?"

She felt her cheeks burn with shame at his reference to the previous night. Would she ever dispel the memory of his touch? At least today he was dressed in the buckskin trousers and shirt he had worn on their trek. Her attire was also more modest.

"Perhaps, but it is too early to judge. I have read only the first few pages."

"Then I had best be on my guard when you reach the end." He gave a low laugh and eased himself down beside her. "You have chosen a good teacher." He indicated the tome.

She met his gaze without flinching. "I need no text to learn the finer points of treachery."

"Treachery? That is too strong a word." His eyes sparkled with unabashed delight, as if he relished nothing better than a verbal duel. "However, if I stand accused by you, then I accept my guilt."

"It doesn't bother you, then, to know you are contemptible and totally without honor?"

"Did I imply such?" He laughed. "If so, please disabuse yourself, for you have put forth a minority opinion. In all my life, I have met no man who shares it. Nor any woman."

She felt an immediate urge to quash his conceit. "Of what women do you speak? The ones who live a simple life in this village or those you consider part of your social circle when abroad? In any event, are any of those women ever allowed to express an opinion? Or do they only parrot the ones foisted upon them by their men?"

Rive's expression lost its wry amusement. "Sometimes it is to a woman's benefit to defer to the wishes of a man. You would do well to follow that example."

"That is a lesson, I fear, which serves a woman ill."

He uncurled his long frame, rose to his feet, and drew her up with him.

"Shall I take the time to teach you? You will find me quite an adept tutor."

Every muscle in Catherine's body tensed. Too late, she realized where a verbal joust with him could lead. He was not a man one could easily cajole or best with a well-turned phrase. Then why did she persist in provoking him? If only she could find satisfaction in silently berating him. She could be as stubborn and willful as he. Although he had proved a formidable opponent, it rankled her to remain passive. Since necessity had forced her to defer to one man, it left her with no appetite to defer to yet another.

"I have had cause to observe your tutorial skills, and I find them excessively lacking in subtlety. There is no lesson you can teach me that I desire to learn."

She kept her voice steady, although her hands, clasped at her sides, trembled.

He made no move to touch her, but the gaze from his emerald eyes held her as closely as if he had drawn her into his arms.

"Perhaps I can change your mind. Shall I try?"

Her heart lurched, sending the blood rushing to her head with a thunderous roar. Was there no end to his conceit?

"Shall I teach you obedience?" He rested one long finger lightly against her cheek. "Come." He glanced toward the bed. "We shall see what an hour can accomplish."

Recognizing the determination in his eyes, she had the sense to realize no words would sway him. As he reached for her hand, she bolted for the doorway.

Chapter 10

Now, with no sentry to bar her way, Catherine ran away from Rive, heedless of her direction. There were few people about, only children playing a game of tag and a small group of women tending to the corn in the vegetable garden. They went about their work, perhaps having already lost interest in her. She looked over her shoulder and saw Rive standing outside the lodge, slowly shaking his head.

Her flight took her directly to the river, which put her in a less than enviable position. Caught between a wide expanse of water and Rive, she was momentarily nonplussed as to which held more danger. However, it was too late to change course.

Flat ground gave way to a gentle slope. Midway, concentrating less on the terrain than on her pursuer, she tripped and lost her balance. Momentum carried her down the knoll, where she lost her footing. Breathless, she landed on her hands and knees. The thick grass cushioned her fall, but small stones scraped her outstretched palms and exposed knees.

She sat on the downward edge of the slope, collecting her breath. The sky formed a deep-blue canopy, and the river sparkled under the fiery glow of the sun. A light breeze brushed her skin. The scene was idyllic, and might have remained so, had she not spotted Rive easily negotiating the same ground where she had almost broken her neck. She scrambled to her feet and backed toward the water's edge. When it licked against her heels, she stopped.

"Do not come any closer."

"Catherine …." His tone held an implicit warning.

She backed away until the water rose to her ankles.

"I advise you not to venture any farther. There are dangerous currents in this river."

She knew he spoke the truth. The man whose long strides had taken him to within a few arm's lengths of her posed an even greater danger. With no weapons close at hand, she tore off one sopping-wet moccasin and threw it at him. It landed harmlessly at his feet. Her aim improved with the second one, which grazed his chest but did nothing to dissuade him. She backed away until the cold water lapped against her bare legs.

"I'd rather drown," she cried.

"Would you?" He pulled off his shirt then his moccasins and tossed them aside. "Your threat lacks conviction, but its truth is easily put to the test."

She gulped in a deep breath. Good God, was he planning to strip naked? To her relief, he kept his trousers on as he waded in.

His strong hands closed about her waist, and he carried her deeper into the water. In no time it reached his chest, and her feet no longer touched the bottom. She'd never been immersed in anything more perilous than the calm and shallow lake waters in which she had recently bathed or the rose-scented baths she had once enjoyed in London, so her fear was only natural. Not to mention that this man was unpredictable. Soon the river was lapping at her chin.

"This is lunacy." She choked on a mouthful of water.

"Isn't this what you wanted?"

Of course she'd had no intention of drowning herself, and well he knew it. Now he seemed intent on doing it for her.

"Let me go." Even as she spoke, she realized her error.

His lips parted in a wicked smile. "If you wish." Abruptly, he released her.

She sank beneath the surface, with almost no time to panic before he pulled her up.

She clutched wildly at his shoulders. "I cannot swim."

"Shall I teach you, then?" His hands glided to the small of her back, and he drew her toward him.

She shot him a withering glare.

"Take care your pride does not do you in." He lifted one hand, and with his thumb, brushed aside the wet strand of hair that clung to her cheek.

Smarting, she turned her head aside. Only the depth of the water kept her from placing a well-aimed kick. "My pride will still be intact long after you've been sent to the gallows."

"Ah, but many a man has cheated the hangman, just as many a woman has learned the virtue of humility. That, my pet, is something I am determined to teach you." Prying her hands from his shoulders, he held her at arm's length.

"Ponder such in the black depths below, and for once, take care to keep your mouth shut."

The water rose to her chin. Still, she felt little of her earlier fright. Theirs was a clash of wills, and he was not about to drown her to prove the strength of his. She was beginning to feel chilled and much in need of warmth. Still, she did not wish to grant him satisfaction. It did so irritate.

"I concede that you are stronger than I." She clasped his hands and used them to keep herself afloat. When the flimsy lifeline proved too precarious, she made a grab for his arms. They tightened around her, and she let him settle her against him again.

"Physical strength is not at issue."

She clung to him, her fingers seeking the shallow ridge between his neck and shoulders. "All the more reason you should fight fairly."

"But, *ma belle*, what has given you the idea I wanted a fight?"

As if to prove the point, he slid his hand beneath the hair at her nape. His fingers caressed her skin then slowly splayed through the wet, wild, tangle to her scalp. Cupping the back of her head, he brought his even closer, seeking the underside of her ear with his lips and brushing her skin with a kiss no woman would consider chaste.

"Please … stop." She breathed the words against his cheek, fighting the honeyed thickness that invaded her tongue.

His answer came without words, but with a prolonged exploration of her throat, where he planted a trail of kisses. He teased her mouth with his, parrying lightly, then exerting just the right amount of pressure to lure her into a response to his kiss. He parted her lips and used his tongue to plunder at will.

She melted against him, intensely aware of the outline of muscle and bone where her breasts pressed against his chest. Quite clearly, she remembered how he had felt the previous night without the layers of clothing. At least now, they formed more of a barrier between them. She tried to free her lips before her body betrayed her into enjoying the deliciously wanton sensation spreading through her scalp and down into her toes.

His thumbs glided across the slick surface of her arms. Then his hands lowered to her waist, probing, defining each indentation, before moving over the rounded swell of her hips.

Her breath caught, sounded a ragged echo against her ears. No sooner had she recovered from his devilish caress when his hands moved still lower to lift her up and tightly against him. It occurred to her that perhaps the clothing separating them was merely an illusion. He held her for a long moment before lifting her into his arms, carrying her to shore, and retracing his steps to the lodge.

It was cool inside with a breeze filtering through the roof opening. He set her down then knelt to light a fire in the open pit in the center of the room. When the flames shot up, she watched them with longing. Instead of edging closer, she stayed near the wall, hugging her arms around her shivering body.

"Come here by the fire."

"No." She wished he would leave. She didn't trust him. Even worse, she didn't trust herself.

"Don't be stubborn. I'm certainly as cold as you, so you need not fear me."

She grasped his meaning but still remained apart. Finally, with a sigh of exasperation, he took her by the arm and steered her to the fire.

He lightly fingered the deerskin that swathed her hips. "You'll warm yourself a lot faster if you remove some of your clothing." He spoke as if theirs was a close and consensual relationship.

Catherine swatted his hand.

He threw both of his up in surrender. "It was merely a suggestion made only out of concern for your comfort."

It was on the tip of her tongue to lay blame for her lack of comfort and to *suggest* he return to his lodge and warm himself by his own fire. It seemed wise to refrain, however, so as not to provoke him further. Instead she extended her hands toward the heat. When he moved closer to the flames—most likely to hasten the drying of his clothing—she did, too.

He made no further effort at conversation. The minutes passed, and she allowed herself to luxuriate in the enveloping warmth. She turned her back to the heat and wondered if, at some point, he planned to leave her alone.

Then he said, "Are you hungry?"

"Yes." Having eaten sparingly all her life, she wondered that her appetite was now so extravagant. When was she not hungry?

He left, and was gone so long, she wondered if he were preparing a feast or if he had forgotten. Then he returned with a shallow basket containing the same kinds of food she had consumed earlier in the day. He also brought an odd vessel filled with water that he described as a dried, hollowed-out vegetable called a "gourd." He also brought two similar but smaller shallow bowls. Then he placed everything on a woven mat and sat down near the heat. Without having to be coaxed, Catherine sat beside him. They ate in silence. After they finished, he poked at stray bits of wood with his fingers and brought new life to the fire.

Turning her back to him, she tucked her knees under her chin and wrapped her arms about her legs. The heat from the fire soothed her limbs, and she breathed a quiet sigh. A languorous feeling crept into her body. Satiated from the food, her energy spent, she rested her cheek against her knees and closed her eyes. She listened to the crackling of the wood and tried to pretend she was home in London, sitting before the fireplace in her father's house and shut away from the rest of the world. Drowsiness overcame her, and she gave in to it gratefully, surrendering her mind to the blissful drug of forgetfulness.

A DELICIOUS TINGLE CREPT ALONG CATHERINE'S SKIN, rousing her to a half wakeful state. For a moment, her mind groped for the source of the sensation that sent ripples of delight across her flesh. The impulse to probe was swept away by a swelling tide of intoxication. Her lips parted in a soft sigh, and she stretched lazily, arching her body, bringing it closer to this newfound source of pleasure.

Still half asleep, she tried to open her heavy lids but succeeded only in parting them a fraction. Through the web of her lashes, she watched a man's face take shape. Then, as if caught in a dream yet somehow outside it, she watched herself extend her arms to him. His lips brushed her cheek, sending a delicious shiver through her body.

Even as a distant alarm sounded in her mind, she fought to hold on to the sweetness of the dream. Slowly, her eyes opened, but reality had not yet fully intruded, and she saw she was lying in the man's arms. She felt herself slipping, down, down. Then, suddenly, she came awake.

"You," she gasped, pulling herself away from Rive. "If you touch me, I'll …."

"What?" He grinned and came to his feet. "If you threaten me with the noose again, I shall have to grow another neck to satisfy your honor."

His grin broadened into a smile. It had melted many a woman's heart, no doubt, but not hers. Never, never hers. That must become her creed. Although her body might betray her, she pledged to keep her heart steeled against his artful ways.

Perhaps her expression sounded a warning he chose to heed. He sauntered to the doorway.

"*Au revoir*, then. I shall leave you to the solitude you crave. But think upon this as you lie alone in your bed tonight. Your destiny and mine follow a common course that was plotted long before we came together on that dark country road."

Catherine, in no mood for mystical incantations, searched for something to hurl at him. Before she could lay a hand to anything, he slipped into the gathering darkness.

Chapter 11

O N THE AFTERNOON OF THE TWELFTH day of Catherine's captivity, Rive appeared at her lodge. Dressed only in what she had come to learn was a breechcloth, he settled himself cross-legged on the floor and proceeded to rub an oily mixture along the shaft of a short, stout wooden stick. One end resembled the crook of a branch. This, in turn, supported an interlaced network of leather strips attached to form an elongated cup of sorts.

"What is that?" She put aside the book of poetry, one of the pair she had commandeered.

Without looking up, he continued to work at his task. "It is a lacrosse stick."

The rag he used looked suspiciously like the torn-off ends of her shirt sleeves, confirming it was Rive who thought to make her attire more modest.

"What is its purpose?"

"It is for sport. You will see shortly. Now go back to your reading. Or perhaps you would care to read aloud to me. I believe toward the back of the volume you will find several poems of, shall we say, an amorous nature."

At his remark, a hot flush worked its way up her neck and into her cheeks. "Perhaps I shall recite one to you while you await your turn at the gibbet," she muttered before hiding her face behind the book.

He laughed too loud and far longer than she thought her gibe warranted. Then he fell silent while he concentrated on preparing the lacrosse stick. As the minutes passed, she continued reading.

"In a few days we leave for Quebec. The timing is poor, but I cannot delay any longer." He gave no further explanation, as though none were necessary.

"Quebec!" Catherine jerked her head up and stared at him as if he had just announced that it might snow the next day. "What devilish business are you about now?"

"The business of war. You claim to be a student of history. Need I remind you the war between France and England has spread to the eastern reaches of New France?"

War, other than her own private one with Rive, had been far from her mind of late.

"Why Quebec?" She snapped shut her book and put it aside.

"New France is threatened as never before. If Fort Niagara is taken, the Ohio Valley will fall securely into British hands. It is the same everywhere. Your general, Amherst, laid siege on Carillon, forcing the French garrison there to mine the fort and blow it up rather than surrender it. A British army has landed unopposed on the Île d'Orléans, making Quebec extremely vulnerable. If Quebec falls, the conquest of New France will follow."

"I should think your effort comes somewhat late. Or do you believe your presence at the eleventh hour will turn the tide in your country's favor?"

He shrugged. "I cannot argue with that."

"Then why get involved?"

He regarded her with mild exasperation. "My dear Catherine, I have neither the time nor the inclination to recount my past efforts in this conflict. Let us just say I have been very much involved until recently. However, it is time now to put aside personal considerations. The loss of New France, along with the British conquest of the Ohio Valley, will have a lasting effect, in many respects, upon my family. I owe a debt to someone in France. It is time I resumed my part in fulfilling my obligation to him."

She wondered if he referred to his uncle in Paris, the man Louis had mentioned earlier. In that case, his participation was certainly a noble gesture. Yes, she would grant him that, but there was nothing noble in his dragging *her* along with him.

"I will not go with you. You cannot force me."

Rive set aside the stick, which he had oiled to a glossy sheen. "You will, and I can. God in heaven, Catherine, I do not want to go to war with *you* over it."

His hands, resting on his knees, drew her attention. His fingers, long and tapered, were very strong as she had learned through physical contact with him. Those fingers would have no difficulty hefting a sword or firing a weapon.

For a fleeting moment, an image formed in her mind of a battlefield like the ones artfully sketched in her history books. It was not at all difficult to project Rive leading a charge in the forefront of such a field, scattered with cannons and stout defenses. She imagined him fitted out in a white and blue uniform—why that color, she could not explain—seated upon a spirited black horse, his hat cocked at a jaunty angle. As he rode into the fray, he brandished a sword above his head.

However, glory was often illusion and reality usually of a less kind nature. In truth, he might be killed. The prospect should have lightened her mood, and it was with a great deal of surprise and confusion that she found the opposite true. She frowned and was still pondering her conflicting emotions when she became aware of his fingers beneath her chin. Gently, he tipped her face up to meet her eyes.

"What is it?" The tension in his facial muscles made his concern evident. "You look like you are about to face a firing squad. Your life will not be in danger, if that is what worries you."

The intensity of her feelings frightened her, and she felt on the verge of tears.

"What is it? Tell me, Catherine."

Betrayed by her emotions, she could not speak. Nor could she tear her gaze away.

His eyes widened, as if he sensed the truth behind her anxiety. "Don't tell me you are worried for *my* safety?" His dark brows rose in shock. He looked as if someone had dropped a bucketful of icy water over his head.

Finally, his words penetrated Catherine's almost trance-like state. "No. Why would you imagine such a thing? You are too conceited. If anything, I should pray for your swift demise."

He traced the underside of her chin with his finger. "I think the lady doth protest too much."

The gold band placed on her finger by Jeremy Flint bit into her flesh, reminding her of where her allegiance lay. She must not allow Rive to cart her off, like a camp follower, to Quebec. The consequences to her family were too severe, should Flint discover she was no longer within his reach.

"I protest only your insistence I should accompany you to Canada."

"I cannot leave you here."

"And if my husband has abandoned me? What will you have accomplished?"

Rive hefted the lacrosse stick and examined it. "Any man who abandons you would be a thousand times a fool. Is Flint such a man?"

Catherine's lips curled into a bitter smile. "I cannot say. I knew my husband less than a month before I agreed to the marriage."

The green eyes shifted to hers and narrowed in speculation. "It appears, then, you did indeed act in haste."

"Perhaps no more so than yourself."

"I believe my actions are open to argument." The statement was no sooner made than he laid a finger lightly against her lips. "Don't take that as an invitation."

She turned her head aside, away from his touch. "You seem so certain."

"He is possessive of you, as any sane man would be. In his arrogance, he must feel stripped of pride. He will come for you."

"What if he considers his life more precious than mine? Do you not understand? He might even have forgotten me by now."

※

DID SHE KNOW SO LITTLE OF men? By Satan's horns he had misjudged her innocence. Yet, how could he not when first he saw her with Flint? She had married him. Was it possible she had entered such a union out of love? The very idea seemed preposterous. Flint must be at least twice her age. An arranged marriage, perhaps? It happened frequently. Or maybe the marriage had come about through necessity.

He thought back to the night he had waylaid their coach. Lashed to the top were her two small trunks. At the time he had given no attention to the paucity of her belongings. Now he realized they represented little in the way of earthly possessions. Yes, necessity seemed the most likely reason for her marriage. Given her education and beauty, she should have had her pick of men who possessed not just excellent character, but means. Unless, of course, the family had fallen upon hard times. Often that narrowed the field considerably. At some point in the future, the matter would bear investigating.

Somehow, he would learn the truth of her unholy union with Flint. First he must survive the war. What were his chances now the British seemed to have taken the offensive? He shook his head as if the physical act could clear his mind of dark thoughts.

"Come." He stood and brought Catherine to her feet. "There is sport today. Perhaps you will cheer for me from the sidelines." He pushed her gently to the doorway.

Chapter 12

❦

"Sport, you say?" Catherine glanced at the stick in his hand. It still resembled a weapon more than a sporting device.

"You will find out in just a few minutes."

He led her outside and strode toward a grassy field, where a dozen or more young men were running about. They were equipped with sticks identical to the one Rive carried and used them to scoop a ball into the latticed cup. Amid much jostling, a cracking sound echoed each time someone struck another's stick.

Rive slowed his pace, shaded his eyes with his hand and surveyed the spectators assembled on either side of the field.

"There's Louis." He pointed. "Come, you will sit with him. He will instruct you in the game of lacrosse."

Catherine drew to a halt. She had matters far more important on her mind than games. "You have not answered my question. What do you intend to do if my husband has decided against my rescue?"

He shook his head, and for a moment, his eyes looked weary. "You give me no peace, so let me answer your question and let that be the end of it. As you might wish for my demise, be assured I have no such desire for yours. You will never be harmed by me." Then his eyes took on a sudden sparkle. "There are less troublesome methods of dealing with you."

"What are you up to? What 'less troublesome' methods?"

He searched the field then pointed. "I could give you to Gray Wolf. He has become quite smitten with you."

Catherine's eyes followed the line of his hand. "You mean the boy who guards the lodge?" She watched the same young man, in near-naked splendor, scoop up the ball and race with it across the grass. "You cannot be serious."

"He is not a boy. In fact, he is quite sought after by the ladies. You could do worse." His expression turned playful and slightly mocking.

A brief glance warned of Louis' imminent approach, and Catherine spoke quickly while they still had their privacy.

"In that case, I would rather you end my life. Do not hesitate, though. For if you do, I swear I shall find a way to end yours first."

Rive threw back his head and laughed. "Be on your guard, Louis. This bloodthirsty wench has a heart colder than a witch's kiss." Then he loped off, looking every bit the primitive.

Reluctantly, Catherine's eyes followed him as he ran the length of the field. He was tall and lean, and the muscles that defined his angular body stood out in relief, unencumbered by the scanty attire that only accentuated the sensual movement of his hips. All but naked, his raven-dark hair swinging loose and untamed, he cut a truly magnificent figure.

She tried to imagine him turned out in a satin coat, breeches, and a ruffled shirt, his long legs encased in silk knee stockings, his feet cushioned in pumps sporting a silver buckle. The image made her smile, and she laughed inwardly at her musings. No, a gentleman's attire was too incompatible with a man whose manner suggested surroundings far earthier than a grand palace or a well-appointed drawing room. Yet, for all his wild posturing, he was no primitive. He was too worldly, too self-assured, too well-spoken and informed—a leader, not a follower. According to Louis, he had been to court!

A gentle tap on her shoulder made Catherine start.

"If you follow me, I shall find a place where you will have a clear view of the playing area. Over there the grass is thick. You will be quite comfortable."

She followed him around the edge of the field. When they were settled, he began an explanation of the game in progress.

"It is called lacrosse, from the French *jeu de crosse*, and has been a popular sport among Indian tribes for many years. The object is to net the ball and shoot it between the opposition's stakes."

He indicated the two poles several feet apart and driven into the ground at each end of the field. "The man you see guarding the space between the stakes must try to keep the ball from passing through. If he does not succeed, the other side wins a point. A man may not touch the ball with his hands. However, it is perfectly permissible to knock it away from an opponent. But wait. You will see."

In the melee of flying sticks, it was difficult to follow the game's progress. Then the ball sailed loose and several men scrambled to net it. One succeeded, but not for long. Rive, wielding his stick like a club, knocked the ball from the other's possession. Securing it, he took off at a run.

"It is a very rough game," Louis continued, as if the idea had not already struck Catherine. "Always it ends with many bruises and sometimes, although not too often, a broken bone."

"It appears quite spirited." She smiled in appreciation of the energy displayed.

"It is, *madame*."

She had come to know Louis better over the past several days when he invited her for brief walks by the river. Often they engaged in quiet conversation. He seemed disinclined to talk about himself but did divulge, for many years, that he lived in the wilderness, hunting and trapping. Men such as he were referred to as *coeurs de bois*.

Sometimes, during an especially brutal winter, they would spend many weeks living among the Indians. He also enlightened her as to the purpose of the masks that hung from the wall of her lodge. Those who wore them believed they were potent enough to scare away evil spirits inhabiting the bodies of the sick. She never questioned him again about Rive, sensing he did not wish to discuss the subject. If he behaved as though there was nothing unusual in her being kept a prisoner by his friend, it was, she surmised, not through callousness, but from a genuine desire not to add to her distress. Again, she wondered if he thought she shared Rive's bed. Unfortunately, there was still no delicate way to disabuse him of the notion.

During those walks, Catherine often thought of escape. There were few means at her disposal. She would not venture far on foot, even if she did not get hopelessly lost in the forest. However, there were always canoes beached at the river. Most were of a size meant to accommodate a half dozen or so people. Others were more reasonably proportioned, including some only large enough for three or four. She was no sailor, but the canoes looked simple in design, and from what she had observed, easy to maneuver. There were always paddles lying inside them. Even a woman with no skill might be able to make her way down the river in one. People lived along waterways, used them extensively for commerce and transportation. A settlement, maybe even a small town, might well lie around a bend.

Dare she consider such a venture? The tiny taste of freedom she experienced during her walks only made her yearn for more. Each day, even as she hatched such a scheme, she had to confront the probability it would come to naught. She was constantly watched, if not by Louis or Gray Wolf, then by Rive.

At first, she had been resigned to wait for Jeremy Flint to rescue her. The passage of time dimmed her hopes. She must rely on her own resources. Every hour seemed to increase her peril. Soon she would be beyond the reach of any man, save the one who kept her captive and whose life had become so intricately bound to hers. How long before the heated desire in his eyes overrode the gentleman's code he adhered to with such obvious reluctance? Would he continue to deny himself? Then there was her own hypocrisy. She knew she did not despise him or his touch. Would her own body betray her one day?

In spite of the fracas on the field, Catherine found it difficult to concentrate on the game. The morning's developments had continued to alarm her, and she began to fidget. A few days, and then it would be too late.

The game continued amid much shouting and clashing of sticks. All eyes were turned toward the playing field. Except for Louis, who would notice if she quietly slipped away? Louis remained seated almost at her elbow. Even if distracted, he would shortly become aware of her absence.

The sun beat down, burning her skin and providing her with the perfect excuse. She began to fan her face with her hand. Then she slumped forward just enough to appear weary and discomfited.

"Is something wrong?" Louis asked.

She placed the back of her hand against her forehead. "I'm afraid the sun has made me ill. I would like to return to the lodge if you don't mind."

"Of course." He stood immediately and helped her to her feet. "I will walk with you."

She acquiesced, so as not to invite suspicion.

When they reached their destination, he said, "Is there something I might bring you? Fresh water, perhaps?"

"Nothing, thank you. I think I will just lie down for a while."

He pushed aside the deerskin flap and she entered into the dim coolness of the lodge. When the door covering fell in place once again, she stood perfectly still. Her heart pounded in her chest, and she feared losing her nerve. Mindful that the river posed many dangers and that she had no experience handling a canoe, she still was certain that now was the time to act. There would never be another. Whatever the risks, it was imperative she escape from this village—and Rive.

She let a few moments pass before moving toward the doorway. Had Louis remained on the other side? He had never guarded her before. The raucous game was in full progress, and he was ignorant of her plan, so hopefully he had returned to the playing field.

She moved the deerskin aside the tiniest fraction, letting in a thin sliver of light. She peered through the small opening but saw no one about. Her mouth felt dry, and she held her breath as she inched the flap farther aside. No one guarded the lodge.

She slipped outside and quickly navigated the embankment that led to the river. At any moment she expected discovery, expected Rive to come striding after her as he had the other day. She could still feel the touch of his strong hands as he held her and the hunger in his lips as they sought hers.

Shouts emanated from the playing field, suggesting the game was still ongoing. Ignorant of its length, she hurried to where the canoes were beached and selected the smallest one. It contained two seats, and under each, a paddle. From watching the Indians maneuver them, she felt confident she possessed enough skill to handle one, too.

The canoe was surprisingly light, and she had less difficulty than expected launching it. She pushed it away from shore until the water rose above her knees, gripped one side, and tried to figure out the best mode of entry. Too much pressure, she soon learned, brought it close to the surface and in peril of tipping over. She paused and considered the danger of that happening once the canoe was in motion but pushed aside the dark thought. She must risk it. Time passed quickly, and her only choice seemed to be to just throw herself in if that's what it took to start moving.

On the third attempt, immersed up to her hips, she managed to climb inside and settle onto the rear seat. When she reached for a paddle, the boat rocked dangerously, elevating her fear of capsizing. The air hung heavy with summer heat, and bugs flitted across the water's surface. Behind her, she could hear the shouts of the men on the lacrosse field. Her heart pounded, and she paused only long enough to steady the canoe. Then, with steely determination, she paddled farther out into the river with no mishaps.

Mimicking the Indians, she used her paddle to slice through the water. Remaining on an even keel required special care with every stroke. Out of sight of the Indian village and proceeding at a steady pace, she felt her confidence grow. She floated with the current and stayed close to shore. The nearby land provided a sense of security, although if the boat overturned, she strongly suspected the worst. She would likely drown.

The sun was setting, and birds were circling in a cloudless sky. She had no concept of time, but her clothes had begun to dry. She had probably been paddling in excess of an hour, which would account for the pain that shot through her shoulders and arms. Only exhaustion convinced her to slow her earlier pace. To her regret, she found no signs of human life. She spotted an occasional deer and once a fox drinking at the water's edge. The silence—intense, eerie, and broken only by the muffled splash of the paddle—unsettled her.

One time, when coming around a bend, she almost collided with a pile of logs—what Rive had once identified as a beaver's dam. Consequently, she became more observant and focused less on her physical discomfort.

When large rocks or fallen trees blocked the way, she was forced to head farther out into the river. The boat cut through the surface with a certain rhythm, and she adapted her movements to it. It surprised her to realize she probably had an aptitude for handling small watercraft. As twilight settled upon the land, the river flowed with a swifter current, and it took all of her newfound skill to manage it.

Time passed, and with each stroke of the paddle, she felt more certain that freedom lay just around the next bend.

Chapter 13

"Catherine."

The sound of her name shouted on the brisk breeze was her first indication she had been discovered. There was no need to identify the caller. The voice had become as familiar as her own; it would ring true and clear in her mind for the remainder of her life. The voice of Rive St. Clair.

From the moment she embarked on her escape, she had not allowed herself to think of him. Often, in days past, she had wondered if she would ever not feel his presence, if she would always carry some part of him in her memory: the lilt of his smile, his vexation when she challenged him, the way his green eyes changed color like a chameleon's, his intractable will and mercurial moods.

Now she rejoiced that, once her fear of the river had ebbed, she had stayed away from the shoreline. However, she must deal with the rushing tide constantly testing her. The ache in her arms had intensified. Pain stabbed between her shoulder blades. At least she was safely beyond his reach.

"Turn in toward shore," he yelled. "You do not know the river. There are rapids up ahead."

A furtive glance caught him sitting astride his horse, his long muscular legs bare, as was his chest. He wore only the breechcloth; the horse was unsaddled. In all probability, he had wasted not a moment once he discovered her absence. Riding along the riverbank, he had no difficulty keeping pace with her.

"Do as I say, Catherine. You will get killed out there."

"Go away." She struggled with the paddle. The river, once almost benign, had turned increasingly perilous. What had begun as harmless ripples swelled into frothy waves that compromised the canoe's precarious equilibrium. Carried along on the swiftly moving tide, she expended ever more energy maneuvering through choppy swirls that threatened to spin her around. Still, she was determined to continue.

"You have headed into the rapids." Rive's voice now took on a distinct apprehension. "Beyond them are the falls."

Water splashed over the front of the canoe, settling in chilly pools around Catherine's feet. Her breath wheezed with every stroke as she battled the churning river. When she could no longer steer a straight course, she conceded that she had lost control of the boat. Fear blossomed like a poisonous bud in the pit of her stomach.

Glancing quickly toward shore, she watched Rive spur his horse on and ride some distance ahead. Then in one swift, fluid motion, he dismounted and dove into the water. With powerful strokes, he cut through the rapids. When the canoe reached the point where he could intercept it, he grasped hold along one side. The boat tipped to within inches of the surface. Catherine shrieked as she was thrown off balance. Then one of his long muscular legs gained purchase, and he seemed to roll up and out of the water. She dropped her paddle and grasped the sides of the rocking craft.

"You are beyond stubborn," he rasped from behind her, "as well as impossible and completely reckless."

She turned her head and saw him sitting with his back against the rear of the craft. He had managed to secure her paddle and was using it to steady the canoe. Up ahead, the river gave off a thunderous roar. The air was thick with mist, and a steady spray of water lashed out at her.

"Get back here with me," he shouted. "In less than a minute we are going over the falls."

She froze. Almost immediately, a powerful arm snaked around her waist, and she was abruptly yanked off the seat and pulled backward. She landed between Rive's thighs, the little breath she had left knocked from her lungs.

"Stay put," he ordered.

He anchored her hips with his legs and tossed the paddle aside. The river roiled about them, and she thought it nothing short of a miracle they did not capsize.

"We are heading over the falls," he shouted. "Quickly, place your legs under the seat and hold on to me. Do not let go."

For once, she did as he ordered. He gripped the sides of the canoe and held on tightly enough to make the veins in his hands bulge. Then the river dropped away and they were pitched into nothingness.

Catherine closed her eyes and screamed. Her stomach seemed to no longer reside where nature had intended it, resettling in her throat. Spume slapped her face. The roar of the falls deafened her, and she expected to be hurled from the canoe at any moment and carried away on a great tide of water.

They landed with a tremendous thud, upright and—mercifully—not completely swamped. After an initial rush, the tide slowed and the river, having expended so much power, once again turned calm.

They drifted on the current for several minutes. Catherine's head rested against Rive's shoulder, and she kept a tight grip on his legs. His breath came in short bursts, and she could feel the rapid rise and fall of his chest against her back. Then he placed his hands on her shoulders and leaned his head against hers.

"Oh, my foolish … headstrong … Catherine," he rasped against her ear.

She wanted to tell him she was *not* his, she would *never* be his, but she was too exhausted to do anything beyond lean against him and fight to catch her breath.

He brushed the wet hair from her face and wrapped her in his arms. "Promise this is … the last time … you ever run away from me."

Fright and frustration brought her to tears.

"Promise you will never … do anything this dangerous again."

When they drifted close enough to shore, he stepped out of the canoe and beached it. Then he lifted her out and set her on her feet. Her clothing was soaked through, but her arms and legs had nearly dried. Still, her eyes continued to mist.

"I don't believe it. Are you crying?"

She sniffled once, then again. "Yes."

Placing a finger beneath her chin, he tipped her head back. "Tears of gratitude, I trust."

She pushed his hand away. "Gratitude?" She gave another sniffle. "What are you talking about?"

"I saved your life. Or hadn't you noticed?"

"You are presumptuous to take credit for my rescue, when what you deserve is blame."

Daylight had begun to fade, and the air had turned cooler. Catherine rubbed her arms briskly in an attempt to create a tiny spark of heat.

Exasperated, he pointed to the canoe. "Did I place your body in that craft? Did I force you to go off on a misadventure which, in the end, would have gotten you killed?"

She stamped her feet to coax a bit more warmth into her body. "No, but only in the physical sense. If you had not …."

"I get the point." He cut her off adroitly. "You may argue it all you wish—and I am certain you will—but not now. Not unless you wish to catch a chill."

When the sun arced nearer the horizon, it lost most of its potency. Rive watched Catherine's efforts to warm herself. His anger at her recklessness had subsided, and in its place came a grudging recognition of her courage. Her wet shirt clung to her breasts, outlining nipples that had peaked stiffly from the cold. It took all his willpower to direct his gaze elsewhere, when he desired nothing more than to strip off her wet clothing and hold her close against his body to warm her. That thought no sooner took form when a familiar stirring in his loins reminded him that the impulse, if acted upon, would have nothing to do with gallantry.

Then she sneezed, and his mind cleared of all thoughts except to return to the village and build her a crackling fire. He even thought he could manage a hot bath.

He took her hand and guided her up the embankment and back to where he had left his horse. She was shivering now, and he made haste lest she take sick. If she did, at least part of the blame would be his.

As if holding in his hand a rakish hat festooned with a fine plume, he made a sweeping bow. "My lady's transport awaits, once again." Then he cupped his hands, boosted her up onto the horse's back and swung up behind her.

The sun melted behind the trees, throwing them into deepening shadows. She continued to shiver, and he gathered her in his arms. As he held her close, an unfamiliar stirring took hold of him, a stirring that in no way resembled the one he had experienced moments before on the river bank. No, this time it did not center in that part of his anatomy—the one that grew hard every time he touched her. It took him totally by surprise and should, under other circumstances, have given him cause to rejoice. Not this time. This time she had stirred his heart.

Chapter 14

◦◦◦

Knees tucked under her chin, Catherine sat in her lodge before the fire Rive had hurriedly built. Her shirt, still wet, covered almost every inch of flesh, right down to her ankles. It took little convincing from him for her to shuck the sopping doeskin skirt, and the moment she did, her shivering began to abate. Anyway, if he had it in mind to make love to her, no garment—whether constructed from animal hide or chain mail—would stay him.

She had come to appreciate the freedom of her new garments in comparison to the restrictions of her normal attire. The fashion in Europe demanded that women be tightly laced under clouds of fabric. She doubted the women of this village who cultivated the corn, beans and squash would trade their clothing for even the costliest wares featured in London's finest shops.

She tipped her head toward the fire. Her hair always took far too long to dry. At home, in London, she would sit on a stool before the fireplace in her bedroom, impatiently holding the strands as close to the flames as she dared. Then, when her hair was dry, she would brush it until it shone and fell in waves down her back. She had used the silver comb and brush set—etched with her mother's initials—sparingly, knowing that one day she would inherit it. A year ago she had sold them, along with most everything else of value they could do without. Months before she set sail for New York, she had found a buyer for her beloved pianoforte. Although the money earned was never enough to make a dent in her father's indebtedness, it went toward the purchase of much needed necessities.

"I have brought you something."

Rive had entered so quietly, she had no idea how long he had stood there. The night air was chilly, and he was dressed in buckskin trousers and a shirt.

This time she hadn't let the warmth emanating from the fire lull her into sleep. After the other night when she had awakened in his arms, she found it prudent to stay alert after sundown.

He placed the bottom half of a stout wooden barrel near the fire. Then he left, only to return several minutes later with two buckets of steaming water. He repeated this action two more times. When finally he had emptied all the water into the barrel, it was filled nearly to the brim.

"My lady's bath," he announced. "Alas, there is nothing at hand with which to perfume it. Still, it should suffice."

Catherine gaped at him. Ever since he'd abducted her, she'd had nothing remotely resembling a hot bath. True, in this settlement, water had been provided each morning, but it was never hot and never so abundant. Had he been in possession of this tub all along? Perhaps he had been luxuriating in hot baths, leaving her to make the best of her rudimentary implements.

"Where did you find this barrel?" She fully expected him to confess he had been hoarding it for his own use.

"That is one question you do not want answered. It's clean now and seems watertight enough. At least I believe it is."

She stared at him with the expression of someone who had just bitten into a wormy peach.

"If you don't want it, I'll not let it go to waste." He dipped a finger into the water. "Just right." He began to pull up his shirt.

"Don't you dare." She waved him away. "Get out and give me some privacy."

He dropped his shirt back in place, but to her consternation made no move toward the doorway. Instead, he leaned over and proceeded to gather up her hair. From somewhere on his person, he produced a leather thong that he used to bind the thick, unruly strands and affix them atop her head.

He accomplished his task adroitly. Evidently he had had much practice assisting a lady at her bath. Too much, no doubt, for nothing about him suggested inexperience with women. At the mere pondering of it, she felt herself blush right up to the roots of her hair.

He rested his hands lightly on her shoulders. "If I may be of any further service—" he whispered against her ear.

"You may not." Naked beneath the shirt and wrapped almost as effectively as a mummy, she found her movement restricted to all but her arms and hands. She waved him away. "The water is getting cold."

A few moments passed before he straightened to a standing position. "So it is. I shall leave you to bathe."

He had approached the doorway when she remembered something she wished to ask. "How did you find me today?"

"Leaping Stag saw you. He's only four years old but understood the danger. He told his mother that the woman with sun in her hair was out on the river in a canoe. By the time word reached me, you were halfway to the rapids."

Given the golden hue of her hair, Catherine saw the aptness of the child's description. She rather liked it. Her lips tipped upward in a smile.

"Later, I told him that in the future he must think of you with a new name."

"It's beautiful. Why would you tell him otherwise?"

"Because 'Woman Who Has Lost Her Senses' suits you better."

Catherine shook her head with such force, her hair threatened to come unbound. "Is there no end to your torments? Get ... out!"

He ducked through the doorway, his laughter ringing in the gathering dusk.

Keeping his eyes to the ground, Jeremy Flint followed the trail of fresh footprints he had picked up only a few minutes earlier. Slowly, he raised his arm and reined in his mount, indicating to the men who rode behind him to do likewise. Then he slipped from his horse and dropped to one knee, sifting the dirt, dried leaves, and pine needles between his fingers. His recollection of the exact location of the Indian village had dimmed with the years. Still, he remembered it was on the river somewhere northwest of here, perhaps a half day's journey.

He hunkered lower, squinted, and debated the merits of following this particular trail. Perhaps it would lead him to the village, or perhaps, like so many others, it would end nowhere. Studying the soft impressions on the forest floor, he became convinced that they had been laid by an Indian. He allowed his confidence to rise.

Chapter 15

Catherine awoke from a dreamless sleep at the sound of her name. A hand gripped her shoulder and gave it a firm shake.

"Get up. Now." The voice was low and unmistakably urgent.

Still half asleep, it took a moment before her head cleared. When she opened her eyes, she found Rive leaning over her.

He thrust a bundle of clothing onto the bed. "Get dressed, quickly."

In the gray light seeping through the roof opening, she could barely make out his features. She guessed it was not yet dawn but close to it.

"What is it? What has happened?"

"There's no time for explanations. Get dressed." He pushed aside the fur pelt that covered her legs and pulled her upright. "Hurry."

His tone, harsh and demanding, frightened her. What could be serious enough to bring him to her lodge this early in the morning? Then the answer rushed at her in sudden comprehension, jolting her wide awake.

"My husband is here."

"Not yet. But close. There are no less than thirty men with him. They're rough types, probably recruited in the taverns near the New York waterfront or from the docks. We picked up their trail less than an hour ago."

Thoughts, most of them ominous, swirled through Catherine's head.

"You have ten seconds to get into these clothes or you will leave this lodge dressed as you are." Grasping her arms, he set her on her feet.

She craved further explanation but recognized none would be forthcoming. Her skirt and moccasins lay on the bed where he had dropped them. Obediently, she snatched them up and hastily donned them. A moment later, they were outside in the gloomy half light.

Silver mist hung over the river. The coming dawn brought the barest illumination, just enough for her to notice the fires burning in open pits. At first, she thought the women were preparing the morning meal, but there was no evidence of cooking pots. Also, she saw no sign of the spitted meats whose tantalizing aromas never failed to whet her appetite. Only the dogs, who scavenged for morsels, engaged in their usual morning ritual.

Smoke hung in the air. In the murky light, small knots of men congregated around the fires. Unaccountably, grass burned along with the wood, intensifying the smoke. In some instances, an Indian sat just outside his lodge. After the urgency with which Rive had roused her, it seemed odd that no one else shared his concern. Then, peering into the gloom, she saw a large group heading in quiet haste away from the village and toward the forest. Used to the shouts and squeals of children and the unintelligible conversations of their elders, she was unnerved by the silence. Neither the young ones being led by hand nor the babes in arms uttered a sound. Coldness crept up her spine.

Cupping her elbow, Rive hurried her along. They approached the first figures hunkered down around a fire pit. Fully clothed in buckskin shirts and trousers against the morning chill, the men sat cross-legged. The same scene repeated itself a half-dozen times throughout the village, giving the impression of people going about their normal routine. Yet, there was something amiss. Why had those men not joined all the others? Why had they abandoned the comfort of their lodges?

She walked quickly beside Rive and toward another group. When they drew close to the men, she realized exactly what was amiss: they were not human. Bundles of slender twigs extended from tunic sleeves. In the dim, smoky light, long spears of grass gave the appearance of human hair. They hung from the backs of carved wooden masks, like the ones mounted to the wall in her lodge. The tableau appeared both imaginative and frightening.

She knew better than to question Rive as to the purpose of this ruse. She hurried to keep pace with him, and they shortly joined the band of Indians on foot. Moments later they melted into the protection of the trees.

"Stay with the women."

"Why are you doing this?" Certainly blood would be spilled if the deception—and what else could this be—failed. "Let me go to my husband. Surely your need for revenge cannot outweigh the value of human life."

"It is not my need alone. Had it been, I would have killed him when first I spotted him on the dock. Many here seek the same retribution. Flint will pay the penalty for his treachery."

Catherine clutched his arm. "You must tell me what he has done."

"You'll learn everything in due course. I promise. Not now."

As the women guided their children beyond the periphery of the forest, she made no move to join them. "You know he is close. Why draw him here?"

"To avoid bloodshed. We will avoid it once their gunpowder is spent. You will see what I mean. Trust me."

He brought Catherine to the cluster of women and children, but she edged forward the moment he joined the men, who formed a half ring within the trees' perimeter. From her vantage point behind a stout tree, she could just peer around it enough to spot the chief—surely too old and frail to engage in battle—beside Gray Wolf. Then she saw Louis standing close to Rive. Only a few men possessed muskets; everyone else carried a knife. They waited in utter silence while tension rent the air.

The invaders came with a rush of horses and a crack of musket fire. Impervious to the danger, Catherine continued to move forward. With Rive and Indians crouched low to the ground, she had a clear view of the village. Her heartbeat pounded in her ears. The reek of gunpowder sullied the air, and the thunderous noise from the many weapons being discharged almost deafened her. No doubt those men assumed what she had earlier—that the figures hunkered around the fires were human. As the attack continued, several figures toppled sideways and fell perilously close to the flames. Mounted men broke from the group and charged the lodges, their horses trampling those seated in front. They fired into the dim interiors. The air became thick with clouds of dust, which partially obscured the scene. The shouts of the invaders and the discharge of weapons echoed throughout the valley.

As the commotion abated, Catherine wondered if the attackers expected no defense. Then one of the men finally suspected the truth and poked at one of the buckskin-clad figures with the barrel of his musket. It toppled forward into the flames. Moments later came a shouted warning that they had ridden into a trap.

Catherine let out her breath in a rush of air. Jeremy Flint must be somewhere among those men. As she searched for him, Rive and the Indian men silently advanced and swarmed out of the forest.

The rising sun spread a carpet of pale light. Catherine moved ever closer and continued to watch from behind another thick tree trunk. The element of surprise enabled Rive and the others to safely reach the attackers. Some hastened to reload, but too late. Pulled from their horses, they were thrown to the ground and kept immobile by a well-placed knee to chest or back. Indian knives flashed and fully loaded muskets took aim. Rive, in the thick of it, leveled his pistol at a man's head. Hadn't he spoken to her about avoiding bloodshed? From the scene unfolding before her eyes, she fully expected to witness carnage.

The maneuver, carried out with speed and cunning, remained bloodless. As the sun rose over the mountains, bringing further illumination, she witnessed defeat in the postures of the men who lay still, no doubt terrified of being massacred. Horses galloped off or were led away; weapons were hastily collected.

The chief came forward, escorted by two of the older men, both of whom held muskets at the ready. He approached Rive and spoke with him. Rive pulled his prisoner to his feet and turned him over to one of the braves. Then he and the chief walked among the defeated men, searching their faces.

Dawn gave way to morning, but even in the growing light, Catherine could not distinguish one man from another. Some wore buckskin, others homespun shirts, breeches, and knee-length boots. Certainly, Flint must be one of them. If so, she could not readily identify him.

She could see that Rive had no better luck. After examining the last of the men, he shook his head in anger.

"We have no quarrel with you," he called out. "We wish you no ill will. Who will speak for you?"

No one answered.

"If you cooperate, every man will leave here unharmed. I'll ask once more. Who will be your spokesman?"

Finally, someone shouted, "I will."

Rive approached a young, sturdily built man being held at knifepoint. He clasped him about the arm and pulled him to his feet.

"What is your name?"

"Benton, sir." The answer came in a quavering voice.

"Where is Flint?"

There was a long pause, as if the man weighed the advisability of answering.

"He must have led you here," Rive said. "Am I right?"

"Yes."

"But he waits at a safe distance. Does it make sense to owe allegiance to a man who would let others take risks while he hides from danger?"

"Well ... n-no," Benton stammered. "He swore that, at the first sight of 'im, 'is wife would be killed."

"Mrs. Flint will come to no harm. As neither you nor any of those other men have been harmed. I give you my word."

Then someone shouted, "Tell him."

"That is good advice."

Benton nodded. "Mr. Flint is waitin' maybe a quarter hour's ride from here."

"How will he know of the success or failure of your mission?"

"I was to give 'im a signal."

"What kind of signal?"

The man paused a moment. "After things got quiet, I was to fire two shots, then wait a minute, or thereabouts, and fire one more. Then wait the same amount of time and fire the last two."

"Your signal will bring Flint here?"

Benton gave a coarse laugh. "No, sir. He ain't comin' here 'til I ride out and bring 'im the final word."

"Well, then, we must not keep him waiting."

Rive fired his pistol then quickly primed the weapon and fired again and again until he had duplicated the five gunshots. Then he spoke at length to one of the Indians—words Catherine could not hear. Even if she could, she was still powerless to influence the course of events. Darkness crushed her spirit, and she slumped against a tree. Flint's imminent demise brought her no joy. She could not bear to think of its consequences.

Two horses were brought to Rive. He mounted and indicated for Benton to follow.

"Don't do anything foolish. I shall be close enough to keep you in sight." Then, with Benton in the lead, Rive and a small complement of Indians rode out of the village.

Chapter 16

Her energy spent, Catherine paced inside her lodge too disturbed and restless to remain still for more than a few minutes. She had no concept of how much time had elapsed since Rive left, only that the pale sky, visible through the opening in the roof, hinted at an early morning hour. The food Louis had brought shortly after escorting her back to the lodge lay untouched in bowls on the floor. Even the sight of it sent her stomach into rebellion.

Gray Wolf once again guarded her door. That much she could see through the tiny chink in the deerskin. To keep her mind from spinning gruesome scenarios, she had taken to counting her steps. After every twenty paces, she went to the doorway to spy. An eerie calm had settled over the village. Even the children, normally active and boisterous, appeared subdued. Their elders, at least those within her cramped view, went quietly about their morning tasks. She suspected they, too, were drained from the earlier events.

Her first hint Rive and the Indians had returned was a piercing yell. Catherine hurried to the doorway. Gray Wolf still stood sentry, although not in such close proximity as before. Making a slightly larger opening expanded her view, and she glimpsed the remaining Indians, who gathered and chattered excitedly. Then, as they rushed forward, the commotion increased to an ear-splitting level.

Emboldened by Gray Wolf's semi-abandonment of his post, she allowed herself an even larger slit from which to spy. Staying out of sight, she waited for the assemblage to pass back into view. When they did, she immediately spotted Rive. However, she could see nothing of Jeremy Flint. Had they killed him on the very spot where he waited for word from his cohort? Whether captured or killed, he would have set into motion the event she feared most: her father's imprisonment and her mother's destitution. She felt despair even greater than when she had agreed to marry him.

As the morning waned and the heat began to escalate, Rive came to her lodge. Completely drained, Catherine sat on the edge of the bed, her hands clasped tightly in her lap. He looked weary, and when she searched his face for signs of triumph, she found none.

"Is he dead?"

He shook his head. "Your husband has much to answer for. Before he forfeits his life, he must face every accuser."

"You mean a trial?"

"No, at least not in the way you think, but an accounting. He sees no evil in his past deeds."

He drew Catherine to her feet. "Come, we will walk for a while. You are owed an explanation, and now I shall give you one."

She stepped out into the bright sunshine. Light stabbed at her eyes and she raised a hand to shade them. As they crossed the village, she asked Rive where they held her husband prisoner.

"He is in a lodge under guard. He won't escape."

She didn't ask if he had been in any way abused, although it would not have surprised her. Whatever his crime, he had sowed much hatred among these people. She could feel no pity for him.

Rive walked with his usual brisk strides, and she had to hurry to keep pace. She had many questions but knew by now he would impart information only when he was ready.

They proceeded in silence, walking beside each other until they reached the edge of the village. Then they entered the forest. Here, the density of the trees made it almost impossible for Catherine to see far ahead. Light turned to shadow and the crisp, cool air came almost as a shock. In the eerie quiet, only their footsteps and the occasional chirp of a bird, along with the quiet murmur of the river, broke the stillness.

When Rive led the way onto a narrow path, she followed close behind. In spite of the coolness, moisture dotted her palms, her pulse quickened and her muscles tensed. Where was he leading her? Why must they go so far afoot before he was willing to shed light on the past? The forest appeared ever more mysterious and haunting in its beauty.

Suddenly, she wished to turn back. "Rive," she gasped, thoroughly unnerved. For the first time she addressed him by his given name.

He turned around swiftly, his eyes scanning the abundant growth around them. Then he touched her reassuringly on the shoulder.

"Are you afraid?"

"Yes."

"There is nothing to fear. Few people come this way."

She did not confide that her dread grew not from their surroundings, but from what he would reveal. After her many questions, she was unprepared for the answers. And why bring her here? Why had he picked this isolated spot?

They continued walking in silence for some minutes. Then he held up his arm and stopped in a clearing where the sun spread a misty pool of light. It dappled Catherine's cheek and somewhat demystified the area.

"We can go no farther." Rive stood by her side and pointed ahead. "It is a burial ground. It is forbidden to walk there."

Catherine's gaze followed his outstretched arm. Feeling very much an intruder, she stood quietly, listening to the sound of the river that flowed somewhere beyond her sight. Whatever Rive's thoughts, he kept them hidden for now. Death, she felt ever more certain, formed the core of his coming revelations and lay at the root of his hatred of Jeremy Flint.

She recalled the night of her abduction. Unable to sleep, she had listened to the conversation between Rive and Louis. Louis had admonished him to believe that the dead were at peace. Perhaps she was soon to learn which dead.

Rive took her hand and led her to the trunk of a fallen tree. They sat beside each other, and the minutes passed almost as if he had had a change of heart. Sunlight splashed warmth onto her back, dispelling some of the chill.

"This is very difficult." He leaned forward and braced his elbows on his knees. "I have not spoken of this to anyone since I was a boy and, even then, not in its entirety."

He stood and walked a few paces toward the burial ground, then returned to where she sat. "Do you come from a large family?"

The query surprised her, and she could not tell if he sought to delay speaking of the past or if his family had some bearing upon it.

"On the contrary. There is just my father and mother. There were two babes born before me, but they died in infancy. My uncle and aunt, along with my three young cousins, live in the far north of England. So we are exceedingly small in number."

He nodded. "So it is with the St. Clairs. I understand they were quite prolific at one time. Now all that remains are my uncle, André, and his family in Quebec, and Uncle Hubert in Paris." He paused a moment, then seated himself beside her again.

"When I was fourteen, I lived for a short while with André. Then he sent me to Paris to Hubert and his wife, who were childless." He leaned his head back for a moment and a slight smile parted his lips. "Their task became twofold: to civilize me and provide for my education which, up until then, had been somewhat rudimentary. To everyone's surprise, they succeeded in both endeavors. So it was deemed I would eventually enter the family business.

"Time, however, exposed me as a restless and impatient fellow—like my father, everyone said. So it was decided that, upon completing my studies at the Sorbonne, I would study for a year in England, become proficient in the language and then enter a military college and devote my life to the service of France."

He paused, and his gaze shifted momentarily away from Catherine. "I am getting ahead of myself. In any event, my life during that time would hold no interest for you."

It should not, and yet it most certainly did. In the space of a little less than two weeks, she had come to accept the incontrovertible fact that everything about Rive St. Clair interested her.

"For generations the St. Clairs made their living in the fur trade. My father was the youngest in the family, and he, my mother and I lived just outside of Montreal. We owned the trading post where Indians and trappers—men, like Louis, who lived in the wilderness—brought in beaver pelts in exchange for knives, bolts of cloth, needles, beads, even cooking pots. Muskets, of course, were very much in demand. The pelts, transported by river to André in Quebec, were in turn shipped to France and sold through the family firm run by Hubert. A very profitable enterprise, you might say.

"Fortunately my father had a trusted employee. So when competition grew stiff in Canada, my father left him in charge and forged a relationship with the natives here. He made the journey each spring, and this suited his temperament well. Sitting all day in an airless room poring over account books was not for him."

Catherine understood that Rive must be very much like his father. She could not imagine him stuck away in a dusty cubbyhole totaling up the day's receipts. Yes, the military sounded a much more suitable occupation. Given his participation in the war, he had clearly followed that course.

"My mother died the year I turned eight," he continued, his tone softened, perhaps, by her memory. "Shortly thereafter, I made the journey to this village for the first time with my father. We stayed for two months and brought our trade goods in three canoes. Always scrupulously fair in his dealings, my father was accepted by the Indians as their brother."

Catherine remembered the affection with which the natives had greeted Rive. At least now she better understood his close relationship with them.

"We came every spring until my twelfth year. That last morning, we planned to leave for Montreal with enough beaver pelts to fill our canoes. I had just carried the last bundle down to the riverbank when I heard musket fire. It was just before dawn. A thick mist shrouded the river, so I never saw the men until they were upon us. I came to understand later they were a militia, organized in the colony, peopled with a few British soldiers, and led by an army scout. They attacked without warning, emptying their guns into the old men, women, and children, firing into the lodges. Anyone unable to escape perished."

He sat quietly for a moment, and Catherine could see the tension in his jaw. She waited for it to ease. "Today, you counted on them striking in exactly the same manner?"

"Sixteen years ago, it was a very effective strategy. Yes, I counted on Flint's memory. At any rate, we could not take the fight outside the village this morning. As you saw, Flint's men were mounted and carried muskets or pistols, which most here do not possess. Believe me, it is unwise military practice, when you are on foot, to attack a mounted man who is carrying a fully loaded weapon. Once it is discharged … well, you observed for yourself what happened."

She supposed they taught such tactics in a military academy. If so, Rive had learned his lessons well.

They sat quietly for a while, and she wondered if he had imparted all he planned to divulge. He must not stop, for she guessed he had come very close to the reason for his hatred of Flint.

Then just as she was about to urge him to continue, he said, "They went about their bloody business and set fire to the lodges. I heard someone shout my name. I turned toward the sound. My father materialized through a curtain of smoke. He was tall and powerfully built, and I wanted to believe he possessed the ability to single-handedly quell the slaughter. As I ran toward him, a man grabbed me by the shirt and held me. My father ordered him to release me. They were the last words he ever spoke. The man drew a pistol and shot him dead."

Catherine was shocked at his revelation. She could only imagine the horror of that day. Just as she would have wished to comfort the boy, she ached to place her hand over that of the man who sat beside her. She knew such a gesture to be unwise. Instead, she waited for Rive to proceed with his narrative.

"I struck at the man who held me, but to no avail. 'Yer worth ten pounds to me, boy, dead or alive,' he told me. 'Makes no difference to me how I collect it.' Then a British soldier approached and addressed him as Flint. 'See if you can get the boy to talk.' "

Catherine's fingers tensed, and her nails dug into her palms. She should have foreseen Jeremy Flint's role in that nightmare. She turned toward Rive, but his gaze, once again, was focused on the burial ground.

"Flint pulled out his knife. He held the point against my throat and asked me where the young men hid. At the time, I spoke just a little English, but enough to understand him. I told him they were not hiding. They had set out two days before to hunt for game."

Rive turned toward Catherine. "It is their custom to hunt for several weeks and bag enough game to see them through the winter. To fall short of food is to perish. Flint should have known. It's common to all tribes. Perhaps he did know and didn't care. Nevertheless, he accused me of lying and pressed the blade deeper. I thought he was going to slit my throat.

"Then a soldier dragged a young girl, who shook with terror, over to Flint. The chief's granddaughter. The soldier ordered Flint to question her. The soldier took hold of me and, although I tried, I was not strong enough to break his grip. Then Flint …."

Rive shook his head. "You do not need to hear any more."

Catherine searched his face and saw the pain that opening this wound had inflicted. Tears gathered behind her lids and she blinked them away. "I want to hear it."

Rive crossed his arms over his chest and tipped his face toward the sun. He sat still for a long moment, his legs stretched out before him.

"Then I will make it brief. He used the girl brutally. When he finished, he took his knife and brought it to where her hair swept back from her brow. I guessed what he had in mind. Somehow—maybe I was on the brink of madness—I managed to break the soldier's grip and lunge at Flint. I grasped his hand, the one holding the knife. I was unable to drive the blade into his heart. It cut just below his jaw instead. Then someone delivered a tremendous blow to my head. Later, I was told it took many days before I regained my senses. Also, according to some of the survivors, Flint returned late in the night and made off with our three canoes crammed with beaver pelts."

After so harrowing a tale, Catherine could not bring herself to utter a sound. Minutes passed.

Rive seemed disinclined to resume his tale. Nor did he make any move to return to the village.

She was desperate to learn what had happened to him afterwards. "How did you come to be brought to your uncle's home in Quebec?"

Her query elicited the barest hint of a smile.

"During my second year of living among this tribe, a French trapper arrived to spend part of an especially brutal winter with us. Upon talking to me, he professed knowledge of my family in Quebec. He had lived there in his earlier years. When spring arrived, I undertook a journey with him, a journey that saw me delivered to my Uncle André, and one that completely changed my life. The man I speak of was Louis, and he has remained a close family friend ever since."

Chapter 17

THE SUN HAD DIPPED FARTHER TOWARD the west when Rive and Catherine returned to the village.

"Where have you detained my husband?" she asked.

He pointed to a lodge where an Indian stood guard. Ignorant as to what had befallen Flint at the moment of his capture, she suspected he must now be incapacitated and no longer a threat to anyone. Yet he remained an even greater threat to her parents, for it was apparent Jeremy Flint would never leave here alive. It became imperative she speak with him. Perhaps, having been forced to face the horror of his past misdeeds, he might somehow find within himself a spark of humanity. Already the words she must say to him were forming in her mind.

"I would like to see him." She laid a hand lightly on Rive's arm. She anticipated his objection. "Do not deny me this one request. It can do no harm. I must speak with him one last time."

Rive waited a moment. "It will bring him some measure of comfort." He frowned and seemed on the verge of refusing.

"Please. In this regard, I will ask nothing further of you."

He did not reply at once. "I suppose every man deserves some solace, no matter what his transgressions."

"I cannot offer him solace."

"Then why this request?"

"It is a private matter between … Mr. Flint and myself. Please." She spoke quietly, but with urgency, nonetheless. "It will in no way change the circumstances in which he finds himself."

He appeared to weigh the merit of her plea. She searched his face and tried to read something in his expression. Finally he nodded and led her to a lodge. He spoke briefly to the Indian on guard.

"I will not stay long."

"That would be wise." He turned and strode away.

Indeed she must keep the visit brief. Even then she realized the enormous challenge she faced in trying to conceal the utter disdain in which she held Flint. Condemning her father to a debtor's prison, leaving her mother destitute, were acts every bit as unconscionable as murdering Rive's father. She must know if Flint sent word to his London agent to cease payment to her family. Or had he, in his arrogance, assumed he would return home a victor? If the former, she must shortly confide in Rive and press upon him the immediacy of her returning to New York City and booking passage from there to England. His return to the war in Canada would have to wait.

Then again, for the past few days, she had been thinking of the quill and small inkpot, along with the blank parchment sheet, she had discovered in Rive's pouch. She had been curious as to what use he had put them, but not enough to provoke him with further questions. Now she sought an avenue by which they might be employed for her own purpose if she could convince her husband. Considering his plight, she did not expect to find him sympathetic. A refusal, however, would add little to her mounting anguish. She must make the attempt.

She entered the lodge. Flint was seated on the dirt floor, his body slumped forward. He wore only dark breeches. As she drew closer, she saw his hands were bound and tethered to a tall stake driven into the ground behind him. His legs were stretched out in front, his feet secured in the same manner as his hands.

At her approach, he straightened and looked up through eyes rimmed with dark circles. His face appeared thinner, making the cheekbones protrude with startling prominence. His mouth, a thin slash, turned into itself in a tight, twisted line. His teeth clenched. There, along his jaw line was the wound Rive had inflicted so many years ago. Until her abduction, she had never felt a moment's curiosity about the scar, nor about Flint's background. Had she thought on it, she could never have imagined what horrors he concealed.

"Water." His voice sounded ragged, barely above a croak. "Get … water." The order seemed to deplete what strength he still possessed, and he slumped forward again.

She could find no pity in her heart. Yet she had not the will to inflict further cruelty by refusing his request.

Nor must I anger him.

"Hurry," he begged.

A cursory search turned up an empty pottery bowl. The lodge appeared stripped of anything that once might have made it habitable. Even the grass mats had been removed from the dirt floor.

"I shall have to seek water elsewhere. Perhaps the Indian who guards the door will allow it, but I cannot be certain."

Flint's lips moved again and she bent lower to hear.

"No need … a jug … somewhere. Find it." His head flicked toward the darkness beyond.

She moved farther into the interior and found a gourd containing water. She poured a healthy draught into the bowl and brought it to him. As she held it to his lips, he fell upon it, sucking up the water in noisy gulps. No animal had ever approached a trough with greater need, nor had she ever imagined a man reduced to such a wretched state. Numbed by the day's circumstances and revelations, however, she felt drained of all emotion.

When he had drunk his fill, he turned away from the bowl. Looking up, his eyes bored into Catherine's with a feverish light. "Good. You're here. I counted on you finding a way." Now his voice grew stronger, and, even though he was so miserably confined, he still managed to sound arrogant, as if he were in command.

She replaced the bowl then stood quietly, searching for words that would neither offend nor give false hope. The implication behind his words was unclear. Had he referred to her presence or did he believe that somehow she might find a way to alter his fate? She had been honest with herself in that her visit had naught to do with his plight, but everything to do with hers.

"You seem dour. Yet, as I watched you enter, I told myself that surely, by now, you had interceded with him and were bringing me good news."

"Good news?" She shook her head slowly. "You must disabuse yourself of such a notion. You will find no one here willing to take up your cause."

"You are wrong, *wife*. Shall I remind you that you enter into treacherous waters when you choose the wrong side against me?" His voice held the same malicious edge. Even on, perhaps, the last day of his life, he could not abandon it.

Catherine fought to keep her composure. "I have said nothing to harm you further."

Flint fixed her with an accusatory stare. "Nor, apparently, have you felt any compulsion to argue on my behalf. So do not pretend this wifely visit has anything to do with duty or loyalty."

She would not lie. "I did my duty once, as you required it of me."

"Now you feel free of any obligation that binds you to me. How fortunate for you, Catherine. What will you do after I am dead? Live with him here?"

"What are you talking about?"

"Ah, innocence. It so becomes you, my dear. Once, I found it quite disarming. I think it has long since faded, along with your modesty. Yet neither seems to distress you." His gaze settled momentarily on her bare legs before moving upward along her body. "Do you lie with him at night?"

His words made her recoil. "Such an accusation is cruel and unjust. There is no truth in it. I was brought here through no misdeeds of my own, but solely through yours." Although mindful that her mission was one of conciliation, she could not stand defenseless before him and allow him to impugn her character.

"And that absolves you from remaining loyal to the oath you swore when you became my wife?"

"Our marriage lacked a mutual devotion and came about for only one reason." She spoke with a calm and even tone, fighting to suppress any hint of the biting recrimination she felt.

"Yes. I should have guessed what brings you to me now." His voice was sheathed in ice. "Obviously, it was not to ease *my* dilemma but to petition for an end to your family's."

She looked directly into his eyes. "What satisfaction can you possibly derive from seeing my father spend his last years broken in health and spirit, or denying my mother refuge? They have caused you no harm. Indeed, they have been true and kind to all who have known them. Tell me. Have you sent word to London to cease payment?"

His eyes narrowed. When he spoke, he did not give the answer she sought. "Perhaps it is still possible for your parents to pass their final years in comfort. However, *you* must bring about such a resolution."

"If you are suggesting that somehow I might alleviate the seriousness of your situation or the peril in which you find yourself, you must take no heart."

Flint's face creased into a web of fine lines, and his eyes gleamed with suspicion. "St. Clair has filled your ear with poison. He has turned you against me. Have you managed to bewitch him as well?"

Catherine allowed a moment to pass before she trusted herself to speak. "You have accused me of wrongdoing and I have refuted it. So, if you persist, then you must believe whatever you wish. It is of no consequence now. You and I both know what brought about this turn of events."

He eyed her closely. "What has he told you?"

"He has spoken what I believe is the truth."

Flint gave a thin, reedy laugh. "Your belief in the truth is misplaced. You would do better to accept it from your husband and not a cutthroat who is no better than the savages he surrounds himself with."

As Catherine's eyes sought Flint's scar, she thought of Rive and what he had witnessed as a boy before making his wild plunge at his father's murderer.

She could neither condone nor excuse her abduction, but neither could she condemn Rive for seeking retribution.

"Well? What will it be?" His voice, raised in anger, brought the Indian guard into the lodge. At his sudden appearance, Catherine's heart leapt in her chest.

Several moments passed in which the Indian shifted his gaze away from her and to Flint. Then, perhaps satisfied that whatever had alerted him posed no danger, he grunted and returned to his post.

Catherine released the breath she had been holding. "I have no wish to argue with you. Nor is it my place to sit in judgment."

"How solicitous." Flint's tone was ripe with sarcasm. "Before blame is laid and judgment passed, let me tell you what St. Clair has, no doubt, failed to disclose."

To Catherine, it seemed natural for Flint to wish to soothe his conscience. Perhaps, in unburdening himself, he might come to perceive the events of which Rive spoke, and the central part he played in them, as they really happened. Perhaps he might even feel some remorse.

"I will listen to you, but I can offer nothing more."

His head snapped down toward his chest, then up to meet her gaze. A pleased expression flitted across his face, as if satisfied to have her once again capitulate to his wishes.

"Sit by me." His voice sounded as dry as dust.

Catherine sank onto her knees then settled back, keeping space between them. To sit close to him repulsed her.

"This happened years ago, too many now for me to remember. I was an army scout, a good enough occupation, I suppose. Back then, I had few opportunities, and I learned to live by my wits. That's something you'd never understand, having spent your childhood spoiled and coddled. Sometimes it required a man to be harsh, even cruel. You either learn how to survive or your scalp could wind up dangling from some savage's belt. They're heathens." His tone was heavy with derision. "In spite of the priests who bring them the Word of God."

Words that have apparently escaped the attention of Jeremy Flint. Her face remained expressionless; she felt no sympathy.

"That is why they'll attack a settlement with no regard for human life. Ask a woman whose husband was murdered or children were snatched up before her eyes. That was the kind of threat we had to stop."

He gave a vicious yank to the cords binding his wrists. Whether through hatred for the natives or from the frustration of being so incapacitated, she could not decide.

"The settlement was two days' ride east of here. Small, maybe twenty, thirty families. Indians came down on them so fast the men barely got off a shot. They killed all but one man, the one who lived to tell about it. Took the women and children who weren't massacred."

She could see and hear the absence of feeling behind his words. It was merely a recitation; she suspected he had given it many times over the years.

"We weren't about to let that stand." His voice, which had begun to rise on a wave of anger, was quickly brought under control. His gaze shifted to the doorway as if he expected the guard to reenter. "Took some time, but we found what we were looking for. At one of the villages, they hid the men. We found their women and children. Then …." His lips parted in a pleased expression.

"Wait. You said 'one of the villages.' Are you telling me you attacked more than one?"

"Just what do you think they did, *my dear*, left their calling card on a silver tray? What did it matter? It had to be one of the tribes from around this valley."

Briefly, Catherine closed her eyes then opened them again to stare in horror.

"*One* of them? Do you mean you were not certain who bore responsibility? You attacked a village, nay, more than one, where innocent people lived, without proof of their complicity? Do you even speak the truth of such a massacre?" His recitation sickened her.

"Oh, I speak it." His eyes stayed riveted on her face. Then he took a deep breath and leaned his head back against the pole to which he was bound. "Someone had to pay in blood. That's how you teach people a lesson. For God's sake, they're filthy savages. There was the bounty. Do you know what a male scalp was worth?"

A shudder passed through Catherine. Had she not already been seated, she feared she would have fallen.

It was as if he had not spoken with such brutal disregard. "So now, wife, you must decide. Either you help me or stand warned of the consequences of a refusal. It will fall heavily upon you and yours."

Slowly, she shook her head. "There is nothing I can say to alter your fate."

"Oh, but you have led *too* sheltered a life." His lips parted in a thin brittle smile.

"I am glad of it, although it has no bearing here."

He inched closer to her, straining his bonds. "Perhaps St. Clair cannot be swayed with words. Neither could I were I in his place and he in mine. You say he has not bedded you. Don't think for a moment he is satisfied. You can bargain with him. You can bargain with the one thing you possess that he, no doubt, most desires."

His words cut as sharply as if he had scored her flesh with a knife. For a moment she could find no words with which to answer him. "I know little of Rive St. Clair, the man of whom you speak. Yet, I can tell you without hesitation that neither the temptations of the flesh nor all the riches of this earth will sway him from the course he has set. As for myself, I shall not bargain with my own body. Henceforth, I shall share no man's bed in the absence of mutual love and respect."

"You are very high-minded, *wife*. Perhaps you have forgotten one of the conditions set when we married: Should I predecease your father, all payment will cease. He will end his days in Newgate Prison. I hear it is exceedingly damp and cold within its stone walls. The meager bread ration is stale and the drinking water foul. The place is infested with rats."

"You can prevent it." She begged him to allow her to write instructions she might deliver to his agent in London to continue the deposits to her father's account. Flint had yanked enough at the leather thong that bound him to allow for enough play to affix his signature. "Can you not find it in your heart to show mercy?"

He narrowed his eyes. "Go to St. Clair. Make one final bargain to spare my life. Otherwise, bear the consequences."

"Even if I were so inclined, he will never veer from his course."

"Oh, but you sell yourself short, my dear. He will bed you. You might even enjoy a tumble with him. Go to him."

She wondered if he had gone mad. She could say nothing further. She rose to her feet.

"I must be guided by my conscience." Her hands trembled, but she managed to slip off the gold wedding band he had placed on her finger a mere two weeks earlier. She dropped it near his feet.

"Goodbye." She walked to the doorway.

"Catherine, wait, please."

She turned back toward him.

"Will you perform a small act of charity?" Arrogance no longer commanded his voice, but a wheedling, uncharacteristic tone. "It will make no demands upon your principles. I ask only for a few sips of water."

She turned toward him, then walked back, refilled the bowl, and held it to his lips.

When he had drunk his fill, he said, "Will you leave it here, close to me, so I might lean over and drink again? They will hold a council to decide my fate. It could be days."

He spoke quietly with what seemed like resignation. This time she felt the tiniest stirrings of pity and placed the bowl beside him. Then she went to the doorway and, without a backward glance, exited the lodge.

Chapter 18

After Catherine left, Flint waited and silently willed the guard not to check on him again. Although anxious to set into motion the plan he'd devised only seconds before, he allowed several moments to pass before moving. Then, recognizing the danger of pausing too long, he leaned toward the water bowl. Using his elbow, he moved it closer. When able to grasp the rim with his fingers, he tipped and emptied it, then drew it next to his body.

Earlier, he had tested the stake, the narrow trunk of a sapling shorn of its bark. It had been driven too deeply into the ground to uproot. However, that also meant he had something sturdy against which he might crack the bowl. Too hard a blow and the sound might alert the guard. The next few minutes called for the utmost caution.

He grasped the bowl and lightly tapped the rim, its weakest part, against the stake. Then he paused and listened for noises from outside. Satisfied he went unheard, he tapped again and continued until a section of the bowl gave way and produced a shard of clay. Several minutes later, he had another, larger piece. Now, using his hands, he broke apart the remainder. He took the largest shard and ran his finger along the jagged edge. Then he cut into the leather strips binding his wrists. The clay held together well, but when it finally disintegrated, he found another piece and continued cutting. When he had only two shards left, the leather thong gave way, freeing his hands. Quickly he went to work on the bonds that tied his feet.

Finally freed, he sat quietly and listened. Sweat ran down his face. He sucked in air with shallow breaths while he planned his next step, eyes never leaving the doorway. The guard must still be outside, suspecting nothing. Flint gathered up the leather strips and selected one whose length appeared sufficient to use as a garrote. Then he came to his feet. Calling upon all the skill he had acquired as a scout, he soundlessly approached the doorway.

A narrow band of light shone beside the ragged edge of deerskin. Staying close to the inner wall, he peered through the slit. To succeed, he must overpower the guard without being observed; therefore, he was forced to take a dangerous risk. Without hesitation, he slightly enlarged the opening. He noticed activity at the river. Then he silently changed position to spy from the other side. He saw no one close by.

He wrapped the ends of the leather thong around his hands and pulled it taut. Then he launched himself outside. With raised arms, he brought the garrote over the guard's head and drew it against his throat, twisting it into a noose. As he tightened the noose, he pulled the guard backwards into the lodge.

The Indian clawed at the thong and made an unsuccessful attempt to dislodge it. His choking sounds encouraged Flint. Deprived of air, the Indian was unable to sound an alarm. Flint tightened the noose further, and a moment later the guard fell to his knees, then onto his side, where he lay motionless.

Flint paused, listened and waited as long as he dared before slipping outside. Crouching, he walked quickly, and in less than a minute gained the shelter of the trees. He wondered when someone would notice his absence. Soon, if his newfound luck soured. He broke into a run.

Immediately, he began laying a false trail. The terrain became steeper, and he continued to climb, snapping small branches off trees and treading heavily, deliberately leaving evidence of his passage. Eventually he would head for the river. Once near, he must take care to leave no visible sign.

He maintained an exhausting pace. Branches lashed his back; stones cut into the soles of his feet. When a searing pain shot through his chest, he stopped and paused for breath. He dared not sit for fear he might never rise again. Instead, he leaned against a tree trunk, gasping for air.

With luck, he had an even chance of survival. Bolstered by this belief, he allowed his thoughts to turn toward the future. With St. Clair dogging him, he would once again have to start life anew. That would necessitate selling his home in Tarrytown and resettling elsewhere, perhaps London. Why not? He relished the amusements of that city. There he could continue to lead the kind of privileged life he had enjoyed for the past sixteen years.

He remembered that first year when he sold the stolen pelts and moved to New York City. He had taken care to observe how men of means comported themselves. He refined his speech and learned how to dress impeccably. His life was comfortable; still, he was not satisfied. He kept a sharp eye out for vulnerable enterprises, either poorly run or plagued by bad luck. Those that were ripe to be plucked by a shrewd businessman. His small infusion of cash was always welcome and, once established as a partner, he exploited every weakness. Eventually, after he managed to take control, he would offer a pittance to buy the concern outright. His offer was almost always accepted. That was how he had acquired his first ship, West Wind. He chuckled inwardly as he recalled how he had arranged to have the ship pirated and its cargo stolen. He'd made a tidy profit. On the brink of disaster, the owners were eager to sell. Yes, he had coveted the West Wind, the same ship that delivered Catherine to him in New York.

Thoughts of Catherine, and the risk he had taken to once again possess her, jolted him back to the present. Was she gone from him forever? Perhaps, but only if he wished it. If he still desired her, he felt certain he could find her again. On the other hand, if he chose divorce, he could enjoy seeing her and her family suffer. He laughed softly. Either way, he would break her spirit.

He pushed himself away from the tree and listened for the sound of footfalls. Hearing none, he struck out again at a brisk pace. As he continued to climb, he thought it best to traverse the mountain before doubling back toward the river.

Evening approached and clouds gathered. Keeping up a steady pace, even after night closed around him, he managed to cover more ground. Finally, having pushed himself almost beyond human limit, he could no longer ignore the pressure in his chest and the fatigue in his leg muscles. He saw a bed of ferns and dropped into them. He must rest, if only for a few minutes.

HE AWOKE TO THE SOUND OF rain in the treetops. Dawn had not yet broken, and darkness still shrouded the forest. A low mist clung to the ground; the strong scent of pine needles hung in the air. He sat up with a jolt when he realized he had been asleep, perhaps for hours. He cursed himself. With stiff limbs, he struggled to his feet and set off again. His mouth was so dry that he could barely swallow. Obstacles loomed in his path: loose stones, fallen branches, exposed roots, jutting rocks. Gray-black clouds churned across the sky, and the ground had turned sodden, making it difficult to gain purchase.

An animal cried out. *Or was it an animal?* He knew the Indians mimicked those sounds and used them as signals. When the cries grew louder, he became alarmed. Certainly, by now, his escape had been noted. St. Clair, and who knew how many Indians, must be almost on his heels. By wasting time, Flint had lost his advantage. In spite of the pain gripping his body, he pushed himself harder.

A flash of lightning split the sky, followed by a crashing roar of thunder. He heard the river gush far below but could not spot it through the gloom. Twice he fell, and pain tore through his knees. He wiped the wet hair from his eyes and fought his body's overpowering need for rest.

He became disoriented. By the time he saw the two dozen or so Indians and St. Clair, it was too late. They had cut off his escape on three sides, their cries loud and persistent. Would they kill him on the spot? He had outwitted the natives before and could again.

Now he saw the river coursing beneath the cliff. It gave off a surging sound as it sped overland. Would he survive a drop of perhaps two hundred feet? It was either that or capture. He decided to risk it.

He stepped to the edge of the cliff and did not wait for his pursuers to charge. Keeping his body straight, he leaped out over the edge. His fall started well. Then his body twisted and he tried to right it. All sense of balance deserted him. When he hit the river, his head and back took the brunt. The incredible force snapped his neck with a distinct crack. It was the last sound he heard before a final darkness engulfed him.

Catherine awakened with a start to weak morning light and Rive staring down at her. She had not heard him enter her lodge but had sensed his presence. His hair and clothes were wet; his eyes bored into hers with anger.

"What is it?" She could think of nothing she might have done to provoke his wrath.

He kept his hands clenched at his sides. Then, without a word, he raised one and opened his fingers. The broken pieces of a clay bowl fell onto the bed.

She sat up. "I don't understand."

"I think you do." His voice held an undercurrent of foreboding. If he had not once pledged to ensure her safety, she would have been afraid. Slowly, she shook her head.

"What do you not understand?"

Again, she searched her memory in vain for some recent transgression. "If you are looking for an explanation, I cannot give you one."

With his finger, he sifted though the shards of clay. "Do you recognize these?"

His words made no sense.

"They are pieces of an ordinary vessel. I have seen many here. Are you accusing me of breaking it?" His reaction to such a middling concern seemed excessive and unreasonable.

"Ah, I knew you would remember."

She looked into his eyes, and the coldness in them frightened her. "Why do you place such value on it?" Then her mind cleared. "That is not what troubles you."

He nodded. "The vessel is of no worth. It is the use you made of it that I must settle between us."

She stared at him.

"Did he plant the seed in your mind? Or did it grow from your own need of him?"

Him. He could only be speaking of Flint. "What has happened? Tell me." Her voice rose, agitated. "Please do not speak to me in riddles."

She saw the slightest shift in his expression as if he were weighing the truth of her purported ignorance. Then the moment passed and with it his uncertainty.

"Someone provided your husband the means of escape."

Anxiety stabbed at her chest. "How is it possible? I left him securely bound."

"Did you?"

His cold tone made her cringe.

"The bowl from which he was given water served to provide the means." He kept his voice low. "This bowl. It was placed far away from him. Someone shattered it for him. It made a very effective tool to cut through his bonds. He then used them to attack the guard. Mercifully, he survived."

Catherine became alarmed. Now she remembered her husband's entreaty that she leave the vessel within his reach.

"He begged for water. It was a simple request. I saw no harm in it."

"Did you love him that much?"

"Love him? I did not love him at all." She was on the verge of tears.

At her revelation, a surprised look crossed Rive's face. "Yet you helped him."

"Not by design. It was nothing more than an act of charity. When he asked for water, I could not refuse. I offered him no other assistance. Do you not see? Had I done so, I would be with him now."

"That is one fate I believe you would not wish to share."

She let out a long breath. It took a moment for his words to give meaning. "He's dead, then?"

"Yes."

She wanted to feel relief, but her family's circumstances rendered it impossible. Still, in all truth, she knew Flint had not deserved to live.

"Did you kill him?"

"He died, but not by any man's hand. We found him downriver with his neck broken. Perhaps we should have left him as carrion. Instead, we buried him."

An act of benevolence, from a man who had every right to withhold it. She waited for him to say what he intended to do with her. Since that was now on her mind, she suspected it must also occupy his. There was no longer any reason for him to keep her there. He must realize it. Time passed and still he remained silent. Much of his anger had dissipated, and she could read nothing in his expression except a profound weariness.

Finally she could bear the silence no longer. "I wish to return to the City of New York and book passage to England. It is imperative that I return to my family in all good haste."

"New York?" He gazed at her with an odd expression. "Travel is not possible at this time."

"Why is it not?" Dread built in her chest.

"For several reasons, not the least of which is a nearby column of British soldiers on the march. No, Catherine, you will stay with me a while longer. At a more opportune time, I will arrange for your transport to New York or wherever you wish. So prepare yourself. We leave for Quebec in an hour."

"You cannot …" she began to protest, then left off. She knew he would not reconsider. If she had learned anything about him, it was that once he made up his mind, he could not be persuaded to change it. He had already reached the doorway. Just before he exited, he turned back to her.

"Gray Wolf will be disappointed when he finds out his guard duty is soon to end."

Then he stepped outside, leaving her still a prisoner.

Part II

Quebec, New France
July 1759

Chapter 19

❦

Catherine's first glimpse of Quebec came after days of traveling in a birch bark canoe on a network of rivers and lakes with Rive and Louis. Therefore, it came as no surprise she must suffer the last portion of her journey cramped, along with a trio of wooden casks, in a small wagon drawn by dogs.

"Don't look so grim. It's not the most elegant mode of travel, but it has certain advantages over walking. I'd have thought you would appreciate the trouble I went through to commandeer your transport." Rive kicked a large stone out of their path. She watched it hurtle down the steep slope that dropped away from the road.

He referred to the miles they had trekked from one waterway to the next. He and Louis carried the canoe—they called it "portaging"—while she hiked alongside. Now, in no mood for conversation, she remained silent, her eyes on the steep, treacherous road pocked with holes. Even had she wished to respond, the bouncing and jostling that threw her continuously against the sides of the cart made speech all but impossible. When they reached their destination, she was sure to appear not only disheveled but bruised.

Earlier, she had questioned Rive as to where he intended to lodge her. He announced she would reside with his aunt and uncle until passage to New York could be arranged. He had ignored her protests.

"Besides, it cost me twenty *livres* to convince the boy to leave the last few water barrels behind." He didn't seem at all put off by her silence. "In dry weather, the springs and wells in the upper town produce barely more than a trickle. This is still the only way to haul water to the heights. So do not sneer at your transport, *ma chère*, for you may well be depriving some merchant of his bath tonight."

Catherine refused to acknowledge that he was part of her shabby retinue. Instead, she gazed back to the river below. The memory of crossing was still vivid. Having learned something about canoes and their lack of stability, she had clung to the sides of theirs, frozen in fear, as they navigated the treacherous currents. Despite Rive and Louis' expertise, every untoward movement convinced her they were about to capsize and drown. When they finally reached what Rive referred to as the lower town, he had to lift her bodily from the craft, for she could barely stand upright.

After seating her on a low stone wall, he had dashed into a nearby tavern fronting the unpaved street and returned with a snifter of brandy. Sitting beside her, he held the glass to her lips. Somehow, she forced a few drops down her throat, mindful of the spectacle she must have created. A woman caught imbibing spirits on a public street in London might well be hauled before a magistrate. Here, no one seemed to give them a second glance.

Of course, the townsfolk were probably occupied with other more serious matters; evidence of the war was everywhere. In the harbor, ships lay damaged or partially sunk in their berths. Fires had blackened and gutted many of the commercial buildings near the wharf—a certain sign the town was under siege. Not so the people, apparently, for the streets were crowded with gentlemen in elegant surcoats, ladies in fashionable gowns, and priests in black robes. Most curious of all were the men dressed in rough homespun shirts and moccasins and wearing woolen hats Rive called *toques*, which covered most of their pigtailed hair. There were military officers as well, dressed in oyster white uniforms faced with blue. The uniform she had once imagined Rive wearing.

Through Louis she had learned about the two towns—one on the narrow strand between the river and the cliff, the other on the promontory several hundred feet above.

"To live on the heights is a luxury only the Seigneurs can hope to attain. They are families of considerable wealth, most having acquired their fortunes in the fur trade. Their style of living is as grand as that of their counterparts in France, in spite of the wilderness that lies just beyond their doorstep. So, Madame, you will be housed in comfort with Rive's family." The reminder that she would soon arrive at the home of strangers, and with Rive, served only to heighten her anxiety.

The wagon stopped abruptly, jolting Catherine into the curved ribs of a barrel. They were at the crest of the cliff where the outskirts of the upper town began.

"It was once very beautiful," Rive said after they were underway again. Louis had remained in the lower town where he would lodge with family. As she and Rive entered the city, she could not totally tamp down her curiosity. She turned her attention to him. "Over there is the Chateau St. Louis, where the

Governor General resides." He pointed to an enormous building constructed of stone. "The walls are over two feet deep, but you can see the cannonballs have taken a toll. Still, it appears habitable, at least for now."

As they proceeded, he gave a running account of the buildings: the Jesuit college, its steeple fronted by a clock whose hands were frozen in the past; the convent of the Ursaline nuns; the Hotel *Dieu*, another large and rather imposing stone structure that served as a hospital; and, finally, the Bishop's palace, which, in Catherine's opinion was grand but certainly nothing to rival Windsor. However, with their suggestion of wealth, the homes impressed her most. Composed of stout timber and stone, they looked out onto well-tended gardens and lawns dotted with shade trees.

They passed a public square where people strolled in the late afternoon sun or sat beneath leafy maple trees. Even in wartime the inhabitants, including finely arrayed ladies, seemed to go about their daily routines.

Catherine gathered the folds of her soiled gown in her fingers. Before they left on their journey, an Indian woman had returned it along with her shift. Although wrinkled, the garments were clean. Perhaps the woman had washed them in the river and spread them out to dry. Unfortunately, additional stitches in the hem had torn loose in several places. She concealed herself as best she could by shrinking into the cramped corner of the wagon.

Concerned about events that had brought her north, she nonetheless clung to one tiny spark of hope; it could be weeks before anyone missed Jeremy Flint. Since he had never spoken of family, she felt certain he had none nearby in New York. However, his absence would eventually be noticed and, she suspected, an investigation conducted. Twice he had reminded her that in the event of his premature demise, his agent in London was to be notified immediately to cease payment to her father. That notification would take months. So time, once her enemy, might now prove her ally.

"Have you grown so accustomed to that deuced wagon you would not trade it for a hot meal and a warm bed?" Rive's voice cut into Catherine's thoughts. She hadn't realized they had stopped. He clasped her about the waist and lifted her from the wagon.

They stood before a two-story stone house, one of several on the wide street, set amid a wide expanse of lawn. Mullioned windows, thrown wide to catch the breeze, flanked a massive oak door. Several chimneys sprang from the pitched roof. A highly polished brass door knocker and knob glinted in the sun. Neatly trimmed shrubs lined the path leading to the house, whose front was bordered by colorful summer flowers. The residents took great pains with their garden and were clearly people of taste.

"Where are we?" Catherine asked.

"This is the home of my uncle and aunt, André and Lise St. Clair. They have lived here for almost thirty years." He tried to nudge Catherine forward, but she refused to budge.

"Why do you hesitate? They will more than welcome you."

She gritted her teeth, making a sound like a muffled growl. "I am sure your family is most hospitable, but is there nowhere else for me to stay? How are you going to explain my presence, or do you usually turn up on their doorstep with a disheveled Englishwoman in tow?" She pushed a tangled clump of hair back from her brow and shook dust from her skirt.

"Whatever my explanation," he was clearly impatient, "let me assure you it will be circumspect enough to preserve your dignity."

Catherine remained unconvinced. "Perhaps you can engage a room for me at an inn. Or at the convent. As you pointed out earlier, surely the holy nuns would not be averse to taking in a lodger for a few days."

Rive's eyes lit with amusement. "You were never meant for a convent. Not even for a short time." Leaning close, he brushed her cheek lightly with his thumb, which then strayed to her ear and lingered just behind the lobe.

Heat built where he touched her. In that moment she chastised herself for allowing him to affect her, still, and turned her head aside. "You are impossible." Even to her ears her words lacked conviction.

"You are taking yourself far too seriously." With a firm hold on her arm, he coaxed her alongside him, up the walk. "Now behave like a lady, or you will disgrace yourself without any help from me."

She was about to make a retort when his hand grasped the brass knocker and rapped it against the door.

A servant, dressed in a simple gray gown and crisp white apron and cap, answered the summons.

"Ah, Monsieur Rive." She dipped into a slight bow. "It is a pleasure to see you visiting again."

"Thank you, Cecile. It is good to be back, even if only for a short while."

After the brief exchange, she led them into a large drawing room.

Although the servant gave no indication of shock at her unkempt state, Catherine had no such guarantee the mistress and master of the house would be as nonchalant. She smoothed her dress. Without a comb, her hair would have to remain in its present disorderly state.

"I shall tell Madame and Monsieur you are here." The servant bobbed another curtsy and left.

While she struggled to manage her distress, Catherine surveyed the room. A fireplace, sheltered by a heavy wood mantel and gleaming brass fittings, occupied one wall. A cream-colored rug, its edge patterned with blue and rose flowers, covered part of the highly polished floor. Two settees, upholstered in pale blue velvet, faced each other near the fireplace. A desk, two wing chairs and a table whose surface held two silver candlesticks—one on either side of a vase of fresh summer flowers—completed the décor, a perfect blend of style and comfort.

Before Catherine could speculate further about the woman whose taste she admired, the door opened and a short, plump matron entered the room. She was dressed in an ivory taffeta gown, her graying hair mostly covered by a white lace cap. She was followed by a man, equally well-groomed in black breeches, a coat, and a crisp white shirt. Their faces reflected their obvious pleasure at the sight of Rive. The woman swept closer, opened her arms, and clasped him in an affectionate embrace.

"I can hardly believe you are finally here," she said in French. She stepped back and surveyed her nephew. "It has been too long since your last visit, but now you are with us and as always most welcome. After all, your Uncle André and I still think of this as your home. Why, only last week we were remarking how empty the house seems now that Philippe is with his regiment most of the time and Francoise is married and living in France."

A man cleared his throat and stepped forward. He stood a good bit taller than the woman and weighed considerably less. "Do not go on so, Lise." He studied Rive for a moment. "You are looking well, nephew."

Standing to the side, her head pounding from an acute case of nerves, Catherine barely heard the exchange of pleasantries, nor Rive's hasty explanations. She wished desperately to disappear like a puff of smoke. All too soon, however, she felt their attention shift to her. For a moment, her eyes lost focus, and she took a deep breath to steady herself. Then Rive was standing beside her. His arm brushed her back and his hand came to rest familiarly on her shoulder. His voice faded in and out, and it was all she could do to force herself to respond with a weak smile.

"I present you with Madame Flint," he told the couple. To Catherine, he said, "This is my uncle, André St. Clair, and his wife, Lise."

A look passed between husband and wife at the mention of the name "Flint." Then a soft, plump hand was offered, which Catherine managed to clasp. That was soon replaced by the strong firm hand of André.

"Welcome to Quebec." André switched to heavily accented English. "My wife and I extend to you the hospitality of our home."

"Thank you, Monsieur, Madame. You are both very kind."

"And you, my dear young lady, must be exhausted from your ... journey." Lise put her arm around Catherine and exchanged a wary glance with her husband. "I have, how do you call it, the perfect remedy. Come, let us sit for a while. André will bring the brandy. Then, after we see those cheeks with a little bloom, the housemen will prepare a hot bath and you will have a good soak. Then we will dine."

When they were seated beside each other on a sofa, Lise brushed the tangled hair away from Catherine's brow. Then, shaking her head, she made little clucking sounds with her tongue. "How long has it been since you sat down to a decent meal?"

Catherine sought an answer, but how could she possibly respond to such an innocent question? The truth would shock this good woman out of her senses. Fortunately, Rive spared her from having to fabricate a reply.

"If you are referring to a repast such as *you* are accustomed to, Lise, I would judge it to be somewhat past recent memory."

"That is no kind of answer at all." Lise held her nephew's gaze and tilted her head to the side. "Well?"

Rive folded his arms and moved to the window. Leaning against the frame, he gazed out into the twilight. "I assume Madame Flint dined most heartily with her late husband some weeks past." He turned toward his aunt. "Since then, her diet has lacked variety. However, I trust you will bring about a change soon enough."

André returned with a tray holding crystal goblets and a bottle covered with a fine layer of dust. He wiped it clean with a small linen towel.

"This bottle arrived by ship from France not two months ago. I paid far too much for it, but then, we do for everything these days. With French ports blockaded, we are fortunate if any goods slip through at all. If it were not for the privateers …. Ah, well!" He sighed. "It does no good to complain." He poured the brandy and handed each a glass.

Unaccustomed to spirits—especially twice in one day—Catherine sipped slowly. The brandy had a smooth quality and slid down easily, spreading warmth throughout her body. Across the room, she heard Rive's voice, low and melodious, as he engaged his uncle in conversation about the progress of the war.

"We heard some news in New York City," Rive said. "Nothing, of course, since."

"Not much to be alarmed about, yet."

"Your optimism astounds me, Uncle. They have all but brought the city down around your heels."

"It's Pitt. I'd like to put my hands around his throat for just one minute …. If he thinks he is going to crush French power on this continent, he will find that it takes more than a war to accomplish his ends."

Catherine held her glass in her lap. She'd barely touched her brandy, but the tiny amount she had consumed left her feeling a bit tipsy.

"Better now?" Lise asked.

Catherine nodded. "Yes, but I hope I am not putting you to too much trouble." She smoothed the folds of her skirt, noticed a splotch of dry mud, and covered it with her hand. "I … I must look a terrible sight. But you see …" she stopped abruptly, not knowing how to continue. Still, she felt the need for some explanation. "I became separated from my baggage and, having just the one gown, was unable to prepare myself for … for a visit."

Lise squeezed Catherine's hand. "There is no need to apologize. My daughter, Francoise, left behind several gowns and some linen. Fortunately, she takes after her father, so I doubt any alterations will be necessary."

"Thank you." Catherine wondered how much Lise understood of her circumstances and if Rive's brief comments earlier had clarified her whereabouts during the last three weeks.

"Well, then. Let us not delay. I shall have Cecile order your bath and freshen the gowns. They have not been worn for several months, but …."

Before she could continue, a high-pitched voice came from outside the room. Then the door burst open and a young girl swept inside.

"*Maman*, why did you not tell me cousin Rive is once again …." Then she looked at Catherine and her voice died away.

"Marielle," Lise said sharply. "How many times have I told you never to enter a room in such a manner?"

"Oh, *Maman*, I am sorry. I … I did not realize, I mean, Cecile did not say there was someone else." The girl was obviously at a loss. Then she spotted Rive, who had turned at the sound of her voice, and broke into a wide smile. With hands outstretched, she rushed to him.

"Cousin Rive," she squealed. "You have come back. I am so glad!"

He picked her up and swung her around in his arms. Then, with an amused grin, he set her down and stepped back.

"Surely this is not little Marielle who, only last year, played with dolls?" He turned to André. "Tell me, who is this young woman I find masquerading as your daughter?"

André beamed with obvious pleasure.

Marielle was *not* pleased. "I have not played with dolls for years and well you know it," she pouted. "Also, I have been quite grown up for some time. If you had stayed with us longer at Christmas, or come back more often when I am not at school, you would have noticed."

"It is a wonder I did not. In the future, I promise to be more observant."

Marielle dipped into a low bow, her raven curls bobbing. She lowered her lashes, hooding her large brown almond-shaped eyes. Then she raised her head and looked at Rive with naked adoration. "I shall see that you are."

Why, she's in love with him, Catherine thought, and as open about it as only a child can be.

However, closer inspection confirmed that Marielle St. Clair was no longer a child, not if the breasts that filled out her bodice were any indication. Somewhere she had learned how to flirt and was making a success of it.

"Marielle, speak in English, please, and come here and greet Madame Flint. She is to be our guest … for a little while."

Lise's command was accompanied by a sharp clap of her hands.

"*Mais oui, Maman.* I mean … yes, Mother." She glided across the room and presented herself to Catherine. "I am pleased to make your acquaintance." Her voice was distinctly flat as she stared openly at Catherine, idly fingering her own spotless rose silk gown.

Catherine forced a smile and felt her embarrassment return under the girl's scrutiny.

Wrinkling her nose as if in distaste, Marielle seated herself on the settee opposite Catherine. "Are you American?"

Catherine shook her head. "No, I am English."

"Oh? I should not have guessed. I thought all English ladies were supposed to be … pallid."

Catherine had no adequate response. Her recent trek for hours each day had indeed caused her to gain back much of the color she had acquired during the days immediately following her abduction. She could only wonder at the girl's reaction had she appeared in her native attire.

Ignoring her mother's glare, Marielle continued as if she had not made a gaffe. "Do you live in London?"

"I did, with my family."

"What brings you to Quebec?" Marielle abruptly shifted her gaze to Rive.

"That is Madame Flint's business and none of yours," Lise cut in sharply. "Really, Marielle, for a girl soon to turn fifteen, you sometimes show a distinct lack of manners."

"I was merely curious. Madame being English …" Marielle's voice trailed away and she again laid eyes on Catherine. "We had an English mistress at school one year. She taught us to properly speak your language. She married a Frenchman and went to live in Paris." The girl's lips curved upwards in a coy smile. "I suppose you are married to a proper English gentleman. Are we to make his acquaintance while you are visiting us?"

"Marielle, enough!" Lise snapped. "I forbid you to subject our guest to an inquisition."

Catherine's fingers tightened around the stem of her glass. She watched Rive disengage himself from his uncle and cross to where the women sat. Most likely, he was prepared to weigh in with heaven only knew what explanation. Wishing to make his endeavor unnecessary, she determined to end the interrogation herself, once and for all.

"I am afraid that will not be possible. You see, my husband met with …

an untimely death a number of days ago." Marielle's face seemed to crumple. Her mouth opened as if she were about to interrupt, but Catherine cut her off adroitly. "I am a stranger in this part of the world, as you have guessed, with neither family nor friends to whom I can turn. Therefore, I accepted … your cousin's offer to accompany him to Quebec. At the time it seemed the only possible solution. Naturally, I am most anxious to arrange transport to England. Your cousin has graciously agreed to do all in his power to facilitate my travel. Hopefully, that will ensue before too long." She glanced at Rive. As she expected, he looked none too pleased with her pronouncement. Tilting her head to the side, she smiled at him.

"If Madame will but exercise patience, everything possible shall be done to provide her with safe passage out of Quebec," Rive said. "But, alas, the war might not permit it for some time."

For a moment, Marielle looked stricken. "Cousin Rive, you must find a way, somehow. After all, Madame has suffered … her husband … and being without protection." Her slim, delicate hands fluttered and her cheeks flared a bright red.

"Calm yourself, Marielle," André ordered.

Rive positioned himself behind Catherine and placed his fingertips on her shoulders. Although his touch was light, it delivered an immediate infusion of heat right through the layers of her clothing. She wondered if the warm flush that settled on her cheeks was visible to the others in the room.

"No harm will befall Madame Flint so long as she remains under this roof," he said. "As to her being without protection, I hereby renew my pledge to keep her safe and, whenever possible, under my watchful eye. I shall do everything necessary to honor my pledge." His words, punctuated with the slightest pressure from his fingers, might have seemed meant for all ears. Only Catherine recognized their hidden message and knew they were intended solely for her. As he leaned forward, his hands glided over her shoulders to her upper arms. "Whatever she requires," he was so close she felt his breath against her hair, "I shall consider it a privilege to provide."

Chapter 20

"You cannot imagine my surprise, nephew, when the tavern boy brought your note apprising us of your return and that you would be arriving momentarily with the widow of that devil, Flint. The first question I asked myself was if *you* were the one to kill Flint. The second was, if the man were already dead when you encountered him, when and where you made the acquaintance of his widow?"

Rive stood alone with his uncle by the unlit fireplace, his arm propped atop the mantel. "Flint was very much alive when I first encountered him." He proceeded to tell André all that had transpired from the moment he spotted Flint and Catherine on the wharf in New York, including following them to a house on Maiden Lane. There, he intercepted a servant who, for a small bribe, professed to be on his way to fetch the magistrate commissioned to marry Mr. Flint and his lady.

"Since the crime had been committed at the Indian village, it was necessary I draw him there. Their loss sixteen years ago exceeded even mine."

André nodded. "And Madame Flint?"

"Catherine." He savored the word as it left his lips. "There is little to tell, but she bore no affection for the husband. Other than her own admission, she is guarded about her past." As for her reasons for marrying Flint, he kept his suspicions to himself. It would serve no purpose to engage in speculation with André or anyone else. It was a private matter, which he intended to investigate if he survived the war. He fully intended to survive, just as he fully intended to do everything possible never to lose Catherine. How did a man go about wooing a woman he had abducted on her wedding night? *Slowly and with the utmost care.*

The men lapsed into momentary silence. Then André said, "She is well spoken and appears to have good breeding. Not the type of woman one imagines consorting with Flint."

"I quite agree, Uncle."

"She spoke of returning to New York City. Was there no way to arrange transport while you were in the colony?"

"At the time, none."

André finished his cognac and put the glass aside. "I suspect you did not wish it." When Rive was about to respond, André held up his hand and waved him off. "I will not delve into your personal feelings for her. To me they are obvious. As to whether they are reciprocated by the young woman, only you can judge. What you do about them in the future is between you and her. I shall offer no interference or advice."

"I appreciate your discretion."

André went to the window and looked out for a moment. Then he turned back to Rive. "Lise has become more insistent about returning to France, primarily for Marielle's sake. No one can predict what conditions will be like if the colony falls to the British. Also, the extended disruption in the fur trade has made the business less than profitable. Hubert and I agreed almost a year ago that we should concentrate more on shipping and banking since we are already well established in those ventures. You'll find the money there these days. You need not worry about the shares you inherited from your father. I am confident their worth will continue to rise."

Rive nodded. "I have the greatest confidence in you and Hubert, of course."

"In the meantime, there are other important matters."

Rive drained his glass and set it on the nearby desk. "You refer to the war, no doubt. It has finally brought itself almost to your doorstep."

"And will be in our beds soon. General Montcalm has made the decision to consolidate his forces here in defense of Quebec. It was a sad day for us when he was placed in command of the army."

Although a captain in the Troupes de la Marine, Rive had no direct contact with the great general. "I gather you do not agree with his strategy."

André slapped his hand down on the desktop hard enough to rattle the glass Rive had set there. "Strategy? The man has not the slightest notion of it. On his recommendation we abandoned the whole of the Ohio Valley as well as Lake Champlain. What kind of war does he think he is fighting?"

"I suppose he conducts it in the way he best understands." Rive shrugged. "Do not be too quick to condemn his tactics. When we crossed the St. Lawrence we happened on a large British force massing close to these shores. The fleet, from what I observed, consisted of several dozen warships as well as countless smaller craft. It looked as if they are planning to land a large army.

I need not remind you, Uncle, that the Americans will fight alongside the British and add considerably to their numbers. Perhaps Montcalm can repeat his victory at Ticonderoga, where he defeated an English army far greater in number. In any event, he will need all the troops he can muster just to defend Quebec. He cannot spread himself too thin."

"Oh, don't listen to me complain. It has been nothing but frustration. The defeat at Île d'Orléans, which fell last month, constituted a terrible blow for us. I saw the end in sight. You are correct about the fleet you spotted. British warships do indeed lie upriver, threatening a landing. Here, I will show you." He pulled a map from a desk drawer and spread it out, stabbing at the broad, black lines denoting the waterways. "The British are in firm control of the rivers. That, as anyone save the most confirmed optimist will tell you, spells disaster for us."

Rive leaned over the map and studied it carefully. He had been cut off from the fighting for three months. Since he spoke perfect English, he had been commissioned to impersonate a high ranking British officer and purchase arms in New York, as well as arrange for a privateer to transport them to Quebec. Success was vital, for the ports in France were blockaded and few ships were able to slip through. Although he would have been summarily shot if the deception had been discovered, he readily agreed to the plan. Fortunately, no one questioned the letter of intent he forged to purchase the arms. Had it not been for his commission, he would never have been at the wharf the day he spotted Flint and Catherine.

He continued to study the map. "Wherever they land, it will be difficult for them to scale the heights." He pointed to an area a mile or so beyond the city, where the steep cliffs, rocky and hazardous, fell in an almost straight path down to the river. "If I were General Wolfe, I would pick a spot such as this. By appearance it seems the least likely choice. Possibly not as well defended as the more logical sites. What do you think, Uncle?"

"If I had an answer, I would be in command in place of Montcalm."

Rive threw back his head and rocked with unrestrained laughter. "A pity you were not blessed with the gift of clairvoyance. A word from you and the illustrious Marquis would find himself demoted to the lowliest position in the infantry." Rive's words elicited a weak smile from his uncle. Clapping André on the back, he continued, "Try to look on a more positive side. Before winter comes, the rivers will freeze. Even if King George were to float every ship in the Royal Navy on these waters, they will have no more effect than so many stumps of dead wood."

André shrugged, appearing somewhat mollified. "I hope you are right, if we can hold out until winter." He picked up the cognac bottle and poured a small amount of the amber liquid into both glasses. "Now, let us toast your return and continued safety." He clicked the rim of his glass against Rive's. "Let us drink, also, to the successful routing of our enemies. May we send them back to Britain like whipped curs with their tails tucked firmly under their bellies."

Catherine ran her fingers over the lovely apple green silk gown the maid had laid out on the bed earlier. On the floor nearby sat a pair of cream kid slippers. After the woman left, two housemen brought in a commodious porcelain tub that took several trips to fill with hot water. Now, alone in the room Lise St. Clair said had once belonged to her daughter Francoise, Catherine pulled off her soiled gown and shift and stepped into the tub.

Sinking down until the water lapped against her throat, she leaned her head back against the rim. She closed her eyes and rubbed her skin with the perfumed soap Lise had generously supplied. To bathe like this amounted to sheer luxury of the type she had not experienced in the several months since she'd left London. Not even the hot bath Rive had provided for her on the day she made her futile escape attempt in the canoe could begin to compare.

Rive. He had not been long from her thoughts. The distraction of the tub being filled and the maid arriving with the gown and a fresh shift lasted at most a half hour. So, as happened all too frequently when she had only herself for company, she could not prevent every physical attribute he possessed from sprouting in her mind like fertile seeds—his face, his voice, the startling green of his eyes, the midnight black hair and long angular lines of his body. These images appeared too often in her dreams, as well. Mercifully, she rarely remembered what occupied her during her hours of restless sleep. Sometimes, upon awakening, memory evoked a mosaic of images, images on which a chaste young woman had best not linger. She did linger at times, indulging in a guilty pleasure that, thus far, had never strayed beyond the familiar to *that*.

She sat up so quickly that the water slid toward the rim of the tub and almost spilled over. She didn't need a mirror to confirm the flaming red of her cheeks, which she clasped between her hands in dismay. She knew so little of lovemaking beyond the half-hearted explanation her mother had provided in an attempt to prepare her for marriage. An explanation so woefully deficient in details as to leave the subject as mystifying as ever. A man and a woman coupled. That seemed to be the extent of it, although how this coupling was accomplished remained, for the most part, unclear.

"Your husband will teach you everything you need to know," her mother had finally blurted before closing the subject. That left Catherine dependent upon her imagination, which she had no desire to indulge at the moment; not when her skin tingled and the sensation, which went beyond guilty pleasure to the *forbidden*, had once again settled between her legs. She shook her head and willed her body to cease its wanton exercise.

She heard a door open, one nearby from the sound of it. Quickly, she turned her head toward her own door. The key sat in the lock. Had she remembered to turn it? She thought so but couldn't be absolutely certain. Then footsteps sounded and a male voice said, "Ah hah." Rive's voice. From the other side of the wall closest to where she bathed, she heard water splash and guessed the housemen were preparing a bath for him, as well. Several minutes later came the sound of a door closing, then silence.

She sat stone still, listening. What was he doing? In short order the answer presented itself. With only the wall separating them, she heard the distinct sound of water being disturbed, and she guessed he had sunk down into his tub. Then silence again. Was he leaning back with his head propped against the rim as she had done earlier? Had Lise provided *him* with perfumed soap? She still held her bar but feared the consequences to her equilibrium if she were to stroke it against her body. Her mind drew pictures of him reclining naked under a colorless veil of water. She clamped her knees together tightly lest her body invite a return of the wanton sensations to which, lately, she so easily seemed to fall prey.

Then he began to sing in a deep, rich baritone, in French and not too far off key. A rather rollicking song, one she supposed would appeal to a soldier. The tune was unfamiliar and she caught only a few words, considering the language barrier and the wall separating them. He continued on for a while before falling silent. Then, just when she thought his impromptu concert had ended, he resumed, only this time in the slower tempo appropriate to a ballad. And he sang in English.

> Oh, she's had her true admirers
> Both near and far away
> Her kisses sweet, she rations them
> Lest she be led astray
> And though I prize her best of all
> Receive naught but her scorn
> For I am just a troubadour
> Who earns his keep with song.

Eyes closed, she listened intently. Then after another pause, an additional word came through loud and clear: "Catherine."

Her eyes flew open. Was he singing about her? A troubadour, indeed. Altogether too near, as well. If she reached out, her hand could almost touch the wall separating them. With the sound so audible, she had the distinct impression he was at most an arm's length from his side of the barrier. She wondered whose room he occupied and if he knew from the start that she was in an adjoining one, bathing just like him.

"Catherine," he sang, as if in answer to her question. He knew.

Although the water had begun to cool, heat suffused her body; her limbs turned languid. She allowed several minutes to pass before she dared attempt to step out of the tub. A linen towel had been laid out on a chair, and she snatched it up and wrapped herself in it. She needed no prophet to tell her that the odd sensation in the pit of her stomach stemmed from his proximity. Surely it was not caused by longing—not with all the effort she had put forth to guard against it.

She dried her hair as thoroughly as time allowed then pulled the shift over her head. Edging the sleeves was a lace finer and far costlier than that she had torn from her own shift by the stream in the wilderness. Had nearly a month passed already?

Have I been with him for an entire month?

Quickly, she donned the stays, gown, hose, and shoes, grateful that everything fit so well. Velvet ribbons in a deep green secured the bodice, which partially exposed her shoulders. She sat at an elegant dressing table, its oval mirror crowned on top with a cluster of intricately carved rosettes. After months of hardship, she reveled in the luxury of pampering herself. She gathered her hair and wished there were some way to secure it so it did not fall loose down her back.

She opened the center drawer. As she hoped, it contained a simple brush and comb along with a glass receptacle that held several hair pins. Hearing only silence from the adjacent room, she hurriedly arranged her hair into a twist and securely pinned it so it lay against her nape. Her cheeks glowed rosy pink, but not entirely from her bath. She tiptoed to the door.

She put her ear to the door. Hearing no sound, she stepped into the hallway. As she turned toward the stairs, a movement caught her attention. Rive pushed himself away from the wall, linked his arm through hers and twirled her almost completely around. Without missing a step, he opened the door and guided her back into the room. Before she had a chance to utter a word, he pushed the door closed with his foot.

Yes, he knew.

"Mmm. You smell like wildflowers." He stood close enough to make a judgment.

He wore oyster-white breeches and black boots. His white shirt was open at the throat, his blue uniform jacket unbuttoned. His hair appeared slightly damp and tousled as if he had not had her luck finding a comb. Except for his devilishly handsome face, he might have been a stranger.

"You," she exclaimed and took a step back.

He placed one leg before him and executed a deep bow. "Yes and, as always, at your service." Barely suppressing a smile, he straightened to his full height. "You seem surprised. I assure you that a gentleman's dress—in this case the uniform of an officer in His Majesty King Louis' army—is not wholly outside the realm of my experience." As he spoke, he moved closer.

"I have only your word." Having been so effectively cornered unsettled her, and she took several steps backwards. "In any event, I attach little importance to clothing. After all, who can tell these days? Behind a gentleman's finery might easily lurk a backwoods lout." She had not meant to insult him but, as was usually the case, words were her only weapons against his boldness. He stood too close, was too imposing, too confident, too wickedly handsome …. She found her defenses no longer shored up with stone, but with fine-grained sand.

One step and the distance between them evaporated. "I see a proper bath and change of clothing have done nothing to curtail your sharp tongue. Mind, Catherine, that it does not cut too deeply."

Had it?

Can he possibly be sensitive to my opinion?

"Is that a warning?"

"Certainly not. Warning you takes a talent I, apparently, lack." The softness of his laugh indicated that he harbored no real resentment at her words. His fingers closed lightly about her arms. "Shall we put it forth as a *suggestion*?"

"That would be something new for you." The sting had gone completely from her tone.

Somehow he managed to back her against one of the four posts that anchored each bed corner. Her heart began to beat wildly. She reached behind and grasped the post for support; clearly her legs intended to be of little service. His fingertips glided down her arms with the softness of butterfly wings. Then he disengaged her hands and brought them to his chest, keeping his own hands closed about her wrists. A feverish heat surged through every part of her body; her skin was on fire with it.

He nuzzled her hair. "Yes, definitely wildflowers. When I rejoin the battle, I shall carry that scent with me." He bent his head and kissed the flushed skin at her throat. "Along with the feel of you." His face was a hair's breadth away. "The taste of you." His lips moved over hers.

The kiss, though deep, lasted but a few seconds. Then his fingers left hers to pluck the few hairpins from the twist at her nape. He dropped them onto the bed.

"Your beautiful hair. Don't ever hide it." His fingers combed through the long, thick strands. "If I fall in battle, my last thought will be of you, looking exactly as you do at this moment."

She felt the rise and fall of his chest and looked into his eyes. She saw no fear of death. As she had suspected weeks ago, he would never shrink from leading a charge into the enemy's lines. Musket fire would never stay him. A maudlin thought and certainly not the last she wished to have of him.

"You are far too ornery to be felled in battle"

He pressed a fingertip lightly against her parted lips. "Let us not speak of my past transgressions." His finger moved from her lips and glided over her chin. When it rested in the soft flesh beneath, he tipped her head back.

His eyes expressed his desire, and she sensed his wish for them not to argue. This she could not deny him. Yet she must choose her words with care, must give no hint that if he died in battle her heart would wither. Her family obligation was clear; her destiny lay elsewhere. He could never become a part of her life.

"I had thought to say only that I wish you Godspeed, as I would wish it for any soldier. My hope is, when this conflict ends, you will be delivered safely to your family."

If he expected a more affectionate declaration, he hid his disappointment. He took her hand, turned the open palm upward, and brought it to his lips.

"Au revoir, then." He released her. "I think it is not yet over between us. That is my hope. Perhaps time will prove me right."

"You are mistaken." Catherine spoke in a surprisingly steady voice. It masked an overwhelming sadness, one which she could never confess. "What you are suggesting will not come to pass."

She did not think he would stop her from leaving the room, and he proved her correct. Still, she was wise enough to turn her gaze from his. Walking quickly to the door, she almost ran from her own heated denial.

MARIELLE STOOD WITH HER BACK AGAINST her bedroom door, her features pinched into a scowl. The ten minutes she had spent with her eye to the keyhole confirmed her worst suspicion: Madame Flint and her cousin were much more than traveling companions. She wondered if they were lovers and decided that in all likelihood they were. Why else would he be welcomed into her bedroom?

Why did he have to bring her here? Why, especially when she, Marielle, wanted nothing more than for him to pick her up and twirl her around, even tease her like he usually did, which showed he cared something for her?

She would never understand why he chose to spend his precious time with another man's widow.

On the verge of tears, she stamped her foot, not once but several times. Her father *must* find a way to deliver Madame back to New York and out of their lives. He simply must. And quickly.

Chapter 21

※

In the two weeks since Catherine's arrival in New France, her days and nights had been fraught with anxiety: the fear that her return to England would never be accomplished, the British barrage on Quebec, and Marielle's persistent questions as to Catherine's relationship with Rive. She had seen nothing of him since the evening in her bedroom. At dinner, André announced Rive had left to reestablish himself with the French forces. Because no news to the contrary had reached them, she assumed he was safe. However, news might be difficult to deliver in the midst of a war.

So, at night, when she tossed alone in her bed, she tortured herself with the thought that perhaps he lay wounded in a makeshift hospital with neither adequate food nor medicine. She had made light of his falling in battle, but whenever she thought it a real possibility, pain squeezed her heart. Although most nights she slept poorly, when she did dream, he still played a central role.

Usually, after dinner, Catherine returned to her room to snuggle deep into the feather bed. Propped against a pair of plump pillows, she read until the candle on the nightstand was nearly extinguished. André had an extensive library and invited her to avail herself of it. Literature had always been a great source of enjoyment and now, more than ever, she welcomed the escape it provided. Sometimes, when she found sleep elusive, she would read long into the night, immersed in the flowing passages of the French philosopher and author, Voltaire. Also, she tried never to intrude on Lise and André. They had treated her with warmth and kindness, insisting she call them by their given names, as they did her. Marielle, to the girl's consternation, had been instructed by her mother to always address their guest as Madame.

One evening, during her third week in Quebec, with the early August weather favorable, Catherine was walking in the secluded garden behind the house. Neatly trimmed shrubs, tall trees and colorful flower beds spread across the grounds. In their midst sat a small gazebo, its latticed sides painted white, with seating inside.

Her anxiety had been especially acute that evening. Although the garden provided a haven of serenity, she felt beset on all sides by circumstances that seemed calculated to shatter her tenuous calm. Each day brought ever-increasing concern for her parents. When would the news of Flint's death be dispatched to London? Perhaps it already had been. She felt it ever more critical that Rive arrange her travel to New York.

She stepped into the gazebo and sat quietly, her head bent and hands clasped in her lap.

"My dear, are you not well?"

She looked up to find Lise standing before her. Although she made an effort to appear composed, her anxiety must have showed.

"You look more than a trifle pale." Lise seated herself beside Catherine. "I hope you are not coming down with the fever."

Catherine's throat felt tight, and she forced herself to swallow and make light of her dismay. "It's nothing."

"Oh, but my dear young lady, it is decidedly something. Are you concerned for your safety?"

"No."

"You are worried, all the same. That is quite obvious."

"I was thinking of my parents. I have not seen them for many months." These last words escaped almost as a sob, and Lise gathered Catherine into her arms.

They sat quietly for a few moments. "I am not a meddling woman, but sometimes it is best for the—how do you say it—the *wellness*, yes, that we confide in another person. You are far from your home and family, but I am here and you may say to me anything and know it will remain only with me. I give you my word. Come, tell me what makes a woman so young and beautiful so sad."

"You are very kind." Catherine had a moment's hesitation about unburdening herself. The moment passed, and with a sense of relief, she disclosed something of her family and the circumstances that led to her father's bankruptcy. "Surprisingly, I was able to earn a small amount of money. A woman who knew my mother arranged for me to give piano lessons to a young girl. Twice a week, I walked to her house, where we worked first on scales, then simple pieces and finally more difficult ones. A serious pupil, she learned quickly. After several months, her mother approached me and asked if her daughter might have advanced enough to give a recital in their home. I readily agreed."

With the memory of that night, Catherine's hands clenched and she fell silent.

After a lapse of several seconds, Lise placed her hand over Catherine's. "I think this recital changed your life. *N'est-ce pas*?"

Catherine nodded before turning her gaze toward the garden. "It was the night I met Mr. Flint."

Speaking his name chilled her, and she paused to collect herself. "He had passed the Season in London and was a guest at the recital. After my pupil played several pieces, her mother insisted I also favor them with a selection. Not wishing to take anything from the girl's success, I picked a simple sonata. At its conclusion, I found Mr. Flint at my elbow. He introduced himself, and we chatted for several minutes. When I excused myself in preparation for returning home, he insisted upon delivering me there in his carriage. Since it had grown late, I accepted.

"The next day, his servant arrived with an invitation from Mr. Flint inviting me to lunch. I wrote a polite refusal and thought that the end of it. I was mistaken. Other invitations followed, one to a concert, and another to the theater. Although it had been many months since I had enjoyed such entertainments, again I declined. Several times I observed him walking past my home. I became quite alarmed at his persistence and finally told him outright I would not entertain his suit. That said, he disappeared, but not for long. Then I began to feel afraid."

"Yes. You were right to fear him."

Catherine turned toward Lise, who bore a sympathetic expression. Her hand still rested atop hers, making it easier to confide in her about the night Flint proposed marriage. "He made it clear my refusal would in all likelihood bring about my father's swift imprisonment. He spoke as if he, in some way, might even hastily accomplish it. Deeply in debt, my father's fate would be sealed. Still he would never have condoned my marriage to Mr. Flint under those circumstances."

"So your father never suspected."

Catherine shook her head. "No. The next morning, Mr. Flint, aided by my complicity, obtained his consent to the union.

"Mr. Flint had booked passage to New York and was due to sail with the evening tide. I insisted I could not make ready in such haste. By then, I knew something of him and gambled he would not press the issue too strenuously. I refused to back down. It was the one concession he granted. A month later, I, too, sailed for New York. Before I boarded the ship, I informed my father that my future husband had insisted upon undertaking his and my mother's welfare. Eight weeks later, I married Mr. Flint."

Lise placed her arm around Catherine's shoulders. "Have you told any of this to Rive?"

"No. Nor will I ever. There is no purpose."

"He can help you. He is a man of some means. Under the circumstances, I know he would insist upon it."

It didn't matter whether Lise referred to Catherine's abduction or her parents' financial distress. She must forestall involving Rive. "I know you mean well, but I would never enlist his assistance."

"Why ever not?"

Catherine tried to choose her words carefully so as not to cause disharmony. Certainly, Lise's suggestion had come about through her own kind nature and was offered in all innocence.

"You see, I have already traveled such a familiar route, one upon which I shall never embark again. Not with Rive, nor anyone. Perhaps I am too proud. Having surrendered not just my pride but my liberty to one man, I cannot countenance doing so again."

"My dear, unlike Mr. Flint, Rive would never demand repayment from you, certainly not anything as far-reaching and permanent as marriage." Then, apparently reading the shock on Catherine's face, she immediately clapped a hand against her cheek. "I did not mean to imply he would require … that he would compromise your … oh, what am I trying to say? I cannot seem to find the right words."

Catherine sought to put the woman at ease. "I believe you meant he would expect nothing in return, certainly not …." Here she, too, sought the appropriate language, words more delicate than the ones that first sprang to mind. "He would expect nothing of a *personal* nature."

"Exactly." Lise sounded greatly relieved. "I assure you he is not the kind of man to take advantage. He is … well …."

"A man of high moral character who possesses a keen sense of justice. I have already been apprised by his friend Louis as to his virtues. I understand he has been to court!" She could not subdue the smile spreading across her face, and the two women dissolved into peals of laughter.

"Oh, such nonsense!" Lise composed herself. "If I know Rive, it was only to confirm for himself the excesses of the monarchy and to mock them. You know something of him, enough to see he is anything but a sycophant and a fop."

Catherine felt her cheeks flush. "Yes, he is anything but those."

"So at least we have settled something. Regarding my suggestion, you alone must decide whether or not to seek his assistance." Lise stood and offered her hand to Catherine. "Come inside now. André has some news concerning your departure from New France."

"Then there is a chance?"

"Yes. Nothing is certain. André will explain."

Catherine hurried with Lise back to the house. They found André in the library with a map spread across one of the mahogany tables.

"I wish I had something more conclusive to offer, but at the moment it is only a possibility. Rive sent word he believes that the privateer he engaged in New York to transport munitions to Quebec might still be somewhere in the city. The man has been most effective in slipping through the British blockade, bringing much-needed supplies from the American colonies."

Catherine was cheered by the news. "Is he English?"

"No, no, my dear. He is French. He plies the sea between the West Indies and New England."

A look of confusion crossed Catherine's face. "I am not sure I follow you."

"I suppose it does sound rather complicated." He beckoned Catherine closer to the map. "Do you know anything of the Indies?"

"Only that they are made up of many islands. England and France have staked claims there."

André pointed to several small configurations, some no larger than a dot. "Here you see the principal French islands. In spite of the war, a flourishing trade is still carried on with the American colonies. The islands produce molasses, which is distilled into rum in New England for the western fur trade and the African slave trade. In return, the colonies provide flour, meat, and lumber, much needed in the Indies."

It was an interesting lesson and, at any other time, Catherine would have found herself a willing pupil. Yet the connection between the far-off islands and her own predicament continued to elude her.

"What have those islands to do with me?"

"Everything. You see, it is entirely too risky to arrange an overland journey at this time. So it appears more sensible to concentrate on the sea. The privateer of whom I spoke, Captain Desault, will set sail for the Indies with only half a cargo. The other half, mainly food stores, he has sold here for many times what they would bring in the islands. At the first opportunity, he will return there. Most likely, he would be willing to take on a passenger. Let there be no doubt that such an enterprise is not without its risks."

As Catherine studied the map, her spirits lifted. "I accept the risks and thank you for your endeavors." Then a sudden thought struck her. "If I do reach the islands, how do you propose I proceed from there?"

"You will be put ashore, most likely in St. Domingue." He pointed to a spot on the map east of Jamaica. "The island is settled jointly by France and Spain, but your destination will be French soil. If you reach it—and there can be no guarantee—you will be within one hundred miles of Jamaica. Once there you will encounter your own countrymen. It should be possible to book passage either to New York or England."

"Oh, England, for sure," Catherine's enthusiasm peaked then just as quickly plunged. "You have failed to consider how I might pay for so complex a trip. I have not a shilling to my name."

A look passed between husband and wife, and Catherine thought she noticed Lise give an almost imperceptible shake of her head.

"Captain Desault will expect no payment. He was more than adequately compensated by the government of New France in his most recent endeavor."

"Are you quite certain? I will not countenance a debt on my behalf being incurred by you, nor by anyone else in your family." This last statement she hoped made clear what she had disclosed earlier: under no circumstances would she allow herself to become indebted to Rive. She looked directly at Lise but could say no more without calling into question her and her husband's honesty.

Chapter 22

The next week passed with nary a variation in routine. Catherine kept to herself as much as possible and waited expectantly for word of the privateer. Most evenings were spent her in her room, but sometimes—when overly restless and lured by the pleasant weather—she sought solitude in the garden. One night, after a rare festive dinner of roast hen, carrots, potatoes, and a small sugared cake, she fetched a light shawl and slipped outside unnoticed.

A carpet of moonlight spilled across the gravel path, and stones crunched under her feet as she walked slowly away from the house. The night was ablaze with stars that splashed a silvery-white light across the dark sky. For once, even the British guns were stilled.

Crickets chirped in the lilac-scented air. The only other sounds issued from inside the house, where André's voice, rising occasionally over the softer tones of his wife's, attested to the fact the two were not yet abed. They were engaging in the topic that had held everyone's attention earlier at the dinner table—the endless war. By then, Catherine knew André's sentiments by heart. At his excited words "the damn fool ought to be shot," she could hardly suppress a smile, for the object of his wrath could be none other than the redoubtable general, Montcalm.

She moved farther down the path. Their voices faded, and she settled herself on a bench in the gazebo. Flushed from the glass of wine she had drunk at dinner, she leaned her head back and let the cool night breeze brush her face. She closed her eyes and attempted to clear her mind of all but this rare moment of peace and the sweet scents permeating the garden.

That exercise rarely brought the rewards she sought, and her thoughts consistently drifted back to Rive. Now, approaching mid-August, they'd had only one missive from him. He stated that he was safe and a British assault on the city did not appear imminent. Still, his welfare was uppermost in her mind. Often, she awakened in the night, her skin moist, her heart pounding, worried that his regiment had been overrun or he faced some other serious danger.

"Catherine."

Startled, she opened her eyes and jumped to her feet. Rive stood in the doorway, his hand and forearm braced against the side frame.

"Did I frighten you? I did not mean to."

It took a moment for her to catch her breath. "Must you forever sneak up on me?" Seeing him—not in a dream but very much in the flesh—renewed her caution, lest she fall victim to her own weakness in his presence.

"That was not my intention."

The uniform he wore reminded her of his responsibility as a soldier. "What brings you here? Does not your duty require you to be somewhere else repelling an attack?"

He cocked his head. "Listen."

She paused a moment. "I hear nothing."

"Exactly my point. There is nothing to hear. Since the British have taken a respite, so, I decided, should I. After all, whenever possible, I have given my men short leaves. Some have family nearby. For others it is a godsend just to abandon the hard ground and warm themselves in the mess tent."

"You are generous."

He shrugged. "Some of the men are very young. Many might not live to see a French victory if it comes."

At his words, a wave of sadness swept through her, then fright at the thought that he, too, might be killed. She wanted to reach out and touch him, to make certain he had come to no harm, but she recognized the danger of even the lightest touch.

"You have done them a good service, then."

He smiled. "It is necessary for morale, my own included. So I decided that I, too, should share in the bounty. That explains my presence. However, I did not mean to startle you. You looked so pensive that I could have watched you all night." He stepped into the gazebo. "What occupies your thoughts?"

Tonight his eyes seemed as green and unfathomable as the sea; the light thrown from the pale moon softened his features.

"I was thinking of you." For once, she could not deny the truth.

"Ah." He stepped closer, a pleased expression on his face.

"Let me remind you, lest you take encouragement, that my thoughts can be of a dark and uncomplimentary nature when turned toward you." With mere inches between them, she thought it wise to choose words that disguised her true feelings for him.

"Surely, not always." He reached beneath the delicate tumble of curls that brushed her cheek. His other hand settled against her back. "Can you find no room in your heart for a sweet sentiment on my behalf?"

"You are entirely too conceited." She could only blame herself for encouraging him.

"I admit my vices." His breath fanned her face. "They are many and varied, as you are wont to remind me."

"So do you now seek credit for your virtues? If indeed they exist, I have not yet discovered them." She tried wriggling out of his grip, but he had taken too firm a hold. Then again, should this be their last time together ….

She sighed and stayed her resistance.

A smile parted his lips—a bewitching, breathtaking smile of no mean proportion that could almost make her forget what he himself had referred to as his past transgressions.

"Let me see. Surely some goodness must reside in me." His brows knit together, and he paused as if in thought. "I am an honest man and steadfast in pursuit of a noble cause. Have I not been so with you?"

She kept her hands clasped together at her breast, a tiny barrier against his proximity. "Being honest and steadfast are virtues to which all men should aspire. Yet not all can claim success."

"I believe I have been both in my desire for us to reconcile our differences. It is what I have always wanted and hoped you did, too."

The personal nature of his statement put her on her guard. Instinct bade her deflect it. "I suppose there is no reason why we should not part as friends."

His lips turned down in a frown. "Do not speak of parting."

He must know that any day she might sail for the West Indies. She had been led to understand that he sought contact with the privateer willing to take her on as a passenger.

"It is inevitable." At her words, regret clutched at her heart.

"Inevitable? Perhaps. Certainly not permanent." He stated this with a conviction that left no room for discussion.

She thought it best not to contradict him. When an ocean separated them, he would come to accept the realization, as she already had, that their paths would not cross again.

He opened his uniform jacket, reached inside, and brought out two small leather-bound books. "I want you to have these." He placed them in her hands. "I have given the devil a bad name long enough. It is time I made amends."

She recognized them immediately as the slim volumes of poetry that belonged to him. In the Indian village she had spent much of her time reading from them.

"I cannot accept these. If nothing else, they should provide you with a few moments of quiet contemplation." She tried to give them back but he would not take them.

"Alas, I have no time for poetry. If good fortune turns against me, I shall have no need of it."

"Do not say that." With the books in one hand, she gripped his shirtfront with the other. "Do not even think it."

She felt the steady beat of his heart. Then his long, beautifully tapered fingers closed over hers. His body touched hers lightly, and his eyes shone with the desire she had seen so many times before. She held the volumes against her breast, deeply affected by his heartfelt gift. Had he sought to buy her affections, he would have chosen something of monetary value and not the books he had carried with him since boyhood. She could not hurt him by refusing his offer.

"I shall keep them safe until …." She bit her lower lip and swallowed the remainder of her thought—that she would hold them until he returned from the war. By then, however, she would be gone.

"Until?" He let her wriggle on her own hook as he often did when he accurately read her thoughts.

For a second she felt nonplussed. Then she made a quick recovery. "I shall keep them until I am an old woman. Then I shall make a gift of them to someone who will appreciate them as much as I."

"Hmm." He pressed his lips tightly. This seemed as far as he was prepared to go in calling her a liar. "When you read from them, will you think of me?"

"Yes … from time to time." She could not admit how constant he would be in her thoughts.

"What more can a man ask?" As if in answer to his own question, he gathered her into his arms. He bent his head and brushed her lips with a light kiss—one that might have seemed to lack passion if not for his quickening heartbeat. His hands moved up her back, plucking away her shawl and letting it flutter to the floor. Then they glided to her shoulders and along the sides of her neck, lightly skirting her throat to the underside of her chin. She shivered as his roughened palms brushed her skin. For a moment, her legs proved unequal to the task of supporting her body, and it seemed wise to lean into him for support. Her fingers, which lay against his shirt, moved over a chest that was broad and hard as a man's surely should be, although not so hard she couldn't feel a muscle twitch under her palm.

"Are you cold?" he whispered against her ear.

"No, not at all." A film of moisture flushed her skin where his fingers traced a path along her nape and into her hair. He drew her closer.

His body held few surprises. She knew with aching awareness the hard feel of his hips, the muscular swell of his thighs. One hand still clutched the books, while the other slowly glided over his chest, palm flat against the lines and contours with which she had become all too familiar. Shyly at first, she let a fingertip trail along the opening of his shirt and heard the quick pull of his breath. In all the times he had touched her, she had never touched him back. Tonight she practiced no such restraint; tonight she would follow her own heart. His heart, beating just beneath her questing fingers, gave a tiny lurch, a pleasurable sensation with which she had, over the past weeks, become well acquainted.

He planted a gentle kiss atop her head. Then his lips brushed her brow and her temple where her pulse leapt in wild response. Next, he explored her ear and teased it with the tip of his tongue before catching the lobe gently between his teeth. Her breath quickened. His lips glided along the curve of her jaw and skirted the fragile ridge to find the pale softness of her throat. With an almost languid movement, he brought his thumb beneath the dainty arc of her chin and tipped her head back. Moonlight flooded her delicate features, and he cupped her face with his hands and planted a brief kiss on the tip of her nose. Her breath, warm and sweet, escaped through parted lips. He captured them with his own in a kiss of tender restraint. Her skin held the fresh sweet scent of honeysuckle and dew, her lips, the rich taste of berry wine and sugared cakes.

He ended the kiss. "Let there be no more barriers between us." He tilted his head so the side of his face lay against her hair.

"Oh, those …." She sighed.

He took a half-step back and gazed into her eyes and saw, if not surrender, at least desire. To ensure his cause, he stroked her hair with hands that had never been gentler. A warm flush heightened the color in her cheeks, and he kissed her there in a decidedly chaste fashion, one that did not come easily, but at least came when bidden. Containing his growing excitement, he once again pressed his lips to her hair and breathed in the fresh, clean essence of rose petals.

"I have had a few regrets in my life, but keeping you with me is not one of them." Then his restraint gave way and his mouth came down on hers in a deep, longing kiss that laid bare his need. If she were to be lost to him, he doubted he would keep his sanity. Her lips parted under his coaxing. Then he broke the kiss, lifted his head, and closed his eyes for a second, willing himself not to err in presenting his proposal, which he had rehearsed endlessly all day.

"Ah, sweetest heart … my dearest heart, my love." He had never before felt so strong a need to express himself in some way other than just the physical. She sighed, and he decided that was enough love talk for now. With the tip of his tongue, he tasted the warm moisture clinging to the skin where he had peeled aside one sleeve of her gown.

CATHERINE SWAYED AGAINST HIM. THE HAND that clutched the books rested against his hip, while the other somehow found its way around his neck. *Just to keep your balance*, she reminded herself, and refused to pay heed to the voice echoing a single word in the back of her mind: liar. When he captured her mouth with his soft lips, he renewed those forbidden sensations she felt ill-equipped to banish, the ones that drove her body hard against his.

His splayed fingers became lost in her hair. Then, drawing back, he looked into her eyes.

"Come with me, if only for an hour. There is a house close to the Jesuit seminary." His words came in a rush. "No one lives there. On the way …."

She pulled her hand away from him with the alacrity of one whose skin had been burned. Then she pressed it firmly against his lips. Even from him, she had not expected so blunt a proposition. *Especially* from him. Weeks ago he could have bedded her with nothing to stop him except, presumably, his conscience. Now, time had become a precious commodity; of that he must be very aware. She had forgotten his determination.

She moved back a step. Not to do so would risk her downfall. "Do not ask that of me."

He removed her hand and held it tightly against his chest. "Oh, my love, I have not put this well at all. What I should have said first is that we can be married by Father Jean at the Jesuit seminary. These are not normal times; the reading of the banns would not be required, only your consent."

At his declaration, her jaw stiffened, robbing her of speech. Never had she anticipated a marriage proposal. Yes, he wished to bed her as, certainly, he had bedded other women. Whatever had prompted him to propose marriage? If it was truly love, she could not face it, nor could she ever declare hers for him.

"I cannot marry you," she said in a staunch tone, turning her face away. How could she agree to marry him in one breath and in the next broach the subject of her family's financial plight? Even if he did not think her calculating—and he would have every right to harbor such a suspicion—her pride had already determined she must never follow the same path again.

"We cannot marry." She tried to slip out of his embrace, but he drew her in closer.

"Why can we not?" His eyes bored into hers. "Tell me you feel nothing for me."

Words of denial stuck in her throat like a stale piece of crust. Her decision, which she knew to be right, was irrevocable. She pushed against his chest. Holding her so close, he had to be aware of the stiffness in her body.

"See? You cannot say it. Do not deny that some true feeling for me resides in your heart."

She strained away from him, refusing to meet his gaze or answer him. Such a course was fraught with danger and would take a stauncher person than she to navigate it. Her future lay not with him, but in England.

A lone candle burned inside the house, left there for her. She felt drawn to it.

"We shall put this aside for now." He brought her hand to his lips and kissed her fingertips. Then he released her.

She heard the disappointment in his tone and knew she would find it in his eyes as well. *If* she dared look at him. Averting her gaze, she turned and hurried back to the house

Chapter 23

Much to Catherine's astonishment, the city of Quebec, perched high above its protective cliffs, continued to hold out, despite renewed efforts by the British to reduce it to a heap of mortar and stone. Each day the shelling intensified. In the waning days of August, Rive sent word that General Wolf had barely a month to successfully conclude the campaign. By late September the fleet would be forced to withdraw, along with the army—which he professed was drastically reduced in number, the men falling victim to dysentery and scurvy. Also—and she could not image how—he seemed privy to the news that the British desertions were rising as their food supply continued to decrease. Of those who remained, barely half were fit for duty. For once the news raised André's spirits.

Along with Rive's missives, André shared whatever news he could garner on his rare forays into the town center. It seemed Montcalm and his troops were entrenched and refusing to give battle, and General Wolfe had been forced to commit his men to suicidal assaults. At Montmorency, an apparently vital area that André pointed out to Catherine on a map, hundreds of British lives had been forfeited. The French had opened fire from atop the vertical cliffs where the bulk of Montcalm's army was encamped. The rain, under which the inhabitants of Quebec suffered as well, had turned the battlefield terrain muddy; still, the British had clawed their way up the cliffs until the steady fire from the French gun emplacements had driven them back.

Catherine found such news disheartening, not because of her British ancestry, but because it distressed her to learn that so many young lives were being lost. It made no difference to her on which side the men fought. She hoped that if Rive was in the thick of those battles the prayers she said for him every night kept him safe.

If the rumors that swirled through the city each day were true, perhaps time favored France and her North American colony. The inhabitants of Quebec appeared capable of surviving the onslaught. When the American rangers swept up and down the river putting farms to the torch, good news followed on the heels of the bad: the colony continued to be supplied by the few French ships able to slip through the British blockade. This greatly bolstered the morale in the St. Clair household—along with the news that even Wolfe's edict forbidding the inhabitants to take up arms under penalty of death was met with derision; boys and men continued to fight alongside the experienced French forces.

However, Quebec and its inhabitants still paid a heavy price. André reported that in parts of the city, flames roared out of control. On more than one occasion, Catherine saw great billows of smoke that portended ill for the city. André also reported that huge furrows had been gouged out of the streets and roads, making navigation extremely hazardous. At that point Lise forbade him to venture far from the house. Lately, they learned the citizenry had fled in increasing numbers, fearful that the routes out of the city would be completely cut off. It had become an increasingly familiar event for Catherine to see carts pitching and weaving under the piles of household belongings as they traveled the streets, the horses urged on by grim-faced men and women determined to escape the ever-increasing bombardments. The route leading to the wharves became ever more crowded with the Seigneurs and their families who had secured passage on one of the few French ships due to return to the home country.

Catherine's own plans to escape to the West Indies had come to naught. When Captain Desault had finally been located, he lay seriously wounded, his ship set afire and scuttled in the river. Her fate was now irrevocably tied to that of the St. Clair's for as long as they chose to remain in Quebec.

As September dawned, the air became noticeably cooler. Peering through a window, Catherine noticed that the ground, at times, lay under a thin layer of frost, and the umbrellas of green leaves began to turn deep red and mustard gold. The arctic winds, not yet frigid but decidedly crisp, often seeped under the front door and around the window frames. This change required André to pile extra wood—an ever-dwindling commodity—onto the fire in the drawing room hearth, the only one kept lit and only by day. By mid-afternoon, on the few occasions Catherine ventured outside, thick streamers of gray smoke belched from a thousand chimneys throughout the city. Obviously, the St. Clair household was not the only one desperately trying to ward off the cold.

During one particularly fierce bombardment, Catherine crouched on the cellar's earthen floor, her hands pressed tightly to her ears. The thunderous reports of the cannons, each time they fired, seemed louder than ever. The massive beams directly overhead creaked and yawned as if at any moment they would surrender the upper stories of the house in one great murderous avalanche. Bits of stone tore loose from the walls. In the adjacent room, the crash of bottles joined in the din as the last of André's wine cellar was reduced to ruins.

Alongside Catherine, the St. Clairs huddled together. Lise offered whatever support she could to her husband, whose skin bore a sickly gray pallor, the result of a mild heart seizure he had experienced several days earlier. Marielle clung to her mother's arm, sobbing quietly.

A fresh volley shook the foundation. Then another, accompanied by a deafening explosion that snapped one of the overhead beams. It crashed down almost at Catherine's feet. The flame inside their one lamp extinguished, pitching them into what would have been total darkness were it not for the bands of weak light issuing in from a pair of small windows.

Then everything grew still, save for the squealing of a rat in some dark corner. Catherine's heart pounded, and she wondered if the shelling had actually stopped or if she were no longer capable of hearing. For the longest time, no one moved. Then she uncoiled her cramped legs and rose unsteadily to her feet. Cautiously, she crept to the foot of the stairs, where she paused and listened for recurring sounds from outside.

"It seems to have stopped." The silence continued. "Perhaps we had best wait a while longer before returning upstairs."

"Pray God there is something left to go up to," Lise cried.

When the silence remained unbroken, they navigated the dark stairs, picking their way through chunks of plaster that had fallen from the ceiling. Embers still burned in the kitchen grate, and André lit the lamp and held it aloft. The room lay in shambles, with pots, pans and broken crockery strewn everywhere. In the front rooms, the damage repeated itself. Almost everything of a breakable nature lay in pieces. The worst shock, however, was the sight of the gaping holes where once the window panes stood.

"*Mon Dieu*," André exclaimed, "it is a small wonder we were not all killed."

Lise sobbed quietly as she surveyed the wreckage. Almost all her possessions lay in ruins. She picked up the pieces of a china figurine and hugged them to her breast, while a fresh spate of tears trickled down her cheeks. Catherine felt a surge of compassion, but there was little solace she could offer other than a sympathetic pat on the shoulder and a mumbled, "It will be all right," which even she did not believe.

Dejected, they repaired to the drawing room. The rear of the house had suffered little destruction beyond a few cracked window panes. At least the brandy decanter had come through the assault unscathed. After the ladies were seated, André poured a glass for each, even allowing Marielle a sip from his. Then he settled beside Lise on the settee.

She put aside her glass, took one of his hands and held it tightly in hers. "We must decide what to do. The house is barely habitable, and who knows what danger tomorrow will bring. We have had a good life here, but it is over. We have remained this long only because of your stubborn pride."

André squeezed his wife's hand. "Sometimes that is all a man has left."

"It has sent more than one man to his grave, and we must think of Marielle. She is young and deserves a chance to live a full life."

At the mention of her name, and seemingly recovered from her fright, Marielle rushed to her mother's side. "I am not afraid, *Maman*. I agree with Papa. Why should we allow the British to drive us out?"

"Perhaps when the roof falls in on your head, you will not be so brave."

The girl made an impatient sound with her tongue. "That is not likely to happen."

Lise raised a brow and glared at her daughter. "I have neither the strength nor the inclination to argue with you. If you cannot be sensible, sit down somewhere and be quiet."

"Oh," Marielle cried. "Why is it every time I try to express my opinion, I am told to sit down and be quiet? Am I to have no say in my own future?"

"And what do you think the future holds for you here? In France you will be able to complete your education. You will have a proper home. When the time comes for you to marry, you will find more than your share of eligible young men from whom to choose. Your uncle, Hubert, has connections at court and will help you make the right match."

Marielle's small hands clenched into fists. "I will not be married off to someone who appeals to you and Papa and Uncle Hubert and whom I shall hate. I don't care if he has the ear of the king himself. You cannot force me."

Catherine watched the girl, so obviously miserable, and guessed the source of her anguish. As long as Rive remained in Quebec, Marielle wished to stay as well. Perhaps she hoped, with the passing of a few short years, he would return her affection and marry her. Catherine sympathized with her, but she could offer no comfort. In the past, every gesture of friendship she put forth had been met with a stiff rebuff.

André glanced at his daughter. "No one will coerce you into anything. What your mother meant was that someday you will wish to marry and have a family of your own. If the young man is well-connected, so much the better. That is years away, so calm yourself."

As if sensing a lost battle, Marielle acquiesced, although she sat smoldering on the edge of a wing chair.

Catherine turned her attention back to Lise and André.

"We are not destitute," Lise insisted. "We have enough money to spend the rest of our lives in comfort. We could live in Paris or, if you prefer, the countryside. It would be lovely to entertain again, see friends and make plans. None of that is possible here. Even with a British defeat, it will take years to rebuild the city. I am too old to start anew." Lise's voice broke and she leaned her head against her husband's shoulder.

"Hear, hear, do not go on so. You will have a house in Paris if it means so much to you. I do not suppose there is much to salvage here." He looked about the room at the accumulation of possessions that represented the last thirty years of their lives together. The portraits of their daughters, painted when they were children, looked down upon them from the walls.

He sighed heavily. "Who could have foreseen such a disaster? I have made a fortune, *two* in some men's eyes. With most of it already invested abroad, we shall not want for anything. I know you have never shared my deep love for this colony, but you have been a dutiful wife. If returning home will make you happy, that is what we shall do."

He rose wearily to his feet. "Since that is settled, I am going to bed. I advise you ladies to do the same. With luck, we shall pass the remainder of the night undisturbed. Tomorrow, I shall petition the Governor General's office for passage to France." Then he turned to Catherine, who had been following the proceedings with great interest. "It seems you are destined to make a sea journey after all. Only this time, I promise you will not be disappointed."

"I am very grateful for your consideration." She made her excuses and left them to go to her room.

The staircase leading to the second story had surrendered whole parts of its wooden banister. Some of the elegantly carved spindles had broken off completely or teetered precariously over the hallway below. In several places plaster had come loose from the ceiling and lay in jagged chunks on the stairs. As she climbed each step, she hugged the wall. Without the banister for support, she might have been skirting the edge of a precipice.

Once undressed and in bed, she lay awake, staring into the darkness. It seemed fate was directing her home after all. More than anything, she wished to return to her family. Together they would face the future, no matter what it held. As for Rive, she would tuck the memory of him deep into her heart. That chapter in her life was, as needs be, irrevocably closed.

Chapter 24

Late one afternoon in early September, Catherine was confronted in her bedroom by a visibly distraught Lise. One look at the woman's face convinced her that something of an extremely serious nature had occurred. When questioned, however, Lise avoided any direct answers.

"André will explain everything." She hurried Catherine out of the bedroom.

"Is there a problem with the ship? Has André had disappointing news regarding the voyage to France? Will we not be sailing after all?" Catherine's stomach tightened and her suspicions grew that she had correctly guessed something of the woman's dilemma.

"Of course we will sail. Everything has been arranged. Nothing, really, that cannot be remedied once we safely arrive on the Continent. Please, do not worry. Now come, we must hasten. They are all waiting downstairs."

Upon entering the drawing room, Catherine felt her anxiety grow. Something serious had indeed occurred. For a moment, it looked as if she had blundered into a tableau. André stood stone still near the window, his hands behind his back, his chin lowered almost to his chest. Marielle sat in a stiff pose on the settee, her mouth a tight slash drawn across her face. One small hand was clutched to her bosom; the other lay closed—fisted on her knee. A man Catherine had never seen before hovered beside André. Small and dark, he had piercing black eyes that seemed to stare right through her as though he had seen something beyond that had caught his interest.

Curious, Catherine turned her head just as Rive slowly unwound his tall frame from a chair against the wall. Trouble tightened his features. At first she thought he had risen to greet her for, indeed, he walked toward her. Then he stopped, stepped away and strode purposefully toward André.

"I suggest we proceed. She has been informed, I trust, or have you saved that delicate bit of business for the last?"

Catherine could not imagine what he meant or why he would appear so uncomfortable. Convinced now the problem stemmed from their plans to flee the colony, she was puzzled by Rive's reaction. Surely, if he had been called upon to assist his aunt and uncle in some way, he would hardly resent it. He had always shown a genuine fondness for them. And, yes, despite his declaration in the garden, she could not believe he would do anything to forestall *her* leaving. No, there was more to it—something that had prompted the presence of the dark little man who stood somberly in their midst.

The atmosphere grew progressively strained. Seconds passed and still, whatever the news, no one seemed anxious to impart it. Was that the purpose of this man? He looked decidedly ill at ease now, as though he wished nothing more than to fulfill his duty and hasten back to wherever he had been summoned from.

"Will you please be seated, my dear." André surrendered his spot near the window and moved to Catherine. As he did, he drew a chair forward for her.

Just before she sat, she noticed a sheaf of papers on a nearby table. Courtesy forbade her to steal no more than a fleeting glance, which was hardly enough to determine the contents. She had only a moment to speculate about them before André once again began to speak.

"Catherine, may I present Monsieur Duprey."

As she acknowledged the introduction, the man edged forward, head bobbing as he bowed.

"Something has ... ah ... occurred," André began, "which was unforeseen and which I assure you has only recently come to light. I will explain everything. Once you are privy to the facts, you will understand why certain measures are necessary."

Before he had a chance to continue, Rive broke in. "Really, Uncle, must you go about this in such a drawn-out manner? If you are unable to come directly to the point, then allow me, as I suggested earlier."

André held up a hand, staying any further protest. Rive shrugged, then went to a window and stared out into the growing dusk.

André cleared his throat and again addressed Catherine. "Now then, as sometimes happens when making plans, unexpected complications arise. In this case, we have a situation that presents a slight annoyance. You see, each individual who wishes to obtain passage on one of His Majesty's ships—a difficulty these days as space is exceedingly scarce—must show proof to Monsieur Duprey that he or she is unquestionably a subject of the king—either through birth or marriage. We are all, of course, French citizens, but that is not the case with you. Under any other circumstances, this rule would not be so strictly enforced. Unfortunately, with conditions as they stand, Monsieur Duprey cannot see his way clear to bend this rule for anyone." André glared at Duprey before turning back to Catherine. "So you see, some unorthodox measures are required in order to remedy the situation."

Catherine's brows knit together in a frown. "I don't understand how such a circumstance can be changed."

"It can, I assure you. It will be perfectly legal."

"You mean I am somehow to become a French citizen?" Catherine glanced at Monsieur Duprey, who nodded his head in agreement. "Surely there is no time. There must be certain requirements to fulfill. I am at a loss as to how to proceed." Her eyes went to the papers just beyond her reach, and she hastily concluded they must be the instrument by which this requirement would be satisfied.

André extracted a handkerchief from his pocket and mopped his brow. Having appeared reasonably calm up to this point, he now gave a different impression. Catherine tried to ease any distress she might have caused. "Of course, I will do whatever you suggest."

Her answer, however, did not bring the expected relief. André still appeared troubled. Even Lise, who sat unobtrusively away from the group with tightly clasped hands, was ill at ease.

"Is there something else?" Catherine was now thoroughly bewildered.

"I wish it were as simple as acquiring immediate citizenship," André continued. "I fear only the king himself could facilitate such a matter with the stroke of a pen. So we must seek other channels by which to accomplish this deed. We … that is … Rive and I have consulted with Monsieur Duprey and come to a conclusion. Our only alternative is to follow his advice."

"Which is?" Catherine was suddenly seized by a premonition it would not be to her liking.

"You must be married at once to a French citizen."

"Married?" At first she thought she must have misunderstood. Then all at once, Lise's reluctance to answer her questions became clear. Now, too, she understood Rive's presence. They … he expected her to marry him. She pushed herself up from the chair.

"I will not do it. I will not even consider it."

Lise rushed forward and put her arms around Catherine. "I understand how you feel, but it is the only possible solution."

"Is it?" She looked from Rive to André. "I would rather stay here."

"That is out of the question," André exclaimed. "You have no idea of the rabble the British have recruited. Don't think for a moment the Americans will conduct themselves like gentlemen if they are given free rein over a vanquished city. No, you must leave with us."

"If Madame Flint prefers the company of the Americans, then I do not think you should force her to marry Cousin Rive." Marielle's voice, high-pitched and tremulous, carried across the room. "I am certain he does not wish it either. I think you are being unfair, and I, for one, shall never forgive you."

During the girl's tirade, Rive vacated his position by the window and stalked over to Catherine. With a firm grip on her arm, he steered her toward the open doorway. Once through it, he guided her to the other side of the house and into the parlor. A chill spread through the room in spite of the heavy drapes kept constantly drawn over the now glassless windows. No fire burned in the hearth; yet neither of these privations caused the coldness that seeped through Catherine's body. Even if sunlight flooded the room, it could not dispel the cold that gripped her.

"You planned this. How could you?"

"Listen to me, Catherine." He spoke softly, but in a serious tone that told her he would brook no contradiction. His fingers gripped both her arms as if in anticipation of her flight. "First, I have no influence upon the decrees issued by the Governor General. Second, and most important, if I were to enter into a marriage contract with you, it would be one that poses little chance of consummation. On that you have my word."

"I do not believe you."

"This is a temporary measure." Underlying the persuasion in his tone, there sounded a clear undercurrent of urgency. "After the marriage is duly recorded, you will be under no obligation to conduct yourself as my wife. When you reach France, the marriage will be put aside through legal channels. It will be as if it never happened."

Catherine's gaze locked onto his. "I have only your word. What guarantee do I have?"

"What more should you require beyond my word?" He sounded almost incredulous that, after all this time, she would question his veracity. "Do you think I would maneuver you into marriage just to satisfy my own desire? You know I wish to marry you. I made that clear. However, your refusal ended my hopes. For heaven's sake, Catherine, do you think me so villainous, so base ...." Suddenly he stopped speaking and just stared at her for a moment. "My God, that's what *Flint* did."

She remained stoic, did not even blink. Her jaw tightened, and she clenched her teeth.

"Oh, my sweet. Why did you not tell me?" One hand came away from her arm to gently cup the side of her face. "*Ma chère.*"

"Mr. Flint has no bearing here." She turned her face away.

"I could not disagree with you more. I shall not belabor the point, however." He dropped his hands to his sides and stepped back from her. "My uncle Hubert will carry out your wishes. On my honor."

She took a moment to decide if he spoke the truth and chose to trust him, for she could think of no instance in which she had caught him in a blatant lie. He was a man who comported himself in a manner he believed justified his actions. He never made excuses, at least to her, for his behavior. She had branded him with many an epithet, but "liar" had never been among them.

"I will agree to the marriage under the conditions you stated. As long as it is understood that I can never fulfill the *duties* of a wife."

"I have no choice but to accept your terms." His expression up to then had appeared dour, but now it lightened somewhat. "However, a wise man once said that it is most impolitic to utter so irrevocable a word as 'never.'" He appeared to smile, although subtly enough as to leave some doubt. "Yes, it can be most impolitic. Can you not, at least on the face of it, see some good advice there?"

"No."

"Ah." He nodded as if accepting defeat.

She remained silent. If she knew only one thing about Rive, it was his expertise at parrying words.

He let a few moments pass. "Come. We had best return to the others before André's heart finally gives out."

When they reentered the drawing room, André stepped forward expectantly. Lise hurried to Catherine. Marielle appeared as grim as if attending a funeral.

"I believe we are ready for Monsieur Duprey." Rive guided Catherine to where the man stood.

"Then I shall perform the ceremony without further delay?" Duprey turned to André. "You and Madame St. Clair will be required to act as witnesses. Do you have a ring?"

Rive reached into his jacket and brought out a simple gold band. When and where he had acquired it, Catherine could not even guess. Perhaps it had been in his possession for some time in the hopes she would agree to become his wife. As Monsieur Duprey's voice drifted over her, Catherine managed to utter the few required words. Rive took her hand and slipped the ring onto her finger. Then there were papers to sign, and, shortly after gathering them together, Duprey took his leave.

Springing up from her chair, Marielle gave in to the misery that had kept her silent during the exchange of vows.

Her eyes swollen and red, she glared at her parents. "How could you? Oh, I hate you. I hate you all!" She dashed out of the room, slamming the door closed.

André and Lise seemed anxious, too, to exit. Making their excuses, they followed on the heels of their daughter. Rive, on the other hand, showed no such haste to withdraw. Quite the contrary, he stayed close to Catherine's side.

"So it is done."

She stood dazed. With great effort, she finally managed to set one foot ahead of the other, intending to take her leave as well. She had gained but a step when he stayed her progress and turned her toward him.

"But not quite." He took her in his arms and brought his mouth down onto hers in a kiss that bespoke the passion of a man finding himself alone, for the first time, with his bride. As the kiss deepened, he parted her lips and coaxed a small response. He moved his mouth in such a way as if to end the kiss, only to resume it with renewed ardor.

Catherine's body went limp. She clutched the sides of his jacket and held on as if her very existence depended upon it. Try as she might to temper her response, the battle had been lost the moment he touched her. Her lips, opened as eagerly as a bud exposed to brilliant sunlight, willingly sought his. All the while her mind, which had temporarily abdicated its control of her body, echoed the imprudence of her actions and sounded a warning that it took all her resolve to obey.

It was he who ended the kiss. Almost abruptly, he set her aside. He raked his fingers through his hair. "Go to your room, Catherine."

She hesitated as if her feet were rooted in pitch.

"Go to your room. *Now*."

His expression indicated he was doing all he could to hold himself in restraint. It finally shook her from her reverie. Slowly at first, then with a quicker step, she hurried to the door. She grasped the knob and could not help noticing the gold band encircling her finger. This one she would keep forever, but tucked safely away from view.

"Goodbye," she whispered under her breath. Then she pulled open the door, certain she had seen the last of Rive St. Clair.

Chapter 25

※

Catherine sat bolt upright in bed, her heart drumming inside her chest, her fingers clutching at the comforter that had dropped to her waist. There was a pounding in her ears from a sound she could not distinguish. She waited a moment until the last vestiges of sleep dissipated and her eyes adjusted to the darkness. The candle beside her bed had extinguished, and no light showed through the chink in the heavy drapes closed against the night drafts. It could be any hour, but she guessed it was probably well past midnight.

She pulled the comforter back up to her shoulders and listened again for whatever sound had awakened her. Now she heard it quite distinctly. Slipping out of bed, she quickly donned her robe. Then she went to the bedroom door and opened it. Frantic shouts, accompanied by fists pounding upon wood, greeted her from somewhere outside the house.

Stepping into the hallway, she fully expected to meet André or Lise, but aside from the disturbance that drew her toward the stairs, the house remained quiet. She proceeded with caution, feeling her way in the dark along the stair wall, until she stood, wide-eyed with fright, at the front door.

"Rouse yourself quickly," a voice cried, before another assault was made upon the stout wood. Fumbling with the heavy lock, she finally threw the door wide.

The moon spread only a faint light, but enough to illuminate a tall, sturdily built youth of about sixteen. He stumbled in, almost knocking her off her feet. His face was streaked with dirt, his clothes in a not much better state. Clutching his side as if in pain, he leaned against the wall, panting.

Catherine stepped back and wondered if admitting the boy had been a mistake. His eyes did indeed look wild. Then she saw his fatigue. If he were bent on mischief, he had little strength left to carry it out.

"Who are you? What brings you here at this hour of the night?"

He took a deep breath and exhaled in a rush of air. "My name is Baptiste. I have been sent by Captain St. Clair to warn you that the British are planning to fire on the city before dawn. He said it will be a heavy assault and much worse than ever before."

She wondered how Rive could be privy to such information. She took the boy's arm and led him away from the door. As yet, she could hear nothing of the coming onslaught. However, if the information proved correct, she did not want either of them exposed to danger. An eerie silence pervaded the streets, which at any moment could be torn apart by cannon fire.

"Captain St. Clair said you understood the steps you must take. The ship lies ready in the harbor. He insisted that you prepare yourselves in all haste. I am to take you there myself."

"What is all the commotion?" André slowly descended the stairs. Behind him, Lise held a candle aloft, her expression as puzzled as her husband's.

Catherine relayed the boy's message and stepped back, leaving André in charge. He spoke to Baptiste for a few minutes before addressing the women, his face etched with worry.

"Dear God, they expect the worst. The British have almost doubled the number of cannons on Pointe Levis. Also, they have increased the complement of soldiers quartered there. Something is in the wind and bodes ill for those who remain in the city. Oh, that fool, Montcalm!" The rage in his voice was fueled by frustration, if not heartiness.

Lise patted her husband's back in an attempt to soothe him. "Do not get so excited. We intended to leave. We shall simply do it sooner."

André shook loose from his wife's hand. "Montcalm is to blame for everything! His self-serving pride has brought this city to an undeserved pass. What will be left even should France prevail? He seems incapable of stopping the tide that pulls against us."

Lise shook her head sadly and walked back to the stairs. "It seems the end might come soon. It remains for us now to save ourselves. I will awaken Marielle. Then we must take what we can carry and make our way to the ship."

It took no time at all for Catherine to collect her few belongings. Unlike the St. Clairs, she had little to salvage. Even the clothes she wore belonged to another woman. Since the servants had been released from their duties days before to return to their families, she helped Lise gather whatever she could— silver pieces, the few items of valuable china that had remained intact, two boxes of André's books, the two small paintings of their daughters and warm clothing for the sea voyage. When at last they were ready, a thin ribbon of light appeared on the horizon. Baptiste hitched up the horses while the four of them crammed their belongings inside the carriage, barely leaving enough room for themselves. What could not fit was strapped to the roof. Then the young man climbed onto the driver's seat and they began their sad procession through the city's streets.

To Catherine's surprise, they were not the only ones abroad. Besides a fair number of militiamen, dozens of wagons and carriages slogged along the road. Their wooden frames groaned, as did theirs, under the strain of unaccustomed loads. Had these people been given the same warning to evacuate? How, she wondered for the second time, had Rive become privy to the British plan to launch a new assault?

Even as she considered this, the thunderous sound of cannon fire erupted in the distance. Having been quiet for the past several nights, it now heralded a fearsome bombardment. The horse shied and the carriage swayed precariously, throwing Catherine into Marielle, who sat, grim and silent, beside her.

Then a stabbing pain shot through Catherine's ribs, caused by a fierce thrust from the girl's elbow. After settling back into the corner to catch her breath, Catherine turned toward Marielle, whose face bore an open look of hostility. All the rage she harbored since the night Catherine and Rive had wed was etched into her childlike features. Catherine accepted the rebuke, for to chastise the girl meant bringing certain discord into the family. Also, once they reached France, her association with Marielle would end.

The carriage gave a sickening jolt and a moment later drew to a halt. Baptiste threw open the door and leaned inside.

"It is impossible to negotiate the street. We shall have to take another route."

"Can you reach the Palace Gate?" André peered through the door opening. "Perhaps we will find less congestion there. If we can make it that far, we can continue on foot."

Lise surveyed the baggage piled up around them and burst into tears. "We shall have to leave almost everything behind."

André took her hand and patted it. "Everything we lose can be replaced. All we need is enough clothing to see us through the journey. We shall take the portraits of the children, of course. In any event, you know how you enjoy visiting the shops. Once we are safely in France, you may purchase anything you wish."

His promise seemed to appease her somewhat. With a sigh, she sank heavily against the seat.

Once again, the horses leaped forward and the coach veered off in a different direction. With deadly accuracy, the cannonballs found their mark. The first acrid waves of smoke drifted in on them, making their eyes tear. The women held handkerchiefs to their noses and everyone was forced to take shallow breaths. Catherine pressed the edge of her cloak to her eyes, but as fast as she blotted the moisture, it reappeared, blurring the landscape.

Twice Baptiste had to stop the coach and maneuver around some obstacle. Miraculously they were able to continue, even as fragments of earth and stone pelted the carriage. However, as they drew closer to the wall on the outskirts of the city, it became increasingly clear the route to the ship would be more hazardous than expected. They halted again, and this time Catherine knew from the miserable expression on Baptiste's face when he looked in the doorway that they could proceed no farther.

"The road is blocked. The militia is waving everyone back. We must continue on foot. It will be dangerous, but, in the end, quicker."

As he spoke, a complement of militiamen approached. Shouting, they tried to urge the people back into the city. Glancing through the window opening, Catherine thought she caught a glimpse of a white and blue uniform, the same uniform as Rive's. Was he somewhere among the troops? When the end came—and it seemed likely it would not be far off—would he find his way to safety? She refused to acknowledge the possibility of his being killed in a final battle somewhere on a blood-soaked field. She blinked back tears.

An angry shout echoed, and a soldier rushed toward them. Gripping Baptiste by the shoulders, he gave him a shove that sent him reeling into the front wheel of the carriage.

"Get this blasted thing out of the road." The soldier advanced on the boy, the butt of his rifle raised in the air. "If you have any sense at all, you will seek immediate shelter for yourself and those in your party."

"Just a moment." André eased himself from the carriage. "There is no need to browbeat the lad. He is merely trying to see us safely out of the city." Hastily, he introduced himself and explained their purpose for being abroad.

The soldier stared at André, then at the three women.

"You are mad, Monsieur, to even consider such an action. The enemy seems bent on reducing everything to rubble, and the roads are nearly impassable. I cannot make too clear the danger in which you place yourself and the ladies if you try to go beyond this point."

Just then an explosion rocked the ground, and a massive section of the wall collapsed under a thunderous avalanche of stone. Although it took place perhaps two hundred yards ahead, the concussion almost caused André to lose his footing.

"Do you see what I mean? The cannon fire is murderous. You would do well to reconsider. Now I must return to my men."

André, head bent, appeared deep in thought. Then he addressed the women, "Perhaps it would be wiser to return to the house, and yet, if we are ever to leave, it must be done quickly. It should not take more than an hour to reach the harbor. That hour might be the most treacherous of our lives."

After a brief discussion, they agreed to go on. Perhaps Catherine's determination decided it, for she steadfastly refused to turn back, even if it meant proceeding alone. The coach, of course, would have to be abandoned and, with it, everything of a frivolous nature. They repacked the clothing into three stout carpetbags, one of which Catherine volunteered to carry. Marielle, sour as ever, was handed another, and André insisted upon taking the third. Baptiste unhitched the horses and gave them a smart slap on the rump. They trotted off through the crowded road.

"They will find their way home." André sighed. "Just as we, pray God, will find our way to France. Now let us be off. Every minute we waste here could cost us our lives."

Once they reached the Palace Gate, it became apparent André could not keep up the pace. His face had turned the color of fine gray ash, and his breathing was becoming increasingly labored. Baptiste, who had gone on ahead to reconnoiter, was nowhere in sight. Finally, Lise insisted they halt for a brief rest before proceeding.

"No need to stop on my account," André gasped. "When we board the ship, there will be nothing else to do but rest."

Lise put an arm around her husband, brushing off his protests. However, they were forced to move on shortly as the sun rose higher in a murky sky.

Catherine trudged alongside André, ever watchful for his flagging energy. With each step, the bag she carried seemed to grow heavier, and she shifted it from hand to hand, often dragging it in the dust. It was impossible to take more than half a dozen steps before stumbling into a rut. Every so often she would feel her ankle give way, forcing her to walk with an uneven gait before managing to regain her footing.

Finally, Baptiste returned. The sight of him, whole and unhurt, made Catherine want to cry out with joy. How easily he seemed to take command, and she felt a rush of gratitude toward Rive for having sent him.

"The road leading down to the harbor has been heavily damaged." Baptiste struggled to regain his breath. "It is still passable on foot if you stay away from the edge. The earth is loose there and whole sections have crumbled away, narrowing the path." At the sight of André, his face filled with worry. "Are you certain you are up to this, Monsieur? I do not wish to alarm you, but it will take some skill and a good deal of strength to complete the descent."

André laid a hand on the boy's shoulder and forced a weak smile. "I appreciate your concern. I have come this far and, by God, I intend to continue." He turned toward Lise as if anticipating an argument. "No one will tell me otherwise. Now if we are ready, I suggest we proceed before some damn fool sends a cannonball into our very midst."

"If you wish to continue, follow me closely." Baptiste relieved André of his bag and stepped through the gate.

Lise took hold of her husband's arm. They began to walk, followed by Marielle and finally Catherine. Just past the wall, Catherine stopped on impulse and glanced back toward the city. Once-beautiful houses stood as ghostly reminders of their former glory, some leveled almost completely, others leaning in an unsteady fashion, supported by the few walls left standing. Great gaping holes, like waterless lakes, dotted the lawns, and uprooted trees lay everywhere. Crimson flames leaped toward a sky leaden gray with smoke. She could have cried for the once lovely city, now in ruins.

For a moment she felt caught in a hypnotic spell, and it took much effort to tear her eyes away. Only then did she realize she lagged far behind the others. She began to hurry and slipped on some loose rocks. She fell, dropping her bag and skinning her palms, which she used to cushion her fall. People rushed by, seemingly oblivious to her presence. Then a man reached down and hauled her to her feet. Without a word, he hurried on, leaving her to make her own way as best she could. She retrieved the bag and plunged ahead, swept along with the crowd, craning her neck for a glimpse of Lise and André.

A sudden explosion hit with enough force to make the ground heave. As if an invisible hand had reached down to snatch her, Catherine was lifted off her feet. She screamed, along with others around her. She slammed down hard and pitched sideways. The bag she had carried careened down the hillside. Suddenly, there seemed to be nothing beneath her except empty space. Then, sliding through a shower of rocks and dirt, pain knifed into her shoulder. Finally, she was able to dig her fingers into the earth and grasp a handhold.

She lay there, below the side of the road, afraid to move and fighting a wave of nausea. Tiny pinpricks stabbed at her eyes. A black cloud seemed to obscure the weak sun. Her ears pounded with a steady drumming that cut off all other sound, and she fought to stay conscious. Through half-lowered lids, she stared at the road. Somehow, she must reach it. Marshalling her strength, she clawed her way upward. As she neared the edge, she became aware of a dark shape looming above her.

"Help me, please," she whispered.

Marielle stooped, bringing her face close to Catherine's. Her eyes burned with the brightness of fever, and a thin cold smile tilted up the corners of her lips. "Do you beg a favor, Madame? Really, how unfortunate. As you have done no favors for me, I feel disinclined to grant you one now." Abruptly, the smile faded.

Catherine thought to reason with her but couldn't form the necessary words. She felt physically and mentally paralyzed, as if she were plunging head first into a dark abyss. She steeled herself for one last effort and raised a hand toward Marielle, who loomed above her, brandishing a stout rock. Then a crushing blow caught the side of Catherine's head, and she was sucked deeper into the black pit.

Chapter 26

As the afternoon waned, a cool breeze rustled through the leafy trees and bent the grass in gentle undulating waves. A welcome silence replaced the din that had enveloped the city hours earlier—a temporary relief, perhaps, almost unnoticed by Catherine, who lay on the scarred hillside.

Still later, as twilight approached, a chill wind brushed her cheek and billowed through her hair. When finally she felt able to move, she rolled onto her back and looked up at the swirling clouds scudding by under a gray sky. Her body ached and a searing pain tore through her head. Fear mingled with the cold and held her limbs stiff and immobile. For a moment, she could not remember what had brought her to this bleak, wind-torn spot, but after a while, her memory returned. Once again she saw Marielle's face, shorn of all innocence, as if she still hovered within sight. She must have left the scene long since, having inflicted what she no doubt considered a fit punishment for an imagined betrayal.

A cold drizzle began to fall, chilling Catherine further. Struggling to sit up, she peered through the mist. Like a sheer, gray curtain, it almost obliterated the landscape. Somewhere below was the harbor and the ship. In spite of the approaching darkness and unfamiliar terrain, she knew she must try to reach it.

Calling upon her last bit of strength, she gathered her cloak about her. Turning onto her knees, she edged toward the roadway. It felt like an eternity passed before she managed to pull herself onto its muddy surface. The front of her gown was hopelessly soiled, and her cloak—wet and caked with dirt—hung heavy and useless from her shoulders. The wind whipped her wet garments about her legs, and she peered at the ominous shapes—abandoned carriages and ruined homes—rising from the gloom.

"What the devil?"

A thin sliver of light broke through the mist. Catherine looked up at a man's dim figure looming above her. He lowered a lantern until it shone in her face. Then he stepped back as if he had seen an apparition.

"*Mon Dieu*," he gasped. "What are you doing out here? Are you trying to get yourself killed?" He raised the light and peered about the empty street, then helped her to her feet.

Grateful for his support, she allowed him to lead her away from the roadside. When they stood in the shadow of the wall, he studied her in the flickering light. His face remained perplexed.

"What is your business here?" He had a kind voice. At her hesitation, he added, "Come, come, you can tell me. I am not going to harm you."

Short and spare of frame and dressed in soiled breeches and coat, he did indeed look kind, although shocked at finding a lone woman on the road.

"I was traveling with the St. Clair family. We have passage on a ship bound for France." She recounted all that had happened, careful to leave out the incident with Marielle.

He shook his head slowly. "I am afraid fate has been unkind to you. The ships have all sailed with the tide. So you see, Madame, it is pointless for you to continue on. You must return home. Under the circumstances, there is nothing else for you to do."

Catherine slumped against the cold, rain-soaked wall. "Are you certain? Is there any chance you are mistaken?"

"I wish it were so, but my information is reliable. My brother was at the wharf. He helped load the ships and stayed until they cast off."

To give herself courage more than to ward off the increasing cold, Catherine hugged her upper body. There seemed no recourse except to return to the house. Darkness had not fully set in, and the fires that still burned through the drizzle provided some light.

"I would take you there myself, but I am on watch for several hours yet. Can you find your way alone?"

The rain fell heavier now, and she was anxious to start back before nightfall. "I shall manage." She thanked him for his assistance. She turned away but had gone only a short distance when she heard footsteps close by. She felt something thrust into her hand.

"Can you fire a pistol?"

Catherine's fingers closed about the weapon. "I don't think so. I have never tried. Why give me yours?"

"I have this other one." He patted a pistol tucked into his belt. "You are a woman alone. With so many houses empty, there has been some looting in the city."

"Surely the soldiers must be able to keep order."

"They have no time for petty criminals. For your own safety, keep this with you." He reached for the weapon. "Here, I will prepare one shot and show you how to fire it."

When she had mastered the required steps, he led her partway up the road. "I wish you *bon chance*, Madame." He then left her to continue on her way.

Once inside the Palace Gate, she quickened her step. A small cluster of French soldiers, along with many more civilians shouldering muskets, hunkered down around open fires. She felt their eyes on her as she slipped past, the pistol concealed in the folds of her cloak. At any moment she expected to be stopped and tried to reassure herself the men meant her no harm. Still, with no other women about, she was acutely aware of the danger. Head lowered, she dared not meet their eyes and prayed desperately that she was headed in the right direction.

Once past the glowing fires and muted voices, she began to run. Virtually alone in the street, she searched for familiar landmarks to guide her back to the St. Clair's home. Twice she had to retrace her steps, but at last she found the house, still miraculously standing. Exhausted, she stumbled up the path to the front door and turned the knob. The huge portal swung open and she hurried inside.

The house lay silent and cold as a mausoleum. For a minute she stood in the entryway, thoroughly bewildered and unable to move. Her sodden clothes sent a chill into her bones, and it occurred to her she had best get undressed before she added an ague to her woes. She ascended the stairs in near darkness and entered her bedroom. Laying the pistol carefully on the nightstand, she removed her cloak and gown and hung them in the armoire. Her shift was at worst damp in spots, and she felt thankful she had one garment fit to wear. Her bed beckoned, and quickly she slipped between the cold sheets, pulled the comforter up to her chin and closed her eyes.

Sleep did not come at once. Although safe for the moment, she turned her thoughts to the St. Clairs. Had they made it safely to the ship? Did they assume she was somewhere in the throng? Marielle, perhaps, declared she had seen Catherine somewhere onboard. They would not worry until it was too late. She could only imagine their concern when they discovered she was not among the passengers. No doubt André would blame himself. She prayed the worry would not affect his heart.

For the time being she had shelter, but no protection. The city had become dangerous to everyone, but especially to a woman alone. She had no money and no means of acquiring any. How was she to live?

Eventually, exhaustion forced her to still her dark thoughts and close her eyes. For now, she was safe. Tomorrow she would turn her mind toward taking whatever steps necessary for survival. A short time later, she drifted off to sleep.

She awoke to the loud chiming of the clock echoing throughout the house and signaling the second hour past midnight. Warmed by the bed covers, she felt somewhat refreshed from her few hours of sleep. Her head no longer ached, and the rain seemed to have stopped. She looked longingly at the grate and wished she had a fire. The remaining logs lay cold and dead, and she did not possess the skill to revive them. If she had a candle, she could go downstairs and forage for food, if indeed any remained. Her empty stomach reminded her that she had eaten nothing since early the previous morning. The prospect of leaving the safety of her room sent her huddling deeper under the comforter.

Gnawing hunger, however, soon outweighed any fear. After chiding herself for being a coward, she stepped out of the bed and onto the icy floor. Immediately, she felt a chill and dragged the comforter off the bed, wrapping it around her body.

The hallway loomed dark, the stairs broken and precarious. She took care not to trip over her improvised cloak. A sliver of moonlight seeped through a kitchen window, enough for her search to yield a small trove of biscuits and a basket containing a few apples. Quickly, she devoured several biscuits, cramming them into her mouth, and followed them with a piece of fruit that proved surprisingly juicy. Realizing her small stock of food would not last long, she satisfied herself with the meager fare. She must ration her provisions, since there was no longer anyone here to see to her needs.

Now, with her hunger satisfied, she carefully retraced her steps, grateful for the tiny bit of light cast by the moon. In the upstairs hallway, she listened intently to the night sounds. Creaks and groans, typical of an old house, greeted her. Then a new sound made her freeze. Directly below, the front door opened and closed. Heavy footsteps echoed as someone crossed the entryway.

Catherine's senses sharpened, alerting her to the danger waiting at the bottom of the stairs. Treading lightly, she tiptoed into her bedroom, tossed aside the comforter, and retrieved the pistol from the nightstand. Then she returned to the landing, cloaked in night shadows.

Somewhere below, a chair scraped against wood, followed by a muttered oath. Then everything fell silent. Catherine's heart beat with terrifying speed. Fear swept through her in an icy wave, and her legs threatened to collapse from under her. She tightened her grip on the pistol and unsteadily raised it.

Without shifting her gaze from the darkened stairs, she crouched against the wall and aimed the weapon toward the narrow space that fell away into the dusky void.

Again, the sound of footsteps carried, this time closer to the stairs. A man's dim shape took form and grew in size as he began the slow ascent toward Catherine, who huddled above. Remembering the instructions, she laid her finger against the lever that released the shot and steeled herself not to fire until he was within range. She wanted to scream, to give vent to the suffocating fear that was slowly choking her. Instead, she clamped her mouth shut and took aim.

A stair creaked. Fearing she would lose her nerve, she slid up the wall, cocked the pistol and fired. The shot went wild, tearing through what remained of the banister and splintering the wood.

"What in God's name?" A deep, masculine voice exploded just as Catherine screamed.

For a split second neither moved. Then, suspecting the man had no intention of retreating, she gathered her wits and through the quaver in her voice said, "Stay back or I shall shoot you for certain this time." Although she'd had only the one shot and her hand could barely stay steady, she made the pretense of taking aim.

"Catherine, is that you? What in God's name are you doing here?"

At the sound of Rive's voice, the pistol fell from her hand, and she tumbled into his outstretched arms. Sobbing, partly from her earlier fright and now with relief, she clung to him, her arms wound about his neck, her face pressed into his shoulder.

"Hush," he soothed. "Do not take on so."

No words could silence her. Neither could the hand that stroked her hair nor the lips that kissed the crown of her head.

"Oh, my sweet, beautiful Catherine," he said, pressing her against him. He lifted her into his arms and carried her down the hallway and into the bedroom. There he laid her on the bed and sat down beside her. Her hands clutched his shoulders, and he leaned in close, kissing her closed eyelids and dabbing at her tears with the backs of his fingers. Stroking her hair, he said, "Sweetheart, you're safe. Look at me."

She opened her eyes. Then she lowered her arms, made a fist, and brushed away the last of her tears. When her breathing began to ease and her awful fear was all but vanquished, she placed her hands against his forearms. "You must think me a hopeless coward." She gave a tiny hiccup and fought back a renewed spurt of tears.

He laughed softly. "I would hardly call you a coward." He eased aside the tangle of hair that had fallen onto her brow and stroked behind her ear with his thumb. "You almost shot me. I can only imagine what you might have accomplished with a little practice."

The tiniest smile tilted up her lips, and she shrugged and swallowed a laugh. Finally, she began to feel better.

He fingered the delicate linen that draped her shoulder and took one of her hands, placed its palm against his chest and held it there for a long moment. "Stay put. I'm going to see about building a fire."

He left the bed and crossed to where the tinder box sat on the mantle. He placed kindling on the grate and spent less than a minute igniting it. The flame grew, and he waited a moment before piling on several pieces of wood.

When he returned to sit beside her again, he enclosed her hands in his. "Why are you still here? Where are the others? Did Baptiste not come to escort you to the ship?"

"He did his best to deliver us safely." She was anxious to absolve the boy from any blame. She told him of the circumstances that led her to become separated from the others but made no mention of Marielle's treachery. In truth, she had already forgiven the girl.

"Oh, my *brave* Catherine."

"Do you think me so?"

He kissed the tip of her nose, and when he turned her palms up, he kissed the scraped flesh. "Yes, I think you are the bravest woman in New France and anywhere else, for that matter. And beautiful beyond a man's imagining. I must have pleased *all* the gods to have found such good fortune."

"Oh? What might that good fortune be?" Breathless, she barely recognized her own voice.

He kissed her lips lightly, and her chin. "You are my good fortune, my brave, sweet Catherine. I thought you would be safely away by now. I only returned here to reassure myself."

"Don't you see? Everything—obtaining my passage, your marrying me—was all for naught."

He opened his hands and brought her fingers to his lips. The tip of his tongue glided down the long slim stem of first one finger and then the other.

"Surely not *all*."

As his tongue leisurely skirted along her skin, leaving a hot moist trail, she felt a little quiver deep inside.

"No?"

"I think we can salvage *something*." He kissed the inside of her wrist where her pulse beat in a quickened rhythm.

She pulled her breath in and out through parted lips. "You do?"

He leaned down and gazed into her eyes. "I most certainly intend to try. However, to succeed will necessitate a joint effort."

"A *joint* effort."

"Hmm. You know. Something that requires the cooperation of two people, usually a husband and wife."

"Oh, you mean *that*." She knew all along where he was leading. She knew, too, she would let him make love to her tonight. What once she had thought of as forbidden fruit had suddenly become a downright necessity. She felt as if she were about to leap out of her skin.

"Hmm, yes, *that*. As I recall, we were almost halfway there on more than one occasion." He gave a slight tug on the satin ribbon that held closed her shift and the bow opened. "Yes, decidedly *that*." He slid the fabric off her shoulder and kissed her there. Then his lips continued along a path down her arm. He began anew at the hollow at the base of her throat.

Her body arched toward his, and she brought her hands up to where his hair swept the collar of his shirt. The first two buttons were undone, and she had no difficulty sliding her thumbs beneath the neckline and across the hard ridge of his upper back. She felt his muscles tense. Shyness no longer seemed in character for her and, needing to explore further, she slipped both hands under the sturdy cotton. His skin felt smooth, taut, and warm against her palms, not as she would have imagined, if she had ever dared allow her thoughts to wander there.

He pulled her into his arms. When his mouth sought hers, she was ready and more than eager for his kiss. Her lips parted, and a muffled groan came from deep inside him. She felt his hand on her hip, where only the delicate linen draped her nakedness, and shivered in expectation of what he would do next. Indeed, the fabric was so fragile he might just as well be touching her bare flesh. Heat flared under his touch, and when he bunched the shift and slid it higher up her leg, she thought him the most considerate man in the world for providing her a cool respite.

"I love you," he said, as his palm skirted her bare knee and the tips of his fingers explored the warm flesh at the crook of her slightly bent leg. When they glided along her thigh, she shuddered. Her nipples peaked, and she felt the stiff, hardened buds brush her shift; she wanted nothing more than for him to touch her there. He was touching her now inside her thigh and she twitched and almost certainly leapt a full half-inch up off the bed.

She wished he would hurry. Each of her senses was focused on the part where he would begin teaching her about lovemaking. No, he was taking all the time in the world, diligently easing the back of her shift up past her buttocks. Why did he *wait*? Did he think she was going to succumb to the vapors if he got down to it any faster?

Then all of a sudden, he stopped.

Chapter 27

"Nooooo!" She hadn't meant to utter a sound, but it slipped out, a great wailing tortured sound. It would probably have awakened the neighbors if, by some chance, there were any left. She pulled her hands out from under his shirt.

He sat up and began to laugh—no wry little chuckle, but a deep throated guffaw. It emerged from him like a small explosion, one that might never stop.

"You're making sport of me."

He shook his head as he sought to bring himself under control. "No, my love. I can think of ten things I would rather be doing with you right now, but making sport is not one of them."

"Then what do you find so humorous?"

"You see before you a man who has just had the biggest shock of his life." His index finger curved over one of her cheekbones. "I thought … I expected, if anything, that you would feel shy."

"I'm supposed to, aren't I?"

"Don't feel obligated on my account. This works perfectly for me."

"Then why did you stop?" She wondered if she would ever understand him.

"I thought we had reached the point where you were almost naked and I wasn't. I was going to strip."

Her mouth fell open, and she stared at him.

"Did you think I was going to make love to you dressed like this?" He tapped his fingers against one of his high black boots.

She shrugged, truly at a loss, having wandered into such strange territory. "Well, I'm not."

He stood up and, without further explanation, dealt with his shirt. In no time, he had flung the garment over a chair. The boots, which required something of a struggle, followed. It was while he fumbled with the buttons on his breeches that she closed her eyes. A moment later she felt the mattress depress under his weight and the long length of his body settle beside hers.

Several moments passed. "Do you ever intend to open your eyes?"

"Possibly not. Is it required?"

He laughed softly. "Yes, definitely." There was a pause. "Have you had no instruction as to how a man and a woman consummate their marriage?

"My husband—you—is supposed to teach me everything about lovemaking. That was my mother's advice."

"Very good advice it is. I suspect, my love, you have a natural ... uh ... *proclivity* for it. However, just to be on the safe side," he brushed her cheek with the back of his hand, "why don't we start with lesson one. Open your eyes and look at me."

There was nothing for it but to do as he bid.

"Now, where were we?" He kissed the tip of her nose. "Ah, yes." He slid his hand up her leg from just below her knee to midway up her thigh, taking the hem of her shift with him.

As he worked the garment higher, completely exposing her legs, her earlier boldness evaporated. The hem barely concealed that part of her body, so intimate and unutterably private, where silky down centered at the juncture of her thighs. She wondered if he intended to expose that, too. Once eager to touch and be touched, she now kept her arms—stiff as broomsticks—close to her sides and communicated only with her eyes. She clenched her jaw. Now, finally, he would do it, but she wished he had not waited so long or insisted upon taking off his clothes. Her moment had passed, and she feared it would not return again.

HE HAD NEVER BEEN SO PATIENT with a woman. Weeks ago, he had determined that if—when—he made love to her, he would practice all restraint, to make her first time as pleasurable for her as he intended it to be for himself. His motive was not entirely selfless. He wished to ensure that the next time, and every time thereafter for the rest of their lives, she would welcome him eagerly to her bed. Now, he suspected her idea of lovemaking bore little resemblance to his own. Being unprepared, she more than likely expected her body, as well as her husband's, would be chastely concealed under night clothes or, in this case, any other clothing they happened to find themselves wearing. Obviously, she had no idea how a man made a woman ready for him. Yet, if ever a woman was created for lovemaking, it was his wife. Had she not demonstrated such only moments ago?

He kissed the side of her neck and felt the vein in her throat pulse against his lips. Then he planted a light kiss on the tips of each breast and worked his way slowly down to her stomach. He felt her give a little inward jump, which he took as a good sign. Edging closer, he draped one of his legs over hers. He was becoming fully aroused, and in no time would be rock hard. Still, he must follow the course he had set. To do otherwise would be a catastrophe. He must place his fate in the hands of reason, for he knew his body would require little, if any, coaxing to betray him. Still, he didn't think he could take all night to go about this.

"Hmm … sweetheart. I think we had best tackle lesson two."

"Oh? And what is that?"

"Lesson two is most clear: nothing should ever come between a husband and his wife."

"Nothing?" She blinked.

"Exactly." He hooked his thumbs under the hem of her shift and slowly began to raise it. It glided over her hips, then her stomach and finally her breasts. She sighed and gave a little shudder, perhaps from the tactile swish of the fabric as it lightly raked her body or, better yet, the renewal of her desire. When he gave her upper arms a slight nudge, she raised them obediently, and he peeled the garment over her head and tossed it to the foot of the bed.

"That, my love," he rasped against her ear, "is lesson two."

He spread her hair across the pillow and kissed her brow. He reminded himself to abandon haste and hold in abeyance the lust that consumed him, although he had not the least inkling how long his restraint might last. Taking her hand, he kissed her wrist and the hollow in the crook of her elbow. Then he stroked her foot with the underside of his. In the glow of the fire, her skin took on the palest pink hue; he wanted more than anything to touch her everywhere. After all, she was his wife and he had the right.

He started by sliding his hands along the outside of her thighs and following the curve of her slim hips and tiny waist. His fingers glided over her ribs, and he bent his head and kissed the silky flesh there. She gave a little quiver, which some perverse god must have instigated to drive him mad. When he reached her breasts, he employed the lightest touch and stroked the underside of each one. Her nipples peaked and she pulled in her breath with a deep sigh. His hands cupped each perfectly rounded breast. Lifting one to his mouth, he caught the nipple lightly between his teeth and flicked his tongue against the swollen tip. She yelped; then her back arched and she pushed closer, as if offering herself to him, and clasped her hands about his arms. Yes, his wife was definitely created for lovemaking.

The slightest movement of his knee opened a space between hers. The flesh inside her thigh was satin soft, and he moved along it with his thumb, gliding slowly upward. He touched her with slow, feather-light strokes, then with more urgency. Where he had found the fortitude to hold back this long and not take her like a randy goat, he couldn't begin to guess. As he probed, she gave a little, musical shriek and, with no bidding from him, opened her legs farther. Could he be so fortunate that, of all the feminine arts, his wife would *excel* at making love? He continued to stroke her with his thumb before probing deeper. His gaze locked with hers and the desire that sent his body and mind spinning almost out of control must have shown in his eyes.

CATHERINE FELT AS ONE MUST AFTER coming into contact with lightning. Little fires flared all along her body. The most exquisite sensation no instruction could have prepared her for spread through her breasts and multiplied in intensity where he probed the deepest part of her. Somehow, her feet had become entangled with his, and still he managed to keep stroking the underside of her foot. She wanted to clasp his hand—the one between her legs—but not to draw him away. No, that would never do, not when what she wanted was to draw him deep inside her. Her blood pulsed in a hot stream, and she felt a deliciously maddening ache tighten every muscle of her body. The ache thrust her closer to him; she could not control the tremble that shook her.

When his mouth moved to claim hers once again, she reached up and clung to his shoulders, fully aware now of the passion she had aroused in him. She answered his passion with her lips, pressing them against his with eagerness, while the kiss grew deeper and deeper still. With renewed boldness, she trailed her fingers over his back. Her leg brushed against him and she felt the hard shaft of his manhood, which came as a bit of a shock. She wished she had not led so sheltered a life, wished she understood the workings of a man. There was no time now to wonder; there was only this moment and what he was doing to her. If truth be told, she wanted him never to stop. Yet, her instinct told her this was only the prelude to something even more intimate, the act by which a woman conceived a child. She could hardly wait for it. Ah, but in the meantime ….

After a long while, he broke the kiss and whispered her name. Then he brushed her cheek with his lips. "I have a hunger that only one feast can satisfy."

Her sigh, a breathy whisper, brushed his lips. "Then take your fill, for there is no one here inclined to stop you."

His hand tangled in her hair, and he combed his fingers through it, spreading it across the pillow. The fire crackled and a log hissed and split, sending a shower of sparks leaping up the flue. He nibbled her ear, teasing the lobe with his teeth. "You invite plunder, and I am not a man to do things by half."

Catherine's fingers swept through his hair. Her lips brushed the vein that jumped in his temple. " 'Tis just as well, for I would have no half measures from you this night."

He moved over her and brought his hands down her sides to clasp her buttocks. When he lifted her slightly and positioned himself between her knees, she shivered.

"I shall try not to hurt you." As he stroked her inner thighs, she opened them still farther for him. "If I cause you pain, it will be for only a short while. Then I shall bring you the most extraordinary pleasure." His fingers probed gently, searching for entrance into the moist warm heat of her body.

His entry, when it came, was unhurried. He paused as if to allow her time to accept him, then pushed deeper into her and stroked with a light touch. Since she was innocent, she was grateful for his gentle thrusts. She dug her nails into his back. After a while, her body began to move with a slow rhythm. When he came across the virginal boundary that set up a wall between them, she felt him push deeper and harder until finally he plunged through. She cried out, and he waited at least for a moment or two until she overcame the shock of it. Then there was nothing to hold either back.

Now, with her complete surrender, his passion spilled from his lips with words no poet had yet set to paper. He rained kisses over her face, her throat, the tips of each breast.

"You are my wife and my true love. No matter what the future brings, I shall never love you less than I do now."

Raw instinct fashioned her response. She tightened her arms and legs about him, and when he brought her to a higher point of arousal, each rippling sensation sent waves of pleasure tearing through her. It amazed her that she could continue breathing. Yet, somehow she managed to whisper her love for him. Then, with her fingers laced behind his neck, she brought her lips ever closer to his. When he kissed her, her lips clung to his, and she gave herself up to the maddeningly exquisite pleasure flooding her body, holding him deeply within her and greeting all he did with an abandon she had not dreamed possible. He lifted her again and again to the brink of passion and she was sucked into the vortex of her own desire.

Chapter 28

A PALE BEAM OF SUNLIGHT SPLASHED THROUGH the open drape and spilled across Catherine's face, half waking her from an untroubled, dreamless sleep. Her lids fluttered and closed again, filtering out the light. Gradually, the warmth that lit her cheeks spread in delicious currents throughout her body. It filled her with a sense of well-being and brought an unconscious smile to her lips. Stretching languidly, she curled her toes around the linen sheet that lay twisted beneath her feet and, arching her back, worked her sore muscles in small circular movements. For a moment, she neither knew nor cared where she was, grateful only that the biting cold had subsided and her earlier fear had vanished.

Still in a state of semi-wakefulness, she sighed deeply and had almost given in to the urge to sink back into sleep when a niggling thought intruded. Once there, it took root until a rush of memory sent her eyes flying open and her hands fluttering to her naked bosom. Everything about the previous night passed before her eyes with such clarity as to deepen the flush she knew must already color her face. Turning her head, she surveyed the empty space beside her in the bed and trailed her hand along the sheet. It still bore the faint impression of the man who had recently lain there. Finding herself alone, she panicked, sitting up with a start and glancing about the room.

Rive stood by the window, hands braced on either side of the frame, staring down into the garden. He didn't seem to realize that she had awakened, for he neither spoke nor moved. He did not give the impression that he felt the least self-conscious standing there stark naked. If so, upon rising, he would have donned his breeches. Now that she had caught him unawares, she let her eyes wander down the long, beautifully proportioned length of his body, as if seeing it for the first time. With her arms propped against her raised knees, she felt content just to watch him, to familiarize herself again with his lean, well-muscled frame. Even in inactivity, he exuded a fierce magnetism. Over the course of the past months, she had oftentimes submitted to his will. His ability to secure her complete surrender to his physical being, bringing her to unimaginable depths of passion, filled her with wonder.

"I was beginning to think you would sleep forever," he said, keeping his gaze on the garden below. Then he turned and walked to the foot of the bed, casting his eyes on her as if eager to devour her naked flesh.

"Lovemaking has turned my wife into a lazy wench." Leaning over, he placed a kiss on her bare toe.

Catherine's blood bubbled and rushed, like a molten stream of lava, to her head. The remnants of her former shy self still seemed to linger near the surface for, in the face of his blatant assessment, her embarrassment returned. He had caught *her* naked. She reached for the sheet bunched at the foot of the bed and began to draw it up over her legs.

He disengaged her fingers and sent the cover billowing to the floor. His hand roved the length of her arm. His gaze clearly implied that he had not yet had his fill of her, nor, perhaps, would he ever.

"Your propriety comes too late. I have been awake these past two hours."

The gist of the remark was not lost on her, nor was the obvious fact that he seemed ready to make love to her again. Now a delicious thought occurred to her. It was *her* turn to play the tease. After all, he was her *husband*, and should there not be some banter between a man and his wife?

"I think you could have found a better way to spend your time than playing the voyeur." She found it impossible to completely suppress a smile. "I had not thought such occupation to be to your taste."

He knelt on the bed, leaned forward, and cupped the back of her head with his hand. His fingers splayed through her hair, sifting the tangle of thick golden curls. "You have judged me correctly," he said, his voice turned husky with emotion, "and must therefore reward my patience."

"Do you seek a boon, sir?" Her lids dropped languidly; then she raised them to stare into his eyes. Their emerald color had deepened, perhaps from his desire. She could not be sure yet. It was all too new for her.

"A boon, yes. Would you deny me?"

Her gaze strayed from his, downward over his well-muscled chest, and down a little farther. "That, sir, I do believe to be pointless."

"Ah, amongst other things, my wife is clairvoyant."

Tilting her head back, he brought his mouth down on hers. Her response was immediate. They tumbled back onto the bed, lips and bodies clinging, breaths mingling with the stirrings of passion. He stroked her back, her hips, her buttocks, sending hot waves of pleasure streaking through her body.

After he freed her lips, she could not resist just one more tease. "I suppose you think yourself quite good at this." That she found the breath to utter these words surprised her.

He kissed the tips of her fingers. "I never gave it much thought. That is something you will have to judge for yourself."

"Oh, I already have, but to ensure no error in judgment will require far more experience than I have had to date. Years and years, I think, in order to give an honest appraisal."

With that he took her mouth again. She greeted him wantonly and heard his sharp intake of breath as her hands traveled down his back and onto his hips. Light exploded beneath her closed lids. Then there was only desire—desire to please this man who had become her husband, this man who had awakened within her a fierce longing and then forced her to acknowledge it.

Rolling onto his back, he pulled her on top of him. Every muscle in her body clenched; her feet arched and her toes curled in anticipation of what was to come. She braced her arms beside his head and leaned down to kiss his throat, scoring the hollow at the base of it with her tongue and trailing the moist tip over his chest. His hips thrust upward and he gave a grinding moan. She had unleashed a demon, indeed, one that would not be put to rest until the mounting desire that surged through them both had been slaked.

Time moved slowly, and it seemed neither of them wished to see its end. After what seemed like an eternity, he tumbled her onto her back. She melted under the heat of his touch while he explored her body, his supple hands lingering on the insides of her thighs, then on her stiff, engorged nipples.

A little humming sound came from deep inside her throat.

"*Mon petit chaton*, are you purring?"

"Hmm. Little kitten, you say." She rubbed her cheek against his and raked her nails across his back. "I am purring, indeed."

Then he touched her again where only a husband had the right and roused her to a pitch that sent her body straining against his. His name fell from her lips, and he silenced her with fevered kisses. He parted her thighs and entered her, gently at first, then with ever deepening thrusts that created and nurtured the most exquisite sensations within her. Her body seemed to move of its own volition, matching itself to the rhythm of his; she felt her skin glow under a thin sheen of moisture. When finally she reached a state of total fulfillment, she cried out and lay beneath him, her body spent, her fingers digging into his shoulders.

He had not arrived at the same place, for what she thought was his withdrawal was only a prelude to deeper, quicker thrusts. They sparked something new in her, for every sensation she thought could not be surpassed flooded her body once more. She brought her knees to the sides of his hips and squeezed hard—rocking, rising, and falling in perfect cadence with his body's rhythm. She thought she could not stand another moment of the intense feeling that sent every part of her thrumming like a harp string. Then he cried out her name, not once but twice. She felt him shudder, and his release came at the same moment as her own. After a while, he rolled onto his back and reached for her. She nestled snugly into his embrace so he could cradle her in the shelter of his arms.

"You please me so." She traced the line of his jaw, the clearly defined bones that sculpted his cheeks, then his nose, his lips and finally the lobe of one ear, probing gently with her fingers as if committing to memory each small detail. "Considering your expertise with a woman—*this* woman, the last you shall ever have—I shall take it as my right to reserve all judgment. As I said, an accurate assessment of—well, you know—will require much more time—"

"A lifetime," he assured her.

"Oh, yes, definitely a full and complete lifetime."

They lay together quietly for a while, and she dozed for a bit. When she awakened, she kissed his cheek and then his lips. She sighed. "Rive, I was thinking …."

He kissed her brow. "What were you thinking, my love?"

She took a moment to search for the right words. In this case it seemed devilishly tricky, so she just blurted out, "About what we did last night and just now—"

"Did?" He glanced down at her. "What we just *did*, my pet, is *make love*."

"Yes, of course, I know."

"How else might I enlighten you?"

"I wondered if that was lesson three? You never did say?"

He smiled at her. "Catherine, my lovely, vibrant bride. It was lesson three, indeed." She thought she detected just the tiniest bit of mirth in his tone.

"I liked it."

"I should hope so."

She scored his lower lip with her thumb. "I wonder, can we do it again?"

He took her hand and kissed the tips of each finger. "Of course we can—countless times and for the rest of our lives."

"No, I mean right now."

He kissed her ear then followed the delicate outline with his tongue. "If I didn't know better, I would think you *were* actually trying to kill me."

With the back of one finger, she traced the contour of his cheek, his jaw, the little bump that stuck out in the center of his throat. "Of course, if you can't …."

He pulled her to him. Before she could go on tormenting him, he eased himself over her, entered her and silenced her with his mouth. He made love to her slowly and tenderly, as if they had been lovers forever.

Later, when she lay contently in his arms, she remembered the wedding ring he had slipped onto her finger just days before. She had placed it inside one of the books of poetry and tied it with a blue ribbon she found in the dressing table. In order to keep them safe, she had tucked them far into the back of the center drawer. Somehow, with the commotion of leaving for the ship, she had forgotten to take them with her. Now, she was grateful for her lapse of memory.

She told Rive, and he rose and fetched the slim volumes. Lying beside her once more, he untied the ribbon. When he opened the book, the ring dropped onto the sheet.

He picked up the gold band and reached for Catherine's hand. "When first I placed this ring on your finger, I was denied the right to declare my love for you." He kissed her lightly and then slipped the ring onto her finger. "So I shall tell you again how much I love you. It is an even deeper love now than on the day we married, if such is possible."

She held her hand aloft and studied the golden circle. Then she touched his face, tracing its contours with the utmost tenderness.

"I love you." She nestled against him.

As the morning hour grew later, he donned his breeches and went downstairs, leaving Catherine curled up in the middle of the bed, satiated and content. He returned with a tin tub and inside it a sizable stew pot brimming with water. He set the pot onto the low flame that burned in the grate.

"Madame's bath," he announced. "If you will wait but a moment, I think it might be satisfactory."

"A bath. Oh, Rive, you are the kindest, most thoughtful husband to have arranged this." She grinned at him. "Such an improvement over your last offering. What did you say the Indians used that barrel for again?"

"I didn't say, and I'd be hard pressed to know what uses this tub had been put to, either."

"I don't care if they skinned a hog in it. It's more than I ever expected."

After a few minutes, he tested the water with his fingers. "It should be just to my lady's liking, neither too hot nor too cold."

He gripped the handle of the pot with the edge of the sheet and pulled the vessel out of the flames. Then he poured the warm water into the basin.

"I wish I could offer you something better, but this will have to do for now. Unfortunately, I could not find even a sliver of soap."

She got off the bed and stepped into the tub, which proved more commodious than expected. Holding onto his hand for balance, she sat and drew her knees up beneath her chin. With her arms resting along the rim, she gazed up at Rive.

"In future, I shall think of you as my Master of the Bath. Seeing as you have been to court, I trust you well know the procedure."

He bent and kissed her shoulder. "I shall consider it an honor. While you bathe, I will see if I can scrounge up something for us to eat."

"There are biscuits and apples in the kitchen. Hurry, please. I don't think I've ever been so hungry."

He left the room and was gone long enough for her to accomplish a rudimentary bath and dry herself with the sheet. Then she laid it over the carpet and fetched her clothes, which had dried during the night in the armoire. She vigorously shook out her petticoat over the sheet and smoothed the folds with her hands to rid the garment of most of the caked dirt that clung to the front.

She gave a contented sigh and returned her attention to her garments. Since she doubted the St. Clairs would ever return to regain their possessions, she commandeered one of the pillowcases, wet a generous corner of it and carefully sponged clean the rest of her gown. By the time Rive returned, she had donned her shift and petticoat and pinned the stomacher to the outside edges of her robe.

"Ah, my Master of the Hunt. What morsel have you brought me?"

He proffered the crock of biscuits that had fallen victim to her marauding the previous night and a handful of apples. Then he produced several carrots that had been stored in the root cellar. He placed the food on the bed.

"But first …." He produced small scissors tucked into the waist of his breeches, selected a poetry volume and, after scanning the pages, tore one from the binding. After fingering a small lock of Catherine's hair and snipping it with the scissors, he wrapped it in the loose page, carefully creasing each side closed until he had made a small packet. Then he bound it with a bit of ribbon he had found on the dressing table.

"A keepsake. I must have one from you, too." She took the scissors, cut a lock of his hair, selected a page of poetry, and repeated his exercise. She tied it closed with another strand of ribbon.

He put the keepsakes aside, and they sat together on the bed and ate ravenously, consuming the simple fare as if it had been a king's feast. When they finished, Rive walked to the armchair in the corner nearest the window and sat down.

"There is something we must settle." His manner was thoroughly at odds with his former joviality.

Catherine waited for him to continue. When he didn't, she sat stiffly with her hands clasped in her lap. He had turned entirely too serious, and for the life of her, she could not imagine what they had to settle. Her spirits sank.

Chapter 29

"Come here, Catherine" he said in a lighter tone, beckoning her to him. "Come over here and sit on my lap."

Still perplexed, she rose from the bed and went to him. He pulled her down, and she wrapped her arms around his neck. They sat like that for several moments, enveloped in a silence broken only by an occasional crackle from the burning logs.

"Sweetheart …" he paused.

"Yes?" She caught a lock of his hair and wound it around her finger and waited for him to make clear what was on his mind. His hesitancy began to unnerve her. Rive was not a man who took undue time to deliberate before stating his thoughts.

It took another moment before he asked, "Do you agree there should be no secrets between a husband and wife?"

"I do agree." She kissed his cheek, then leaned back and looked into his eyes. She felt an escalating sense of unease. He had told her much about his life but certainly not all. "Why do you ask? Have you been keeping secrets from me?" She did not feel at all ready for a disquieting confession.

He shook his head. "No. My life is as transparent as rainwater."

"Oh." So it was not something new about his past that he wished to divulge. Puzzled, she thought a moment. "Oh?" This time she guessed the direction to which his inquiry was headed. She tried to climb off his lap, but he clasped her about the waist and held her fast.

"Don't run away from me. I have had about as much of that as I am willing to put up with."

"I was not running away. However, if I have guessed your purpose, I can answer you better if I am sitting over there." She indicated the foot of the bed, which was not any great distance from where he sat but far enough to allow her to maintain her composure.

With some reluctance, he released her, and she settled herself against the edge of the mattress. She clasped her hands in her lap and dropped her gaze.

"Catherine, look at me."

Her gaze shifted to his. All his love was there in his eyes.

"I must settle for myself what brought about your ... union with Flint. God knows, I can understand why any man would want you, but what I must know is how a man of such duplicity managed to accomplish it. I know you bore him no affection and yet felt obliged, nay ... *obligated* to accede to his wishes."

She did not answer at once, could not bring herself to speak of Flint. Rive deserved to know the truth and so finally she found the courage to answer him. "My father had fallen heavily into debt." She told him everything that had occurred from the moment she met Jeremy Flint. Just saying his name was like dipping her tongue in poison. "There were to be severe consequences should he predecease my father. Also, if I showed a lack of devotion, all payments to my family would cease."

Rive rose and came to her, drew her to her feet and enfolded her in his arms. "Oh, my dearest wife, it grieves me you should have fallen victim to such a devil." He stroked her hair. "He, or his agent, would have carried out his threat of prison. I have no doubt."

"That was made quite clear."

"Were you to share further in these severe consequences?"

"If I had borne him no children, I was to be cast out, which came as no surprise. By then it probably would have been a mercy."

With one hand, he continued stroking her hair; the long fingers of the other splayed across her back. He pressed her close to him. "You are safe now, and in my keeping. I give you my word that no harm will ever befall you or your parents."

She looked up at him with a wan smile. She would trust this man with her life.

"I do not know when word of Flint's death will reach London. Still, I cannot allow you to take on my family's burden. I did not marry you for that reason."

"I know, and I understand your feelings. It is not easy to lose one's pride. If such be the case with you, I will see it returned in full. I swear it. It was through my actions that the situation became dangerous. I bear responsibility and will do everything possible to make things right. I will act on behalf of your parents as if they were my own. In this, I need your agreement."

She laid her cheek against his chest. It took some moments, but finally she said yes.

"The war will not last much longer."

"The war …. You plan to return to your regiment." She stated it as fact, knowing he would abandon neither his cause nor the men under his command.

"To do otherwise would be the act of a coward and a traitor. Would you want your husband to carry such a disgrace for the rest of his life?"

She shook her head and held onto him tighter.

"So, I must carry out my duty to France. She is a jealous mistress and every bit as demanding as a wife."

How she wanted him never to leave her! She could not ask it of him. What would she tell their children when they studied history: that their father shirked his duty because their mother did not wish to be left alone?

He kissed her lightly on the lips. "Now, Madame St. Clair, we must decide what to do with you in the interim. You cannot stay here. It is too dangerous." He thought for a moment. "You will be safe at the Ursaline convent. The good nuns will be well disposed to accommodate you. I do believe Marielle received her education there, and André has been most generous in his support over the years."

"The nuns? Was not it you who once said I was not meant for a convent?"

He smiled down at her and kissed the tip of her nose. "Did you not prove me right last night and just now this morning? Think of it as only a brief respite." He took her hands, brought them to his lips and kissed first one wrist and then the other. "My beautiful, obedient wife, I shall not send you into their care as a beggar. There are more carrots and potatoes, as well, in the root cellar, along with a dozen or so apples and a generous wedge of cheese. I will gather them into a sack, and we will bring them to the nuns as an offering."

She shook out her cloak, then found another ribbon to better secure her keepsake. The tiny parcel with the lock of his hair were tucked into her pocket. It might be all she had to remember him by. She slipped his keepsake into the snug waist of his breeches. Then he took the pillowcase she had stripped from the bed and together they went downstairs. He retrieved his jacket and, while she waited for him, he went into the cellar to gather up the food. He returned with the pillowcase bulging.

He took her hand. "Are you ready, Madame St. Clair?"

"Of course, Monsieur St. Clair. Have I not always done your bidding?"

"Ah, a docile wife." He had a broad grin and more than a trace of sarcasm in his tone. "Whoever could have predicted it?"

Then, hand in hand, they left the house and set off into an uncertain future.

Chapter 30

Wrapped in her now dry cloak and rocking gently to the horse's gait, a sturdy chestnut, Catherine leaned her shoulder into Rive's chest. The commodious pillowcase, bulging with the produce he had gathered and tied with a sturdy knot, lay in her lap, wrapped securely in her arms. It would not do to spill any of the precious cargo. With food stocks low, this simple fare would be seen as a miraculous find by the good nuns. She could not guess how they replenished their food supply, or how they provided for themselves as the war continued to escalate.

Except for the day she failed to reach the wharf and the French ship, she had seldom left the St. Clair property, and she had no idea if the city possessed an open-air market. If it did, would the nuns have provisioned themselves with its goods? She knew nothing of their life behind convent walls but surmised that they could not roam about freely in public. Perhaps, somewhere on the premises, they cultivated a garden, or their needs were taken care of by local folk. How was she to fit into all of this? Would they regard her as just another mouth to feed in spite of the offering she now cradled in her arms?

She snuggled against Rive, who held her securely. Clouds gathered beneath a weak sun that shed its light intermittently; a breeze rustled through the trees, providing the only sound in an otherwise near-silent world. At mid-morning, few people were abroad, and those who were scurried about their business with bent heads. Rarely did anyone exchange words with fellow travelers. Even Rive had fallen silent.

"It is too quiet. I don't know what unnerves me more, the silence or the pounding of the cannons."

He drew her closer. "When the cannons quit, it is usually a sign that something significant is in the works. The British cannot afford to wait before they launch an all-out attack. Autumn is drawing near."

Even as he spoke, she felt a gust of wind kick up and burrow under her cloak. She shivered.

"Why must there be war? Is it something in man's nature, so ingrained he cannot stand away from it?"

"I like to think most men are possessed of a good and kind nature. As to why wars are fought, there are many reasons and none of them good. Mostly they're about power and conquest. Unfortunately, it is the ordinary men who fight in them and gain the least."

"If you feel that way, why do you take part in this one?"

He let some seconds pass. "It is what I was trained to do. However, there is another side to the issue, and that is a man's desire to protect and serve the country he loves. It is what makes a good soldier. Along the way, I have discovered that not every soldier is eager for war."

She heard the weariness in his tone. "You are not eager for it." She felt confident she had guessed correctly.

"No, I am not. Still, I have pledged to protect this colony, and I will do it. But afterwards …." He leaned down and kissed her cheek. "I have a wife now and must endeavor to keep her coddled and in comfort."

"I care little for comfort." She touched his cheek. "Just return safely to me."

"I desire nothing else. You will always be in my thoughts."

As the convent came into sight, Rive reined in the horse, and they sat quietly for a minute. She leaned her head against his shoulder, and he encircled her in both his arms. Then he spurred the horse on, although neither seemed eager to arrive at their destination.

When they reached the convent, he dismounted and relieved Catherine of the sack of food. Then he lifted her down from the horse. While there was still time, he kissed her with fervor, and she wondered if, perhaps, he had changed his mind about rejoining his regiment. She wound her arms about his neck and would have kept them there forever, had he not reached up and disengaged her hands before stepping back.

"It is time I left you in the nuns' care." A wan smile creased his face, and he picked up the sack. He took her hand, and they walked up the path that led to the convent.

The large stone building, although simple in design, was impressive. Three stories high, with rows of windows sheathed from within by heavy dark drapes, it appeared to have escaped any of the destruction. Not so the surrounding lawn, which must once have been lush and green. Now huge patches had dried to a withered brown. Only a half-dozen trees, some as tall as the convent, appeared healthy.

Rive rapped several times on the stout wooden door, and they waited in silence for someone to answer the summons. After a short while, a small door situated at eye level opened from inside. Through a metal grate, Catherine saw a woman who appeared not much older than herself. Stiff white fabric covered her forehead and framed the sides of her face, revealing little of her countenance. A dark veil draped her head and shoulders.

I am Captain Rive St. Clair and this is my wife, Catherine." Rive spoke in French. "It is important that I speak with Mother Superior. Please be sure to tell her it is Captain St. Clair. She will recognize the name."

Without a word, the young nun closed the door. Catherine clung to Rive's hand, feeling anything but brave. A minute or so later the front door opened, and the same nun stepped aside and bid them enter.

"If you will follow me," she said in a hushed tone, leading them into a large entryway. A metal and glass fixture, which held a single candle, hung by a chain from the ceiling and shed very pale light over the interior. A decided chill hung in the air.

The nun, whose light footsteps made it seem as if her feet hardly touched the polished wood floor, guided them down a wide corridor lined with several doors. Paintings depicting what Catherine assumed were holy figures—perhaps saints—lined the walls. Except for her and Rive's footsteps, not a single sound issued from any other part of the building. When they reached a door at the end of the corridor, the nun rapped lightly.

A woman's voice said, "You may enter." After pushing the door open, the nun bowed her head and backed silently away, leaving Rive and Catherine at the entrance to the room.

Diffused light beckoned them forward. Once inside, they found a comfortable room where a fire blazed in the hearth. Heavy draperies closed off the windows to keep the heat inside. Several more paintings of religious figures, mostly executed in dark, somber colors, hung from the walls. The furnishings included a good-sized mahogany desk, an armchair situated behind it. Both sat on a burgundy carpet. A pair of matching wooden chairs, the seats upholstered in a deep blue plush, faced the desk. A large crucifix hung on the wall.

A woman wearing the same habit as the nun who had admitted them rose from the desk chair. Although her face bore the creases of middle age, Catherine suspected that at one time she had been quite comely. Though short in stature and slight of frame, as Mother Superior she was, nevertheless, imposing.

"Welcome, Captain St. Clair," she said in a soft, almost musical voice as she approached from behind the desk, "and Madame St. Clair."

Still holding the sack of produce, Rive stepped forward and dipped his head in a bow. Catherine could hardly suppress a smile at the sight of her tall, stalwart, and admittedly adventurous husband paying obeisance to this petite woman.

"Mother Superior." He set the sack on the floor at his feet. "My wife is in dire need of your protection." In a concise fashion, he stated Catherine's situation. "So, you see, she can no longer turn to my family, and I am extremely reluctant to leave her alone."

"I understand perfectly. Of course we will offer the protection of our convent." Mother Superior smiled at Catherine and continued in heavily accented English. "As your husband has stated, you were born in England. Are you of our faith, my dear?"

"No, Mother Superior."

"Then we will not require you to attend our religious services, unless, of course, you wish to do so. We have a lovely chapel, and you will always be welcome there."

"That is a very kind offer." Touched by the nun's compassion and grateful for the invitation to make use of the chapel, Catherine felt her eyes mist with tears. "I will be sure to avail myself of it, and often."

"We have many duties here, although we do not have any students in our school at the moment, with the situation so critical. We are always grateful for a helping hand. You will find that some of our sisters speak English, which they have taught over the years to our young ladies."

"I speak French, although not as well as I would wish. I am sure I will not have too much difficulty conversing with them."

"That is of little concern," Mother Superior said gently. "Without our students to service, we have become a more contemplative society."

"Contemplation should suit my wife well." Catherine could hear just the tiniest echo of amusement in Rive's tone. "She has often spent time in quiet reflection. So that she not come without dower, we have brought what meager stores we could gather." He indicated the sack.

"All offerings are welcome." Mother Superior glanced from one to the other. "I will give you time alone now. I wish you God's blessing, Captain."

Ramrod straight, arms at his sides, Rive dipped his head in another bow. "Thank you, Mother Superior."

After she was gone, Rive took Catherine in his arms and held her in a tight, lingering embrace, while she clutched the front of his coat and buried her face in his chest. He kissed the tumble of golden hair at her crown, and she turned her face toward his so he could capture her lips. His hands raked through her hair. When his lips left hers, he kissed her throat and cheek and returned finally to recapture her mouth. His kiss was deep, and Catherine could sense all the pent-up longing in it—a longing that matched her own in intensity.

Finally, he stepped back, reached into his coat, and brought out a folded paper. "I prepared this hastily, but it should be adequate."

Catherine felt her face tighten with alarm. "What is it?"

Rive glanced from her to the document in his hand. "I didn't intend to frighten you. Did you think it was my will?" He gave her a familiar look, the one that produced a combination half smile and half frown. "It's not a will, *per se*. It is a set of instructions to my Uncle Hubert in Paris. Do not read them until after I leave." He placed the paper in her hand.

"How is he to receive this?" There were times when her husband made no sense at all.

"It will be delivered to him by you."

Only then did she understand. She could not form the words that swam in her head, could not form any words that spoke of the possibility of Rive dying in battle.

Yet he seemed to have no such qualms. "In the event that something happens to me and I am unable to return here for you, Louis will take up that charge. If he is unable, a trusted fellow officer will come in his stead. Your passage will be secured to France and to my family. Hubert will know how to proceed from there."

She could only stare at him and shake her head.

"I feel confident none of this will be necessary. I plan to come through this war with nary a scratch. Then I shall whisk you away to a place where I can make love to you all day, every day, until we sail together." He kissed the tip of her nose.

She felt tears gather behind her lids and blinked them back. She would indulge in no cowardly weeping this day. She gave him the bravest smile she could muster. "I shall await you here, my love. I shall pray for you in the chapel each day. I shall remind God you are far too ornery to ever—"

His lips silenced her. After he finally ended the kiss, he said, "Wait here while I speak once more with Mother Superior."

He was absent no more than a few minutes. When he returned, he took her hand and they retraced their steps to the front door.

"Now behave yourself," he chided in his teasing way.

"I shall be the perfect guest, so quiet and obedient the sisters will hardly know I am among them." There was a slight catch in her voice. "When you return, you will find a most humble and docile wife who will spend the remainder of her life providing for your *every* need."

"Ah. Is that not every man's dream?" He kissed her once more with tender restraint then opened the door and stepped outside. The wind was blowing harder and sang a discordant strain; leaves gusted across the ground in a reddish swirl. He walked to his horse, waiting until he was mounted to look back at her. "I love you."

"And I you." She managed a weak smile.

As he urged the horse onto the road leading away from the convent, he waved to her. Her fingers fluttered in response, a halfhearted answer to his farewell. She kept the tears at bay until he was so far from sight that his broad back was barely visible. She closed the door and gave into a paroxysm of weeping.

A short time later, Mother Superior sent one of the young nuns to escort Catherine to her room. The tiny cell-like enclosure held a narrow cot, a *prie dieu* on which to kneel in prayer, a commode and simple china pitcher and washbasin. When she was alone, Catherine opened the folded paper Rive had placed in her care. The words were written in French, which took all her concentration to decipher:

> Using monies from my shares in the family enterprises, the debts of Mr. Thomas Bradshaw, father of my wife, Catherine, are to be absolved in whatever legal manner necessary and in the appropriate court in the City of London. Also, my wife is to receive an allowance each month, enough to keep her and her parents comfortable for the remainder of their lives.

There were also several bank notes, of large denomination, both in French francs and English pounds.

After reading the document twice, Catherine put it and the money aside. She recalled Mother Superior's peaceful demeanor and pledged to emulate it while she waited for Rive. Then she lowered herself onto the kneeler and prayed for the speedy and safe return of her husband.

Chapter 31

～❦～

An icy wind, one that would make most men wish for a blazing hearth, swirled down from the north, and sent currents of air skipping over the choppy surface of the river. Dusk had turned the sky to smoke; then, with the passing hours, it deepened into an ominous black. The night welcomed few stars into the dark void, and only a paltry sliver of moon allowed any light at all.

Rive held to the stout wooden frame of the boat as the oarsman sent it forward in ragged spurts. With any luck, they would stay on course and find a safe beachhead at Point Levis, a spit of land across the river from Quebec. Dressed in the scarlet tunic of a British grenadier, he kept a vigilant watch over the river and listened as it beat against the distant shore. There, somewhere in the patchy darkness, the British camp was situated. By all expectations, several hundred men were quartered in preparation for the final assault on Quebec.

The boat cut an almost soundless path through the swells spraying across her bow. At a signal from Rive, the burly man stilled the oars.

"There, ahead are the rocks," Rive said in a voice barely above a whisper.

The man nodded and continued rowing. He knew these waters well, which was why Rive had selected him for the mission. He and his father and grandfather had fished them for over half a century. Just beyond lay a cove that offered the best opportunity for a safe landing.

A cloud obscured the moon then slid by just as the small craft rounded the curve of the rocky outcropping. Dead ahead landfall beckoned, and within minutes, the boat scraped bottom. Rive leapt for shore. After a silent wave of farewell, he immediately abandoned the spot, heading inland with haste, crouching low to the ground. So far his only company was a brace of shorebirds and the merciless howl of the wind.

His progress proved swift, for he dared not stop to ease the strained muscles in his legs and back. When he spotted the flickering lights of the campfires in the distance, he stopped and dropped to the ground. Hard and cold, it nevertheless cradled his exhausted body with no less a welcome than a fine feather mattress. On this night he would find no rest. Exercising caution, he studied the configurations ahead, his eyes and ears alert to any danger.

As he had expected, the camp was large. Numerous tents dotted the landscape. Constructed of drab canvas, they were illuminated by flames leaping from dozens of fires. Coated in the brilliant scarlet of their regiment, the men hunkered close by. Some sang a melancholy tune longing for home; others talked, played cards, or rolled dice. Their voices carried on the wind, and he sought a way to bring about the next phase of his plan: to become one of them.

Then he heard a muffled oath and pressed flat against the ground, breathing in the soil and spiky grass. In the murky gloom, he could just make out a man's tall, lanky form, musket barrel resting against his shoulder, head and body slightly bent into the wind. A sentry and certainly not the only one in a camp this size.

He had been too fortunate; now would come the first test upon which rested his survival. To move in any direction might give his position away. Yet to stay virtually in the man's path was to invite detection.

Seconds passed with dread alacrity. With the barest movement, Rive inched toward the periphery of the camp. A cluster of stones beneath him shifted and slid under his weight. He mouthed a silent epithet. There was no time for care. He must make haste if he hoped to remain undetected.

The sentry halted. Rive froze, then edged forward again and used both forearms to bear the brunt of his weight. He had often employed such a ruse as a boy when he stalked deer and rabbits. He understood the consequences of the slightest sound. Then he might merely have lost his prey; now he would lose his life. The thought was potent enough to drive him forward and carry him away from the sentry.

A ribbon of light spilled from the moon, barely enough for him to gauge the camp's distance. When the sentry turned toward the sea, he quickly gained his feet and ran silently, dropping into a crouch. He skirted the perimeter, staying well away from the huddled figures of the soldiers, whose scarlet coats were identical to his. Briefly, he wondered which of His Majesty's subjects had worn the coat before *he* had relieved him of it and dismissed the thought. The man had been dispatched to where no war would ever touch him again and Rive, for one, had no intention of joining him.

Trusting to luck and his own instincts and skill—he had, after all, accomplished this feat once before at the British encampment on the Îsle d'Orléans—he made a bold dash for the camp, using the nearest tent to shield him from view. Exercising caution, he made his way toward the central area where the voices of the men grew louder. Several soldiers sat around an open fire. Intent on their own needs for companionship and warmth, they seemed not to notice the Grenadier who slipped in amongst them, held his hands toward the flames and, with a grunt of disgust, dropped onto the ground.

AT THE URSALINE CONVENT, CATHERINE QUICKLY settled into a routine that found her emulating the customs of the nuns. Everyone rose shortly after dawn, and after performing a simple ablution, dressed and gathered in the chapel. There an elderly priest, Father Jean—whose name Catherine recognized from the night Rive proposed marriage—often arrived to conduct mass. After this they took a breakfast of thin porridge in the bare, windowless refectory, sitting at a long wooden table flanked by wooden benches.

At lunchtime she often helped sort out the day's rations in the kitchen. With supplies dwindling, the decision of which items to consume and which to keep in reserve became vital. Potatoes were never eaten on the same day as bread; and if a slice of apple was favored one day, carrots appeared on the menu the following day. A tiny wedge of the cheese Rive had brought with them was served either at lunch or dinner, a luxury in the face of certain deprivation.

Weather permitting, Catherine spent part of the afternoon in the rear garden, where the last of the vegetables—potatoes, turnips, cabbages, and carrots—grew. She tended the patch with Sister Nathalie, the youngest of the sixteen nuns in residence. She quickly learned to use a trowel to dig up the root vegetables, wash them and even on occasion cook them. Since she had eventually taken over cooking in her parents' home, she was no stranger to kitchen duties. At other times, wrapped in her cloak, she read from her books of poetry, caressing the soft leather that, not long before, Rive's hands had touched. However, oftentimes she found that the beautiful words left little impression on her thoughts, for concentration seemed nearly impossible.

Nights, however, proved the most difficult. Early to bed, she huddled under the thin sheet and blanket that barely dispelled the ever-present chill. Often she heard the sounds of cannon fire. Those explosions, although distant, kept her constantly on edge. She could concentrate on nothing but her steadily growing fear that Rive might be captured, or worse, killed.

The realization of her deep love for him only increased her anxiety. His own declaration, when she truly became his wife, never strayed far from her memory. When she closed her eyes, she saw his face and, before sleep claimed her, heard his voice saying, "You are my one true love." Lying in her dark little cell, she often recalled their first night together as man and wife. Then the blood would rush to her face. Married woman or not, the memories still made her blush. Still, she held them close. Also, she suspected that this was the first time he, too, had found love.

On Catherine's third day at the convent, there came a break in her routine that brought a welcome but totally unexpected boon. After finishing a meager lunch of half an apple, one biscuit, a wedge of cheese of such small proportion as to only hint at fulfillment, and a cup of tea, she and Sister Nathalie set out into the garden to gather vegetables for the evening meal.

At first Catherine thought the lack of a proper diet had caused her mind to play tricks. However, further inspection proved that she could still recognize a cow, and a reasonably healthy-looking one, when she encountered it. The animal, for its part, having spied the two women, issued a mournful sound. Then it lowered its head to a small patch of grass and continued to graze.

Catherine stared in awe. "Where do you suppose it came from?" Somehow it had managed to make its way into this fashionable neighborhood, in spite of the British bombardment. The mystery it presented might well prove unsolvable.

"It's from a farm beyond the outskirts of the city, to be sure. Either the farm has been abandoned because of the fighting or this cow wandered off on its own."

The animal appeared quite content to go about the business of eating. So it was with a mixture of curiosity and false bravado that Catherine approached. With all due caution, she crept to within an arm's length of the beast. It interrupted its grazing to raise its head momentarily and glance with round, soulful eyes at this uninvited distraction.

"Just what do you think you are doing here?" She rested her hands on her hips in a proprietary stance. It was, after all, the *sisters'* grass the cow so blissfully chewed.

Sensing no immediate threat to its well-being, the animal returned to its solitary occupation.

"Scat. Go back to where you belong." Catherine punctuated the order with a resounding clap of her hands. To no avail.

Time passed, and the situation appeared to warrant some action. However, what form should it take? Never before had she found herself in possession of another's property. While she and the sisters were certainly innocent of any wrongdoing—after all, the cow had come to *them*—she believed some effort probably should be made to determine ownership.

With Sister Nathalie observing, and with good intentions, Catherine slowly circled the beast whose udder, clearly filled with milk, had perhaps approached the bursting point.

"I think it wishes to stay," Sister Nathalie said.

Catherine smiled for the first time in days. "I think you are right."

"Should we keep her, then?"

Catherine supposed that if one wished to pursue the ethics of the situation, a moral dilemma might well exist. The cow, and indeed its milk, belonged elsewhere. Yet it had chosen to take up temporary, if not permanent, residence in *this* garden. With no clear identification—for did not *all* cows look alike?—she could not imagine, even for honesty's sake, parading into the countryside, given the war, to seek out the owner.

Therefore, in all good conscience, could not the nuns be considered interim guardians? Surely, to abandon the poor creature to the street was to invite outright thievery.

She discussed the matter with Sister Nathalie, who heartily agreed they would borrow the cow for the immediate future.

"It is settled then." Catherine reached out and tentatively patted their newfound acquisition on the rump. Her gaze fell again to the full udder. Teats sprang from it like stubby fingers, and she wondered how to get them to yield their milk. Did the task require a light or determined touch, a pull or a squeeze, or perhaps some other mysterious hand motion?

"Have you ever milked a cow?" she asked Sister Nathalie.

"No, Madame, I was raised in the city."

"As was I. I suspect there is only one way to find out. If you will go into the kitchen and bring back a large cooking pot, I'll endeavor to relieve this beast of her milk."

A minute later, Sister Nathalie came dashing back with the pot. She handed it to Catherine, who squatted down and bent to the task, if not with relish, at least with determination. Positioning the vessel beneath the cow, she reached underneath and took one of the teats firmly in hand. Her reward came by way of a flick of the animal's tail against her arm. She jumped up and stepped back, more from surprise than any physical harm.

Cowardice, however, never won the day. This she knew well, and so she took to the quest with new resolve and a far warier eye. Its udder swayed as the cow moved restlessly, side-stepped across the patch of grass, and retreated just beyond Catherine's grasp.

"Come, you will feel so much better if you will just let me …." She grabbed the pot and lunged forward and unerringly her hand found its mark. She squeezed, the cow gave a mournful, throaty "moo" and began the little dance began anew.

"Will you hold the pot?" Catherine asked Sister Nathalie. Then she got down onto her knees and managed to dodge the flicking tail.

With visions of steaming cups of milk wavering before her eyes, she gave a yank. It produced nothing more than another mournful cry from the animal. So she adjusted her motion and worked her fingers as if trying to coax a tune from some thoroughly foreign instrument. After much persistence, a thin white stream shot from the teat, only to find its mark on Catherine's gown. Far from discouraged, however, she continued in the same vein, adjusting her aim until finally a squirt of milk made it into the pot.

"Aha." Using two hands, she guided streams of milk into the pot. For the better part of half an hour, she and Sister Nathalie applied themselves to their task. When the milk level rose almost to the brim and the cow appeared empty of nearly every drop, they pulled the vessel to safety and congratulated themselves for their persistence.

They carried their prize into the kitchen and poured the warm milk into two large china pitchers. Then, looking about her, Catherine put her hands on her hips and gave a deep-throated laugh. By God, she would survive this siege one way or another. If she could master the fine art of milking, no war was going to ever defeat her.

Chapter 32

Having successfully infiltrated the camp, Rive continued going about the business of gathering information. By day, he fell in with the men, performed his duties and did nothing to call attention to himself. At night he joined his fellow Grenadiers around the campfires, listening to their grumbles and posturing. Whenever possible, he steered the conversation toward Quebec, the impregnable fortress across the river.

There were rumors of every possible stripe: the invasion was set for mid-October; no, the date had been moved back, more than likely mid-September; the assault would take place where Montcalm had set up his riverside fortifications, a repeat of July thirty-first, only this time it would succeed; with the first serious turn in the weather, the fleet would be recalled to Britain where it would pass the winter in preparation for another incursion into Canadian waters the following spring.

The night of September twelfth brought the usual gusty winds. The men hung together in their bivouac, crowding about the fires for warmth. Cannon and musket shots could be heard coming from east of the city, where Montcalm's fortifications spread along the shores of the North Channel. Restless and desperate now for some useful information, Rive moved about the encampment. However, nothing untoward seemed to be in the wind. Perhaps the rumor the Beaufort line would be attacked again had proved correct. Each day a flotilla of ships drifted downstream on the ebb tide, only to reverse and float upstream on the flood tide. It seemed the idea was to openly parade before the French but carry out no attacks. Then, after Montcalm and his forces became overly confident, they would launch their assault.

General Wolfe had recently evacuated his camp at Montmorency and taken up position here on Point Levis, only one mile across the river from Quebec. With this in mind, Rive made his way toward the British battery, close to the shoreline.

"You, soldier." A voice stopped him in his tracks.

As Rive turned, his right hand found the pistol wedged under his belt. Of course, he dared not fire the weapon, but a good clubbing to the head would silence anyone challenging his right to be there.

"Do you wish a word with me?" Cautiously, he approached the man. Like some in the company, he had abandoned his regimental uniform for the comfort of a hunting shirt and leggings.

"They need volunteers for the forward barges. The landing is set for tonight."

"It is about time." Rive took care to keep his mounting excitement hidden. "Where did you say the landing is to occur?"

"I didn't say, and neither will anyone else. Only General Wolfe has that information. Not even his generals have been told yet. You never know where you will find a spy these days. If you are in, report to the officer in charge of the Grenadiers. You'll find him forward of the battery."

The man moved on and Rive made a quick decision. If not even Wolfe's own generals were privy to the plan, then *his* chances of discovering the landing site appeared slim to none. The only way to gain any information was to volunteer for a place in the whaleboats.

Without further hesitation, he proceeded to the forward battery. There he found several men padding the oarlocks. He assumed these were the advance boats. No sentry would be the wiser when the vessels silently approached the landing site. He knew he must find a place in one of those boats.

"I was told to see the officer in charge of volunteers," he said to the nearest man.

"Over there. He's wearing the regimental colors of the Highlanders."

A lantern was hoisted in one of the boats, and a pale-yellow sliver of light pierced the dark night.

Rive sought the man out and was quickly taken into the ranks of the volunteers, which numbered about twenty.

"Any word on the landing site?" he inquired casually of the officer.

"You and the others will find out when it is time." The officer looked toward the troops assembled around Rive. "Okay, men, we are to get into that whaleboat." He indicated a craft in the process of being launched and where oarsmen were already in place. Rive climbed aboard and settled himself near the front. Even when all twenty-four volunteers were seated, the oarsmen didn't head out onto the river. They waited patiently, no one uttering a sound. It was difficult to judge time, but Rive thought it must be well past midnight.

He kept his ears cocked for any tidbit of information. Finally, a Highlander appeared. "Make way for the general." A stirring went through the ranks. A man sporting the uniform and trappings of a senior officer, a general, made his way to the boat and climbed aboard, followed by another officer of lesser rank. Speculation began amongst the volunteers. Shortly it became clear that their passenger was none other than General Wolfe. After he took up the most forward position, someone gave the order to proceed.

With little light from the moon, the water appeared as black as mourning cloth. When Rive finally turned his gaze from General Wolfe, he saw the ghostly outlines of scores of British ships appear in the gloom. The advance boats were leading a flotilla that stretched for miles. He was able to make out the Highlanders and light infantry, which he knew would be used to secure a beachhead. Somewhere farther behind, the artillery would sail along with the supply ships. Indeed, the black night was made for the devil's work.

In silence, the flotilla sailed on the ebb tide, skirting the broad plain that spread westward from Quebec City. Slowly the current carried them downstream. The men, crammed together, dared not speak. They knew that only one of two things awaited them: either victory or certain death. Steep cliffs bordered the plain. Rive remembered his prediction when he had studied the map with André. The assault would probably come where the French least expected it. In all likelihood, the landing site was L'Anse-au-Foulon.

The river current carried them on their course, and Rive's mind moved in concert with them. One thought after another crowded his mind, all of them centered on one necessity: he must somehow warn the French sentries atop the cliffs of the approaching danger. How to go about it? Any untoward action on his part would more likely see him carry the news to the bottom of the river.

"*Qui vive*?" a French sentry called down from the heights.

At first there was silence in the whaleboat. Then a Highlander returned the challenge in expert French. "François! *Et vive le roi*!"

And long live the king!

Now. There must be no care on his part for his own safety. He must give an immediate warning. The tide was taking them swiftly downstream. In no time they would be well beyond the sentry's outpost.

"Non!" he stood and shouted, his voice carrying clearly in the still air. "*C'est l'Anglais. L'Anglais!*"

The next second, a blunt instrument smashed down on the back of his head. The darkness around him deepened, and he tried to fight through it and hang onto the last vestiges of consciousness. The last thing he heard was the Highlander's shout assuring the sentry that they were the expected supply ship.

Chapter 33

To the small detachment of French soldiers guarding the cliffs above the plain, there seemed to be nothing unusual about the pre-dawn hours of September thirteenth. Made weary by weeks of inactivity, Louis Villet lounged with a small group, as the black near-moonless night closed about him. Set against this dark background, the white tents of the French force stood out, but there would be little sleep for him and the other men tonight. A week earlier they had shared the same desolate ground with a full battalion. Montcalm, however, anticipating Wolfe, would not abandon the campaign without one final assault, and so had recalled the battalion to strengthen the Beaufort lines. Now he waited, unaware that directly below a flotilla of British landing craft edged closer to the narrow strip of land at the base of the cliff.

It was not until hours later that Louis learned General Wolfe had come ashore and given the order to begin the climb. At first hearing, he found it absurd that such a feat could be accomplished, but the British, nonetheless, had scrambled forward. Not an easy task, he conceded. They had to make the climb with their muskets strapped to their backs, testing their skills against the unrelenting force of nature. Apparently, even as twigs must have snapped and metal clashed against rock, no sound carried to the heights above because no alarm was given. With so complete a surprise, not a single shot was fired until the force reached the summit and overpowered the French, laying bare the Plains of Abraham. Louis sadly conceded that these long, broad plains were the perfect setting for what would later prove to be the final battle for Quebec.

A FIERCE BOMBARDMENT, THE WORST YET, SENT Catherine and the nuns scurrying into the cellar. Pulling the shawl loaned to her by the Mother Superior around her shoulders, she sat hunched in the tight circle of women. As her eyes slowly adjusted to the darkness, she was seized by a shudder as icy as any wind penetrating a chink in the stone walls. Her ears pounded from the cacophony of cannon fire.

For hours they huddled in the dark. By now Catherine was certain that the British assault would bring everything down around them in a shower of destruction. She thought constantly of Rive and railed against the fates, which seemed, indeed, to have turned against them.

During a lull in the bombardment, she gathered her courage and led the way upstairs. Once there, Mother Superior suggested they visit the chapel and pray for the deliverance of the French forces and the city they protected with their lives. She followed the nun's lead, sinking to her knees and offering up prayers for Rive's safety. Sometime later she slipped out of the chapel and stole to a window, where she could peer through a tiny opening in the drape. It was still early morning and she had just taken up her station when she saw a contingent of French troops shuffle down the street.

They were a rag-tag group, hardly more than a few dozen. She scanned each face, hoping Rive would be among them, and had to swallow her disappointment when he was not. Still, it pained her to observe their listless gaits and hunched shoulders. Some trailed their muskets in the dust, and others used them as improvised walking sticks. They had an unmistakable air of defeat. Whatever had occurred, it boded ill for the city.

People left their homes and rushed into the road to cluster around the soldiers. She watched the brief exchanges and, unable to bear the suspense any longer, raced out to join them.

"You, there," she accosted a young soldier. His uniform was caked in mud, his head wrapped in a blood-stained bandage. "What news do you bring?"

"Nothing good, I fear. The British have gained the heights above the Anse-au-Foulon and are routing the French forces. Everything is collapsing. Many of our men are falling back into the city. There have been hundreds captured, even more killed. The enemy is demanding immediate surrender. We shall try to hold out a day or two longer, but they are inside the gates. Without reinforcements, we have too few men to stave off another attack. I am sorry, Madame. It is indeed a dark day for France." His eyes filled with tears and he turned away to rejoin his weary comrades.

RIVE'S FIRST IMPRESSION WAS OF A pair of badly scuffed black boots. Squinting, he cast his eyes over leggings and a sturdy chest draped in a crimson jacket. Lying on his side on the whaleboat's hard wooden planking, he judged himself to be a mere two feet from the man who was ostensibly guarding him. No other soldiers remained in the boat, and he could spot none at the base of the cliff. In the near distance, he heard the roar of cannon and musket fire and guessed the battle for Quebec had already begun. If he were to join in, it must be soon.

A rudimentary plan formed in his mind, and he had no time to tinker with its implementation. In one swift movement, he reached out and grabbed the guard by his ankles, throwing all the strength he possessed into thrusting the seated man backward and off his perch. Before the sentry could recover, Rive snatched his musket and drove the stock into the hapless guard's forehead.

Rive tore off his red jacket and rubbed the back of his head. "You might say I evened the score with that one." He grabbed the musket and jumped out of the whaleboat beached at the base of the cliff.

The sounds of battle erupted from above. It seemed certain that the French had their backs to the city while they faced the enemy across the wide plain. Quebec City lay some distance east. To climb the cliff here would put him in the middle of the British lines. Therefore, he ran along the rocky shore until he judged his own forces occupied the land above. He began to climb and could only hope he would find the French engaged in a victorious rout of the enemy.

When he pulled himself over the crest of the cliff, his hopes died. Glancing eastward, he saw a force of British frigates extending from Quebec to the Beauport fortifications. The sound was intense, as though they were firing every gun.

What he witnessed before him dismayed him further; the French could not hold their ground. White clad soldiers dotted a torn and scarred earth and lay like the last remnants of snow on a barren field. Straight ahead were the brilliant red coats of the British army. Musket fire crackled from the woods, stalling the enemy's advance. But when the smoke cleared, they were once again on the move, drawing closer to the city. It lay all but defenseless. Dashing into the fray, Rive did his best to rally the men around him, a decent-sized company of militia. He could not see General Montcalm but hoped he was somewhere on the plain with enough troops to turn the tide in France's favor.

Chapter 34

Clouds as dull as aged pewter scudded across a leaden sky. The battle had been raging all day with little information finding its way to Catherine and the nuns. By evening, news—most if it disastrous—had spread. Everyone who could mobilize some form of transport removed themselves as far from the advancing British army as possible. It was a disorganized exodus punctuated by occasional shouts and the creak of carriages lurching under heavy loads. Catherine was grateful that the St. Clairs had escaped earlier. She doubted André's heart could have withstood the strain of a French defeat.

On September eighteenth, Quebec City surrendered to the British, and the government of New France moved to Montreal.

The nuns, however, went about their daily prayers and chores and tried to keep their spirits up. That goal had become increasingly more difficult and was made no easier when General Montcalm's body was laid to rest in a bomb crater under the chapel's altar. With each passing day, Catherine's worries grew and, whenever possible, she questioned the returning soldiers about Rive. However, none brought any news of him.

Then, just after breakfast—one late September morning when the clouds gave way to a pallid sun—Mother Superior came to Catherine, who was on her knees in the chapel. Part of the roof had collapsed, carving out a gaping hole above the altar, but the rear of the structure had been deemed safe now that the fierce bombardments had ceased.

"Madame St. Clair, you have a visitor."

Catherine jumped to her feet. "Is it Rive?" She was already dashing out of the chapel when the nun's next words stopped her.

"I am sorry to say it is not your husband. I believe this man might bring news of him. I have asked him to wait in the visitors' room."

Catherine rushed down the corridor. Pulling open the appropriate door, she entered the room with such haste she nearly collided with Louis Villet.

For a moment, she could not find her breath. Then she felt a terrible pain in the pit of her stomach. She remembered Rive's caution: in the event he was unable to return to rescue her, Louis would assume that duty. She bit her lower lip and fought for the courage to accept whatever news he brought. At least seeing her husband's good friend, a man of whom she had grown fond, brought a measure of joy.

"Louis, you are unharmed." She reached for his hands and would have thrown her arms about him, except she sensed that such a gesture would embarrass him. She stepped back and managed a wan smile. "Please tell me Rive has had the same good fortune."

A wooden bench sat against one wall, and Louis led her to it. He waited until they were seated before answering her query. "Rive is alive, Madame. He is a prisoner in the Dauphine Redoubt, a military installation. We have spies about, but they have been unable to learn much about the men held there. Only that Rive …."

Catherine feared his next words would not be as heartening as his earlier declaration that Rive was still alive.

"What is it, Louis? Tell me, please."

"He has been accused of spying. He was recognized as the man who impersonated a British soldier and called a warning to the French sentries atop the cliffs. It was a miracle he was not shot at the very moment he shouted the warning. I suppose they could not risk it, if they were to keep the element of surprise. Rive was imprisoned and, I am sorry to say, condemned to pay the ultimate penalty. A warning, no doubt, to others who might think to pursue the same course as long as fighting continues. The battle has moved to Montreal, but the city is undermanned and not expected to hold out for long."

Catherine's hands had clenched the moment Louis divulged the accusation against Rive. If they had found it dangerous to shoot him dead as he warned his countrymen, they no longer had cause for delay. When she broached the subject with Louis, he did not deny it.

"The verdict has been posted outside all of the British installations and in parts of the city, as well. The execution will take place in two days."

She jumped to her feet and pressed her hands to her cheeks. Tears sprang into her eyes and she brushed them away, loathe to show weakness in the face of her husband's bravery.

"Can we do nothing? Can we not send an appeal to the British? They have been victorious. What do they need with one more death? What can it serve them?"

Louis stood and walked to the window facing the road. He gazed outside for a moment before turning back.

"Although we believed it useless, upon learning the news, we petitioned General Murray, who has been installed as Governor of Quebec, to spare Rive's life. Unfortunately, we have heard nothing in response and must assume the request was denied. Do not lose heart. We have put together a plan. We feel it has a good chance of success."

"A plan …." She breathed a hopeful sigh.

"There will be some danger involved and can only be implemented with your help."

"Anything. I will do *anything*. Just tell me what you wish of me."

He brought her back to the bench. When they were once again seated, he withdrew a folded paper from inside his shirt. He opened it and handed it to Catherine.

It appeared to be an official document and contained three names: Jacques Gillard, Madame Catherine Gillard, and Brigadier General James Murray.

"It is a pass," Louis said, "entitling the wife of the prisoner, Gillard, to a visit with her husband. It is an excellent forgery since we were unable to secure a pass honestly. With this in hand, it is possible the guards at the entrance will not question your having been granted entrance to the redoubt. The pass bears today's date. If we are correct, and it is forbidden for Gillard to have a visitor, it will appear that order had been rescinded."

"This prisoner is Rive?"

"Indeed, Madame. From the start, before he volunteered to infiltrate the enemy camp, he adopted the name Gillard in the event of his capture."

They sat quietly, while Catherine digested this latest information. "I can assure you I shall be most persuasive in convincing the guards I have been granted the privilege of visiting my husband. How may I assist, once I am inside the redoubt?"

Again, Louis reached under his shirt. This time he withdrew a metal file of perhaps five inches in length and sharpened to a point.

"This implement must be smuggled in to Rive. It can be done only by you, since you will not be searched."

Catherine glanced down at the stomacher secured by hooks to her gown. She would secrete the file beneath the stiff backing under the outer silk covering. She suggested this to Louis and he agreed.

"Once you are inside, it is vital you remember every detail: the number of soldiers who occupy the fortification, where they are stationed and most important, exactly where they are holding Rive. We do not know if you will be allowed to see him privately in his cell, or if a guard will be present. No matter, you must pass him this file."

Catherine nodded. "Do not worry. I will draw close enough to him, and no guard will stop me."

Louis' face creased into a tiny smile. "I am certain you will." His demeanor became serious once again. "Also, you must tell him that during the night, when most of the soldiers are asleep, an explosion will tear an opening into the wall farthest from his cell. He will have no trouble hearing it, and it will be powerful enough to draw the soldiers. At exactly that moment, Rive must pick the lock to his cell door."

Catherine's brow puckered. "Will he have enough time before the soldiers return?"

Louis gave a small muffled laugh. "He will do it in less than ten seconds."

"What if the one guarding him stays at his post?"

"Even better, for in no time he will find himself a prisoner and stripped of his uniform. Do you understand?"

"Oh, yes. I shall play my part perfectly."

"Tell him that a second explosion at the rear of the installation will follow exactly thirty seconds after the first. With luck, the additional commotion will leave the front unguarded. In any event, if soldiers remain on guard, we have men nearby to overpower them. Once outside, Rive must head to the woods west of the building, where we will be waiting for him." He handed her the file.

"This afternoon at three o'clock, Baptiste, whom you have met, will arrive here with a carriage. He will take you to the redoubt and wait until you have been admitted. Then he will station himself a short distance away so that he can observe you when you leave and bring the carriage around. You will give him all the information you have gathered concerning the soldiers and Rive's location, which he will pass on to me. There is a house near the Place Royal that has sustained some damage, but not enough to render it uninhabitable. Baptiste will deliver you there. God willing, Rive will join you once he is free."

Catherine reached for Louis' hands and held onto them for a long moment. She wished she could throw her arms about him but once again practiced restraint. Instead, she thanked him and walked with him to the front door.

"*Au revoir*, Madame. We shall meet again in just a few hours." He turned and hurried down the path.

Catherine stood in the open doorway until she could no longer see him. Then she closed the door and returned to the chapel. She sank down, for once unmindful of the discomfort of the hard kneeler. Everything Louis had imparted swirled in her head. What if the guard did not allow her to visit Rive? Or worse, searched her and discovered the file? The pass bore Rive's assumed name. They would know a plot was afoot. Would it hasten his execution? She pushed that thought from her mind, along with the possibility of danger to herself. She must not falter. She must believe the plan would succeed. She and Rive would sail as planned to Paris and then to London for a reunion with her parents.

She clenched her jaw in resolve then bowed her head and prayed.

At exactly three o'clock, Baptiste arrived at the convent. Keeping close watch at the window, Catherine, as nervous as a cat tied up in a sack, was ready to leave with him. She had already said goodbye to Mother Superior and the other nuns and thanked them for their many kindnesses. For their own safety, she kept her mission secret. With Rive's earlier written instructions and the money he'd given her tucked into her pocket, she climbed into the carriage and prayed for the fortitude to implement the plan to free him.

Few people or conveyances were abroad, giving the carriage a clear path. She commented on this to Baptiste.

"The inhabitants who have taken the Oath of Allegiance have been permitted to keep possession of their estates. Perhaps they felt it wise to stay home and guard against any intrusions."

"I suppose." Her mind was not on the estates of the wealthy seigneurs but consumed with her mission to facilitate Rive's escape.

They rode on in silence. At the corner of a wide intersection, Baptiste drew up the horses and climbed down from his perch.

"Look, Madame, there is the Dauphine Redoubt."

Catherine gazed out of the carriage's window opening at a tall, very imposing building. It was set into a wide expanse of lawn that sloped down to thick woods on either side. Impressive in length and depth, it rose up four stories and had a pitched roof from which sprouted a goodly number of chimneys. Jutting from one side were several tall, narrow, windowless extensions. Could Rive be held in one of those?

"I will bring the carriage to the front. There will be a soldier, perhaps two, on guard duty there. You must show him your pass. If he does not question it, there is a good chance it will raise no suspicion from the men inside."

He climbed back onto the driver's seat, flicked the reins and the horse trotted on. The redoubt was situated well back from the road. When they reached the front, Baptiste stopped the carriage, stepped down and opened the door. He pointed to a spot nearby. "I will keep watch from over there. When I see you exit, I will come at once to fetch you. I wish you good luck, Madame."

She exited the coach and walked with determination down the path. A large wooden door had been pulled open to accommodate a wide entry. A soldier, shouldering a rifle and wearing a scarlet coat with a black collar and cuffs, stood guard. He looked neither young nor old, just weary. Showing not the least hesitation, she approached him.

"*Bonjour*. Good day." She proffered her pass. "I speak some English. *Un peu* … only a little, but …." If she had to cajole her way past this soldier, it would have to be accomplished in his language. She prayed he did not speak French.

The guard glanced from her to the pass and back to her again. His brow puckered as if he were judging her right to be there.

"The prisoner, Gillard, does not have visitors." His tone confirmed his uncertainty.

At this first obstacle, she took a deep breath and gazed up into his eyes. "Oh? But you see here the pass. It says I am allowed to visit with him. Yes?" With a delicate finger, she tapped the paper and produced a tremulous smile. "I am his wife."

The guard took a deep breath and exhaled noisily through his teeth. "I do not know. I thought—"

"Do you have a wife, Monsieur?" Her eyes misted, and it did not take much for her to call upon a sudden spate of tears.

"Yes, I do, Missus. Back in England she is."

"I suppose you miss her very much." She hoped the man had been on good terms with the woman and had not joined the army to escape from her.

He nodded and his expression turned wistful. "Aye, it's been two years since I last laid eyes on her."

Breathing a sigh of relief, Catherine dabbed at her tears. "If the situation were for you the same as for my husband … and you faced death, would you not wish to see her one last time to give her your fondest regards?"

"Aye, for sure I would wish that."

"I ask nothing more, Monsieur, only a few scant minutes with my husband." She clasped her hands against her breast as if in prayer. "The general, the new governor of Quebec, understood. That is why he issued the pass. See, he has signed it."

Once again, the guard studied the paper. "It seems to be in order."

"*Oui*." Catherine called upon fresh tears.

"Now, now, don't get all upset. I do not see where a few minutes can do any harm." He handed back the pass. Then he leaned into the doorway and shouted, "Williams, get over here."

A soldier, who looked barely old enough to fight in a war, appeared in seconds.

"Take this lady down to the prisoner, Gillard. She's his wife. Tell the guard on his door she's allowed a few minutes with him. You stay right there. When time's up, bring her back here."

"*Merci.* Thank you." Catherine smiled at him. "I shall pray for your swift return to your wife."

As she turned into the doorway, Williams said, "This way, Missus. Watch your step."

Catherine followed him into the building and down a central corridor. Opened doors exposed small rooms occupied by perhaps two dozen soldiers. Some of the men sat at desks or tables where missives of a sort—dispatches perhaps—had collected. Others milled about and conversed in low tones. Perhaps they were bored. With their boredom might come carelessness. In the middle of the night, their lack of attention might work in Rive's favor.

"Careful, here," Williams admonished. "The steps are plenty dark."

Indeed, he spoke the truth. The only light issued from a pair of lanterns that hung from the ceiling. Also, the steps were steep and much worn. When they reached the bottom, Catherine had counted fifteen of them.

In the lower corridors, lanterns sat in niches carved into the thick walls. They threw off muted light, barely enough for her to see by. Since it was dark and dank, she assumed they were in a cellar. Happily, she spotted no other soldiers. Then they turned down another corridor where a red-jacketed guard sat across from a wooden door. He possessed a large frame, burdened with an over-abundance of girth. His musket leaned against the wall alongside his stool.

"Eh, who's this?" He hoisted himself to his feet.

"The prisoner's wife. She has permission to see her husband."

The guard took the pass and held it toward a dim slash of light. He studied it for a few moments and handed it back. "Got the general's signature, all right." He plucked a round metal ring from an iron nail driven into the wall and inserted the single key it held into the door lock. He gave it a turn and pushed open the door.

The tiniest bit of illumination escaped from the single lantern within to light a small room, containing a wooden bench and not much else. Straw covered most of the hard-packed dirt floor. Wasting not a moment, Catherine hurried into the cell. Seeing her, Rive went directly to her.

"Catherine ... what?" His expression was one of incredulity.

She placed her fingers lightly over his lips. "Shh," she whispered. The door remained open, and she felt very keenly the presence of the two men who stood just outside. Then she removed her hand and placed it against his nape and leaned into him. When he took her in his arms and kissed her, she could not have cared if the entire British force looked on. Still, she dared not allow the contact to last beyond a few seconds.

"Oh, my love," she whispered against his ear. "There is little time. Listen carefully." In a quiet rush of words, she outlined the plot formulated by Louis.

Then she stepped back, leaving only a few scant inches between them. With her back to the guard and Rive's arms around her, she slipped her fingers beneath the stomacher and brought the file it concealed partway up from its nesting place. With his free hand, Rive carefully slid it the remainder of the way. In seconds, it was hidden under his shirt.

"Oh, my beautiful brave wife. You have put yourself in danger."

"No more so than you, my loving reckless husband." Her words were spoken so softly, she could not be certain he even heard her. "I only did what any devoted wife would do to avoid becoming a grieving widow. I had to risk it."

"You could have been arrested."

"And soon released. I am of no consequence." In truth she did not believe the enemy would be so kind.

He gave her a dazzling smile. "Ah, my wife is now a military tactician. Will my good luck never cease?"

"Too often you have done your best to end it. In the future, I would have years and years of quiet living with you. I shall brook no arguments."

"Ah, still you would have the last word."

She brought her lips very close to his ear. "That is only for the moment. However, I'm sure once we are together again—"

"Time is up, Missus." The guard's voice cut short her rejoinder. Catherine turned her head and saw he had entered the cell.

"Just another second, my good man," Rive cajoled. Before the guard could interfere, he once again brought his lips close to Catherine's ear and spoke in French.

"There is a man in the lower town named Henri Zelle. Tell Louis to find him and see if his sloop is still seaworthy. If so, we will need it before dawn. Otherwise, he is to secure another vessel for us, one which can be easily manned. Now go, before the guard becomes suspicious."

The final moment had arrived. Perhaps this might be the last time she ever saw him. She clutched at his shoulders. He bent his head and his lips found hers in a passionate, but all too brief, kiss.

"I love you so," she whispered.

He brought his cheek next to hers. "I shall give you more than ample time to prove it."

"Let's get a move on." The guard's voice held an impatient note.

"*Au revoir*, my love. I wish you *bon chance*."

"You are my good luck." Rive mouthed the words and stepped back.

Once outside the cell, she followed her escort back to the upper reaches of the fortification. With every step, she prayed that, in just a few short hours, she and Rive would be together.

Chapter 35

Baptiste brought Catherine to a house on the shore of the St. Lawrence River. There, in the lower town, so vulnerable to the British assaults, the damage appeared quite severe, even more so than in the heights. Constructed entirely of timber, the house had parted with a section of its roof. It had fallen, no doubt, victim to one of the many artillery blasts, which left the rear open from above to the elements. Still, she did not care about its lack of comfort. It was the place where she expected to rendezvous with Rive, and nothing else mattered.

The thought, at first hopeful, turned bleak. What if he didn't escape? Anything could go wrong. Her heart ached for him. Perhaps the plot had been uncovered, and while she waited in this dismal hut, preparations were being made for his execution. She clasped her hands against her breast and prayed the fates would not be so unkind. Yet, she must face the possibility.

Baptiste suggested they do without a fire or even a lantern. For their purposes, the house must appear uninhabited. Catherine readily agreed, well aware of the danger.

While Baptiste waited for her to become settled, he broached the subject of her failing to board the ship for France.

"There was much commotion and the young Mademoiselle St. Clair stated firmly that she had seen you board. Otherwise, I would have searched for you. I beg your forgiveness that I did not."

Quickly, she absolved him of all responsibility and thanked him again for his further efforts on Rive's behalf. *Poor Marielle.* She felt genuine sympathy for the girl. Unbeknownst to her, she had unwittingly brought about the very event she feared most—the loss of her cousin to another woman.

After Baptiste left to bring Louis the information she had gathered, she huddled in the encroaching darkness wrapped in her cloak. A small hole in the front of the structure that had once held a window pane allowed her to peek outside. Seeing no one afoot, she assumed that many of the inhabitants had fled in the face of the British occupation.

With nothing to fend them off, the late afternoon winds invaded the house, chilling her. There was neither food nor drink. She would welcome a tiny sip of the brandy Rive had forced her to drink in public on the day they arrived in Quebec City. They could do little except wait and pray for him and Louis and anyone else in their company.

A small wooden chair, the lone piece of furniture, occupied one corner. The afternoon continued to wane, bringing on a gloomy dusk. At least the weather remained dry, although the clouds spread a sooty curtain over the town. Seating herself, she leaned her head back against the wall and closed her eyes. The utter quiet unsettled her, but she dozed off and on while the night gathered about her. Once, she awoke with a start and felt her heart race. She listened intently for some uncommon sound but could hear nothing, not even the desultory cry of a bird or skulking animal. Yet *something* had awakened her. She tiptoed back to the window. Peering into the black void, she wondered how Rive fared at that precise moment.

THE EXPLOSION CAME WITH A ROAR from the powder keg set afire. Rive slid the file from under his shirt and sprang to his cell door. He could hear nothing immediately outside it and had no way to judge if the guard had abandoned his post. No matter, he would go about his business in the quietest manner possible.

Taking care, he inserted the file into the lock. After a few jiggles, he was rewarded with a click; the workings had disengaged. He expected the second blast at any moment; however, he did not intend to wait for it. Surprise was important now. With the next explosion, he would be halfway up the staircase.

He grasped the door handle and yanked the portal inward, ready to overpower the guard if he remained at his post. A second later he was outside his cell. He saw no one. He took it as a hopeful sign, although he would have been happier if he had been able to confiscate his jailer's red jacket. No matter, the possibility still might present itself. He was halfway up the dim stairway when another blast rocked the walls. Loose stones showered down on him. He raised his hands, fingers spread wide over his head in case a chunk of the ceiling gave way. It would be a hell of a disaster if he had come this far only to be knocked senseless.

In seconds he was alone in the upper corridor, the front door of the redoubt directly ahead. Looking neither left nor right, he ran as if a whole company of marksmen were on his heels. Then he pushed out the door and made a dash for the woods.

There Louis and a small complement of mounted men met him. Spotting the unmanned horse, he vaulted into the saddle. Less than a minute later they were completely secluded by the trees. No one spoke. Every man knew his job. The others rode off in different directions, away from the route Louis and he would take.

The ground, still wet from the last rain, muffled the horse's hooves. They cut through the woods and stayed away from the roads. When it seemed safer to go on foot, they abandoned the horses and slipped silently through the grounds of the nearby estates, using leafy shrubs and trees for cover. Shouts came from somewhere in the distance, possibly originating from the soldiers in the redoubt. They made all haste for the lower town and the house where Catherine waited.

Catherine. His mind filled with the essence of her; her eyes that could widen in surprise or peer out from beneath thick lashes during the most passionate moments; her hair that fell in golden curls onto slender rose-hued shoulders; her body ....

Abruptly, he forced such errant thoughts from his mind and returned his concentration to where it belonged. They were nearing the steep decline that led to the lower town. What he didn't need was to fall and break his neck. In the pitch dark, it would be easy to lose his footing. No lights shown below; the river was a black silent beast moving through the night. With luck, they would soon be on a boat and away.

CATHERINE ALMOST JUMPED A FOOT WHEN she heard rapping on the front door. She rushed to it, praying it was Rive. Why would he need to announce himself? Anxious, she stood with her ear to the wood. Who else besides Baptiste and Louis knew where to find her?

Hardly breathing, she waited for a further development. Shortly, she heard a man ask, "Madame, are you there?"

She didn't recognize his voice, but then he had spoken softly. Still, she knew it wasn't Rive.

At the moment, she had few choices. Either she could remain quietly concealed behind the door, or chance the man on the other side was a friend and had been sent to assist them. She decided to trust to the latter.

She opened the door and a powerfully built man dressed entirely in black, even to the toque that covered his head, stepped quickly inside.

"I am Henri Zelle. Louis said you would need my boat tonight. It lies ready in the harbor. You are Madame St. Clair?"

Now she remembered the instructions Rive had given her. Louis was to find this man and arrange for his sloop. She identified herself as Rive's wife.

"Your boat is seaworthy, then?"

"Aye, she managed to escape the destruction. Not that the British didn't try to run her aground more than once when we slipped through the blockade with supplies. She runs swift. If we need to hoist the topsail, she can do close to ten knots. She has a shallow draft, and once we're out of danger, we can sail near the coast."

Catherine wished she knew their destination, but at the moment it didn't matter. All that mattered was that Rive and Louis arrive soon.

The wind had stiffened, intensifying the chill in the small room. Occasionally, the squawk of a shore bird cut into the silence. She stood near the window opening and listened for any sound that might herald the arrival of the men. Would they come on horseback or on foot? Or would they come at all?

A slim border of light, so narrow it could have been drawn by a pen, began to peek over the horizon. Dawn would break shortly. She began to pace again, while Zelle waited near the door. The silence was nerve-wracking and almost as intrusive as a mad clanging of bells sounding an alarm. Catherine clasped her hands so tightly she could feel pain in every finger. Time passed and, with it, her hope.

Just then, the door burst open. Rive and Louis spilled inside, so close to Catherine they almost ran her down. In seconds, she was in Rive's arms. For just a moment, neither spoke, nor did the other men. Then Rive took charge, conversing in a hushed tone with Henri Zelle.

"There is food aboard and blankets," Zelle said. "And brandy to ward off the cold. We three will have no trouble sailing her."

"Then we had best be off," Rive said.

They left the house, Zelle leading the way to where the sloop lay at anchor in the harbor. When they reached a partially beached rowboat, he signaled for them to board. Once Catherine was seated, the three men launched the boat. The oarlocks had been padded so they might proceed in silence. With powerful strokes, the men cut through the shallow waters until the boat idled alongside the sloop. A rope ladder dangled down over her side, and Louis quickly climbed it.

Rive clasped Catherine about the waist. "You're next, my pet. I hope you're not afraid of heights." He unfastened her cloak and slipped it off her shoulders.

Then he lifted her up as far as his arms could reach. Louis grasped her upper arms and brought her the rest of the way up and over the rail. Rive and Zelle quickly followed.

After raising the anchor, Zelle indicated a small cabin amidships. Although Catherine appreciated his offer, she stated she wished to stay above with her husband. When Rive fastened her cloak about her shoulders and steered her to the cabin, she did not argue. She understood their haste.

The cabin sported little headroom. There was a bench, however, and from her perch there she watched through the doorway as the men hoisted the sail. Shortly, she felt the boat move. Now they must leave the harbor and gain the river without being intercepted. She heard the wind lash the sail and the creaking of the timbers. She leaned back against the cabin wall and, some time later, dozed.

She awoke to find Rive squatting in front of her.

She put her hand on his arm. "Why do I always sense when you are close? It does not seem to matter if I am awake or asleep."

"That is an interesting observation." He leaned forward and kissed her lightly on the lips. "Do you suppose it is something peculiar to lovers?"

She sighed. "*Lovers*. I do so like that word." There was a slight pause. "And all it implies."

"My luck grows by the minute. Remind me to thank all the gods.

With the wind pulling at her hair and Rive's strong arm around her, she felt hope for the future. Then she placed one of her hands over his and leaned against him, her heart filled with love.

Chapter 36

With the help of a favorable wind, the sloop fairly flew through the Gulf of St. Lawrence and into the Atlantic. As they neared the City of Boston, which Rive stated as their destination, Catherine rejoiced to see the sun shining its early autumn light around puffs of white cottony clouds. The air smelled fresh and clean.

Rive had already explained the procedures they would follow, once they arrived in the city. Their first order of business was to secure lodging at a reputable inn. Then new wardrobes must be ordered. While they waited, he would make arrangements for their passage to London.

As they entered the harbor, she gazed at the thicket of sails that rose up from scores of ships lying at anchor. She had to remind herself that she had arrived in the colonies less than four months earlier. It might as well have been a lifetime ago, for all that had happened in the interval. Nearing the dock, she caught a glimpse of warehouses and just beyond, commercial establishments.

After the sloop was secured at one of the wharves and Catherine and the men had disembarked, she touched Louis on the shoulder to draw his attention.

"Before it is too late, and we must part, I want to thank you for all you have done for me and Rive. I know we most likely will not meet again, but I wish you to know I will think of you often and with fondness."

He smiled and gave a slight bow. "I will think of you as well, Madame. As to our meeting again, there is always the possibility fate will find us together once more."

She could not imagine how that would be possible, for Louis' future lay here on this continent, and hers and Rive's on another. There was no time to question. The three men huddled for some moments; then Rive led her away from the dock and onto the street. They walked several blocks to an inn where they engaged a room. It looked not only commodious, but clean. That evening, they dined on a hearty stew at a nearby tavern.

Once back at the inn, Rive held a candle aloft, and they climbed the stairs to their room. Earlier, he had ordered a bottle of the proprietor's finest wine, which they found waiting for them.

"To the future," he said after pouring each a glass.

Catherine touched the rim of her glass against his and offered her own toast. "To our future together." She took a tiny sip of the deep hued burgundy.

"May it be long and fruitful, and may nothing ever separate us again."

"Very long." And more than likely fruitful. Unless she was greatly mistaken, she would be presenting her husband with an heir some months hence. This she decided to keep to herself until they were ensconced on the ship and en route to London. Then she would let him wait on her and coddle her and fetch her every kind of tasty morsel. But first ….

"Rive, since we are speaking of the future, how, my adventurous husband, do you intend to occupy yourself in order to keep busy? By your own admission, you are not the type to be sequestered in an office paging through dusty account books."

"I have been meaning to broach the subject with you but find my mind occupied with matters closer at hand. With luck we will set sail in no more than a week. Once we reach London, I intend to participate in a happy reunion between you and your parents. If you wish, I shall explain everything to them. In fact, the subject being as delicate as it is, I believe I should."

"Everything?"

"Ah … the more indelicate parts we may, perhaps, glide over."

"I should think so. And then …."

"Then, while we enjoy your parents' company, I will send a dispatch to my Uncle Hubert in Paris to apprise him of my marriage. Also, I will instruct him that a certain percentage of my shares in the family enterprises be transferred into your father's account so that he may draw an income from them forthwith."

Catherine's eyes welled with tears. "You would take on such a burden?"

"I hardly considerate it a burden. After all, have they not given me their daughter, whom I cherish?"

They had been seated on two wooden chairs. Catherine set her glass aside on the table between them and went to Rive. Careful not to spill his wine, she settled in his lap.

"You are the best husband in so many ways that it will take me a lifetime to enumerate them all. For now, you have my gratitude and my love."

"I gladly accept both." He kissed her lightly on the lips.

"Now, husband, tell me. What does our future bring? Will it be in London or Paris?"

"Hmm. What would you say if I told you neither?"

"Neither?" She could barely contain her surprise.

"You see, I have a plan—"

"Oh, dear, perhaps I should take a sip of wine. Your plans have sorely tested me in the past, and I cannot imagine myself so fortunate to find that you would have undergone too much of a change in so short a time."

He laughed softly. "My wife is indeed a clairvoyant." He proffered his glass and each sipped from it. "France cannot prevail against the British. Shortly, the war, in all its manifestations, will end. However, there are some eighty thousand French-speaking residents in New France who are entitled to representation in the new British government. I would like to help make that possible."

Catherine's eyes widened in amazement. "You are planning on entering politics? I cannot believe it. On second thought, I can, for if anyone can convince the victors to share the spoils with the vanquished, it is you, my love."

He reached for her hand and held it tightly. "Then you do not object?"

She smiled and gave the tiniest laugh. "If I have learned one thing in the course of the past months, it is the futility of objecting to whatever you set your mind to." She brought his hand up to her cheek and looked at him. "In this, you will find no objection from me. Wherever you go and whatever you choose to do, I will follow you. For did I not promise to be a docile wife?"

This time his laugh was loud enough to echo through the establishment.

"Did you say *docile*?"

She leaned back and nodded, although not with any great conviction. "I did indeed."

"Then I shall truly count my blessings. If I find an obedient wife under that stubborn exterior, I shall count them twice over."

He put his glass on the table and set her on her feet. Then he rose himself and took her in his arms. "Yes, a wife should be obedient to her husband in all things."

He picked her up and carried her to bed.

Even as a child, **Carolann Camillo** was captivated by words. She would make up plays, collect the props, take all the parts, and direct the action. She wrote poetry and, in high school, several cheers that were performed at basketball games. She acted in school plays and attended the American Academy of Dramatic Arts, appearing as an extra in films and in a couple of way off-off Broadway productions.

Carolann's other novels include *Southern Star, Forever Mine, The Very Thought of You,* and *Eyewitness* (with Phyllis Humphrey). A member of Romance Writers of America, she was a finalist in the Windy City Romance Writers Contest. She won the Foster City International Writers Contest in the children's story division.

Carolann was born in New York City and graduated from St. John's University. She lives with her college professor husband twenty miles south of San Francisco.

You can find Carolann on the Web at www.carolanncamillo.com.

Toni Abbott plays a soap opera villainess. During a late-night photo session, the photographer is shot to death. Toni is knocked unconscious and awakens with only vague memories of the event. With the help of a handsome young lawyer, she sets out to awaken her dormant memory and unmask the killer. Meanwhile the writers are deciding whether to kill off her character. Will life imitate art?

From Carolann Camillo and Camel Press

※

Thank you for reading *The Frenchman and the English Rose*. We are so grateful for you, our readers. If you enjoyed this book, here are some steps you can take that could help contribute to its success:

- Please think about posting a short review on Amazon, BN.com, and GoodReads.
- Check out Carolann's website at www.carolanncamillo.com.
- Spread the word on social media, especially Facebook, Twitter, and Pinterest.
- "Like" Carolann's author Facebook page: www.facebook.com/CarolannCamillo and the Camel Press page: www.facebook.com/CamelPressBooks.
- Follow Carolann (@CarolannCamillo) and Camel Press (@camelpressbooks) on Twitter.
- Ask for your local library to carry this book and others in the series or request them on their online portal.

Good books and authors from small presses are often overlooked. Your comments and reviews can make an enormous difference.

CPSIA information can be obtained
at www.ICGtesting.com
Printed in the USA
LVOW11s1742061217
558856LV00006B/1060/P